BITTER PILL

BITTER PILL

PSYCOP 11

Jordan Castillo Price

JCPBOOKS.com

First published in the United States in 2020 by JCP Books
www.JCPBooks.com

ISBN 978-1-944779-11-5
First Edition
Also available in audiobook

DEDICATION

To Piper Vaughn and Avon Gale
for inspiring me to tell Jackie's story

And Lady Tif for helping Vic look his handsome best

CHAPTER 1

Funny, how heavily I used to rely on Auracel to put a damper on my abilities.

Don't get me wrong. These days, I still saw the appeal. I got a buzz off the pills—maybe not an entirely pleasant buzz, but beggars can't be choosers—and the drug truly did crank down the ghosts. But I'd become more and more uneasy about the thought of some random pill determining what I did or didn't see. And lately, I'd been kicking around the idea that maybe there was another way.

I'd decided to pay a visit to Curious Curios to ask about yoga instead of just making a phone call. What were the chances of me getting a lesson on the spot? Given the clutter, hopefully pretty slim. You know they're ice skating in Hell when I'm actually glad about clutter. But I was still easing myself into the idea. I didn't want to do anything hasty like trying out a pose. Especially not in public.

I forced my way through the consignment co-op where Crash and his beau now peddled their wares, and told myself to buck up and deal with it. If they tried to make me yoga, I'd yoga. Sure, I stunk at it and I'd end up with a charley horse, but in the end, what really mattered was the way it affected my mediumship. Sad but true, in terms of harnessing my ability, putting my body through a bunch of awkward poses had yielded undeniable psychic results.

Fucking yoga.

Several paperwork-heavy weeks ago, I'd wrapped up my first undercover assignment. Since then, my mind kept going back to the fleeting moment of empowerment I'd felt when I stood up from the mat...and realized I could affect my ability with something that didn't leave wicked drymouth and a one-eyed headache behind. And it was time to admit I needed help.

Curious Curios had been in business for a while now, and Crash and Red were looking more settled in. The strange furniture and assorted oddities had seemed random back when they'd first hung out their shingle. Now, the stuff had settled into its best advantage just as seamlessly as Crash and Red had settled into their roles as official boyfriends. Crash had always struck me as too independent to be tied down. And yet, here he was with a guy who not only shared his livelihood, but his bed. And they hadn't strangled each other yet.

Then again, couldn't I say the same for me and Jacob?

Currently, Crash was with a customer. As much as he's always claimed people are a pain in the ass, he's a major social butterfly and an extrovert of the highest order. A certain type of customer always responded to his breezy, conversational, low pressure sales tactics. Red was more thoughtful and deliberate. While Crash talked the woman's ear off, Red was tending to the store by tidying up a display of peacock feathers. His close-cropped hair shimmered in the same opulent, iridescent colors, purples and greens and outrageously vibrant blues. He greeted me with the slow, easy smile that broadcasted the epitome of calm. Which, of course, only made me more self-conscious. Especially when he focused his whole and undivided attention on me.

"What's up?" I went for a fist bump—and since when have I ever so much as attempted a fist bump?—then shifted to a stilted wave.

Red acted like he didn't notice. He's gracious that way. "Our YouTube channel is finally taking off."

I'm about as savvy on social media as a Neanderthal living under a rock. Other than a fake identity constructed by my employers, my online presence is nil, so I don't tend to encounter the types of posts and memes and photos other people share with their family and friends. But I nodded along like having your own channel was a perfectly normal thing that I understood, and Red kept talking. "Are you familiar with ASMR?"

The Association for Some Majorly Random...um.... "Not exactly."

"It's short for *autonomous sensory meridian response*—a feeling certain people get from a variety of different things. The sound of plastic crinkling. The swish of the wind through a tree. And whispers—lots of folks are into whispers."

Oh, that wasn't creepy at all. I brushed a shuddery feeling from my forearm.

"You've heard of it?" Red asked.

"Let's just say the kind of whispers I deal with aren't something a normal person would want to encourage."

As the customer headed out toward the communal register with an antique music box cradled in her arms, Crash slid into the conversation without missing a beat. He eyed me critically and said, "I've always thought *normal* is entirely overrated, but in your case, I could see why you'd be hesitant. But we're just talking a fun frisson of goosebumps, not a visit from beyond the grave." He pulled out his phone and a set of headphones.

"Here, give it a whirl and see what you think. I promise—nothing's haunted."

Crash called up a video. The production value was surprisingly good. Gentle music. Soft-focus flowers nodding in the wind. And then I realized it was just an ad for some over-the-counter herbal remedy. "What's with the ad?"

"A word from our sponsor—that's what pays the bills. And now the fun begins."

The ad ended, and switched to a shot of Red. He was seated at a desk in a dimly lit room with a stack of tissue paper at his side. He looked directly into the camera with that profound, soul-searching gaze of his that left me wanting to slink away and hide...and then he smiled a slow, easy smile and said, "Today we're going to fold some paper." Was that code for something? He said it with such gravity it seemed like it must be. He proceeded to draw a sheet of tissue off the stack and do exactly what he said: fold it.

"I like the blue. It's such a rich and vibrant color, somewhere between teal and aquamarine...."

He went on in that vein, voice low and intimate, commenting on the color, the texture, the sound. After about a minute, I said, "People actually watch these?"

"I know, right?" Crash cracked a grin. "I don't experience the elusive tingles myself—probably too hyper—but Red has some pretty devoted followers."

Red gave a demure shrug. "It's not worth getting a big head over. You know how it is, in one day and out the next."

"And I'm sure most of them are just perving on him," Crash added with a leer. "But editing the video is fun and I dig brainstorming ideas for new content—and most importantly, the sponsors are happy with us—so we might as well make hay while the bandwagon's in town."

I handed the headphones to Crash with a shrug.

"Whatever floats their boats." After all, I saw dead people. Who was I to judge if someone got their jollies from listening to Red fold paper? "So, is this a physical thing? Or psychological? Or—?" Some kind of psychic talent the powers-that-be had never managed to document?

Red said, "There are theories, but nothing conclusive."

Welcome to my world. "Speaking of which...do either of you know why yoga would act as a psyactive?"

Crash said, "I've done plenty of yoga, but only for the least elevated of reasons. I dig the way it makes my arms all chiseled."

Red didn't look like he believed Crash, but was happy enough to let him pretend to be only incidentally spiritual. "I've heard rumors," Red said. "But given how competitive certain New Age types can be, I didn't pay them any mind."

Crash said, "Maybe you need to be at a certain level to tell the difference. Us lowly undocumented peons with no training might not get much of a boost from, say, a ten percent increase. But the walking Ouija board? Look out!"

"Be nice," Red murmured.

Crash was smiling, though, mostly with his eyes. "Vic can tell when I'm just yanking his chain. Seriously, though, of all the things you've tried, yoga's gotta be the most benign."

"Tell that to my hamstrings."

"Let me guess," Crash said. "You want to skip all the rigmarole of maintaining a yoga practice. You want to figure out which particular pose jangled your subtle bodies into alignment and cranked up your inner dial to eleven. And you want to be able to do it on the spot when you're dealing with a scary-assed ghost."

"You don't need to make it sound so unlikely."

"How many times have I told you to start meditating? How many times have I laid out the chakra cleanse? And how many times have you utterly and completely blown off my advice?"

"I...tried. It's confusing."

Red said, "Different practices work for different people, and maybe yoga really is the best practice for you. I could help you. I just took a four-week workshop at Rainbow Dharma."

"That's too much to ask—"

Crash cut me off. "If he didn't want to help you, he wouldn't offer. Listen, if you don't commit to a practice, it's not gonna magically happen. Plus, all that floorspace in your loft is just begging to be put to constructive use. So stop acting like you're not getting exactly what you came here for and just say thank you."

"Okay," I said weakly. "Thanks."

"Cool beans. Now help us knock the cobwebs off the top of that credenza. Neither of us can reach it."

What the heck had I just gotten myself into? The rest of the visit went by in a blur. Not because we were doing anything particularly unusual...but because I suspected that I was on the cusp of taking some real control of my talent.

Either that, or I was about to make myself look like a major, grade-A dumbass.

Once I'd dusted all their highest shelves and eaten half a leftover vegetarian burrito, I was getting ready to leave when Crash said, "Everyone wants a magic pill. But unless your main problem is maintaining a hard-on, it's unlikely you'll find such a simple solution."

Red's brow furrowed. "For a minute there, I thought you were talking about Kick."

I perked up at the sound of a street drug I hadn't yet heard of. Not as an ex-cop, either...but a guy who tends to like pills a little too much. "I've never heard of Kick—what is it?"

Red said, "Short for *psychic*. People say it's like mescaline without the jitters. And for some folks, the visions they have while they're on it come true."

Crash was less impressed with the drug's pedigree. "I'm sure it's nothing but adulterated sinus pills and wishful thinking."

"Don't be so sure," I said. "Psyactives are real. They're hell on your body, for sure—and without Con Dreyfuss handing out drugs like Halloween candy, I wouldn't even know where to scrounge them up—but they exist."

A gaggle of after-work customers drifted in. Red unfolded gracefully from the multicolored embroidered cushion on the floor where he'd been sitting, and Crash hopped down off the credenza. But before Crash joined Red in greeting the throng of shoppers, he leaned in and said to me, "I can see that the wheels are turning, and no matter how I attempt to dissuade you, you'll only be more determined to try it. Just do me a favor. Before you swallow candy from a stranger, have your guys at F-Pimp check it for razor blades first."

CHAPTER 2

I PULLED UP TO Mid North Medical—which I still thought of as The Clinic—wondering if anyone there would be able to tell me more about Kick. Yes, they were all highly trained medical professionals in the field of Psychic Health. But the majority of Psychs I knew personally wanted to dial their talent back, not crank it up.

Then again, I couldn't speak for every level. I'd never once swam in the shallow end of Psych.

I did a little double-take when I saw the new receptionist, even though I'd been encountering him for the past several weeks. All those years of seeing Patrick Barley sitting at that window had left quite an impression. And even though, intellectually, I knew The Assassin was in the wind, part of me still worried that one day he'd pop through the window like a bespectacled jack-in-the-box and blow my brains out. The new guy—Troy something—was forgettable. Fortyish, Caucasian, slightly overweight. But Patrick Barley'd had that "everyman" persona down pat, and he'd been anything but. So Jacob had gone through Troy's records with a fine-toothed comb.

His work history seemed legit—if managing a team of mall

cops is your idea of legit. Maybe his job experience made everyone at The Clinic feel more secure...though you couldn't compare the potential for a hostile anti-Psych mailbomb to a group of teenage girls pocketing cell phone cases at the kiosk....

Troy glanced up as I flashed my F-Pimp ID. Obviously, he recognized me by now, so I just did it as a courtesy. When he saw it was me, he perked up and said, "Oh, hey. Did you catch the new episode of *Ghost Wars* last night?"

"Not...really." I'd told him I wasn't big on TV in at least three prior conversations. Which didn't stop him from giving me a play-by-play of last night's lineup every time I saw him. Every damn time.

"They were off the coast of Maine at a site where at least four shipwrecks were recorded, but there were probably a lot more they didn't know about. And the equipment started to fail just after midnight—"

"Anyway, I'll catch you later," I said, with no intention of actually doing so. Guess the aftermath of Patrick Barley had left me a little twitchy.

Me and everyone else. Word travels in the world of Psych, and as much as Laura tried to keep things under wraps, the staff at The Clinic was fully aware that the current FPMP attention was more than just a routine audit, and they were glad for the backup.

As a patient, I'd always found the medical staff to be professional, if detached. But now, in my official capacity as an agent of the Federal Psychic Monitoring Program?

I actually garnered sustained eye contact and the occasional smile.

In fact, they seemed as impressed with me as they were with Jacob. And given the way people fawn over him, that's saying a lot.

I found Jacob in the records room surrounded by teetering stacks of paper files, picking through for any potential leads on a certain Dr. Kamal. Patient records had been digital since The Clinic was first built a dozen years ago, but admin records? On paper, at least in those early years...the ones when Kamal ran the joint. And the paperwork having to do with Kamal? It was as if it had somehow disappeared.

Imagine that.

Jacob was hunched over the desk with his jacket off and a pair of drugstore reading glasses perched on his nose. He hated the things, but had given up on acting like he didn't really need them to see the fine print. Especially now that he'd gone up a magnification since he started sifting through the haystack back at the end of February. There's no use in telling him he looks hotter than the glasses models on the optometrist's wall when he wears them. Or like a soap opera actor when he turns and whisks them off just so. They make him feel a little self-conscious. And that's kinda cute, too.

He looked up from his work and locked eyes with me. We regarded each other with the satisfaction of knowing we'd managed to shoehorn me into his investigation without raising any eyebrows. All it took was the claim that my car was in the shop. Of course, it actually was in the shop—I'm no dummy. I wasn't about to botch an excuse that was so easy to double-check. The mechanic who dealt with my complaints about "that weird rattling noise" seemed happy enough to keep taking our money, and I now had a valid reason to carpool, so it was a win-win all around.

Our scheme went like this: I showed up to collect Jacob and was admitted on my FPMP credentials. Jacob claimed he just needed "a few minutes to wrap things up." And I got to poke around The Clinic while I waited.

Worked like a charm.

Jacob fell into the ruse easily enough that I should probably be concerned. "Listen, I know it's late, but I've got one more file I need to look at. It'll just be a few minutes."

"Fine." I'm not a stellar actor, but I think I sounded like I thought I was doing him a favor. "I'll just...go say hi."

The women in the office were particularly nice to me these days—probably because I was willing to eat all the baked goods they were constantly plying Jacob with—but instead of ruining my appetite on someone's homemade lemon bars, I veered toward the in-house pharmacy instead.

My federal agent status and my connection to Jacob allowed me a bit of roaming, but the pharmacy was locked up nearly as tight as the automatic weapons armory at the FPMP shooting range. An electronic lock protected a small suite of rooms. The main workroom saw most of the action. From there, one door led to a vault of valuable prescription meds, and another to a closet full of disused medical equipment. The whole thing was tucked away on the basement level, behind an industrial-looking safety cage, just across from the meeting room that served as the building's official tornado shelter.

I found Erin Welch, the pharmacist on duty, shutting things down for the night. She was a quiet, studious woman who looked a lot younger than she actually was. Her straight, dark hair fell forward toward her face. When she tucked it behind her ear, the gesture came off more like a college student than a forty-something professional. That thing about sustained eye contact? I didn't tend to get it from her.

"So," I ventured. "There's lemon bars in the break room."

"Oh. Um...thanks. I was just on my way out."

"Sure, I wouldn't dream of keeping you. I know how it is waiting for a certain someone to finish just one more file."

According to the tradecraft, most people would find that remark relatable. Then again, if she was single, complaining about my superhot future husband could've had the opposite effect. Given the paltry replies I got from her whenever I tried to strike up a conversation, it was too soon to inquire about her marital status unless I was really freaking smooth. And I've never been accused of that.

She gave a nervous almost-laugh and said, "Anyway...."

I stepped aside while she finished keying in some kind of code beside the door, making sure I was looking pointedly at a random fleck of nothing on the opposite wall. It wouldn't do for me to seem like I was trying to rob the dispensary, after all. Especially since I took so few Auracel these days, I'd accumulated a pretty sizable stockpile. What I really wanted was information.

"Say, listen. I was wondering if you've heard of a new street drug called Kick."

She paused and actually looked me in the eye for once. Her brow was furrowed—then again, she was so serious, maybe she just had resting worry-face. "Why would you think that?"

"Because...you deal with psyactive pharmaceuticals for a living?"

"Oh. Right. Just the official medical grade drugs, though."

"Well, if you do hear anything—"

She looked somewhere over my shoulder, not like she saw anything there, but like she was eager to end our conversation. "As I was saying, I was just on my way out. Good night, Agent."

"Have a good one," I murmured. I was about to follow her out when I paused and turned to double-check that there truly had been nothing lingering behind me. Purely the power of suggestion, of course. They've done studies where someone on the street looks up and every other pedestrian in visual range follows suit. When a person looks at something, the rest of the tribe all want to know what grabbed their attention. But just as I'd suspected, there was nothing behind me but a locked door.

I pulled down some white light and looked harder.

Still nothing.

No one had ever died at The Clinic. No one in modern history had even died on the property itself. That's why it was custom-built in that particular spot.

Even so, I wasn't 100% convinced I was alone…but there was only so long I could loiter there by the locked-up pharmacy without revealing that my meanderings were more than just social. So I gave the area one final sweep and moved along.

By the time I'd done my rounds and gone to gather up Jacob (code phrase: *are you through yet?*) the sun had set, the sky was dark, and repeaters had begun drifting into the crosswalks. Even though it meant having to readjust all the mirrors, Jacob drove.

"Well?" Jacob ventured. "Any good gossip?"

We presume the car is bugged, though we're constantly reassured it isn't. It can be so exhausting trying to figure out what you're willing for your superiors to overhear. We'd both decided that chatting about the investigation was fair game. At least unless it implicated someone either of us needed to protect. "Following up on a lead," I said. "Probably nothing."

"Most leads are." Jacob pulled up in front of the cannery with a weary sigh. "Remind me again how I thought I would storm The Clinic, look through a few file folders, and flush out Dr. Kamal from wherever he was hiding?"

That's the thing about investigative work. You're ninety-nine percent struggling through the weeds and one percent stunned it's actually coming together. Come to think of it, that described weddings pretty well, too. At least, I thought it might. We were still hacking our way through the undergrowth in the nuptial arena.

I opened our front door to an alarming slide of catalogs. They started coming after we innocently requested more information on custom wedding bands. Big mistake. Weddings are big business, and the industry was hell-bent on separating us from our hard-earned money by informing us of all the ways in which our special day could potentially be lacking.

The catalog landslide was so voluminous today I couldn't even gather it all in one load. Jacob stooped to round up the stragglers, and we both headed toward the couch to do a quick and dirty sort to ensure we didn't accidentally toss an important bill.

As nighttime rituals went, mail-sorting was a real pain in the ass. Usually when you wind down for the day, it's by doing something soothing—or at least blowing off a little steam. Jacob had been spending his days mired in paperwork, and coming home to more of the same couldn't be any fun. "Here's what I want to know," I said. "Once we do finally get married, how will all the catalogs know to stop?"

Jacob gave me the side-eye. "What do you mean?"

"The deluge can't keep coming forever, can it? Does it time out after a few years? Or after a set number of mailings? Or is there some master list of weddings that will let everyone know to stop burying us in paper?"

I thought I'd been making some wry observation about the state of consumerism and the irrelevance of mail in a digital age, but Jacob didn't seem to find it particularly amusing. "You said *finally.*"

"Finally what?"

"When we do finally get married. That's what you said."

Oh boy.

"Out of the whole spiel I just gave, *that's* the word you pick up on?"

Jacob huffed and pinched the bridge of his nose. "This Dr.

Kamal thing is taking up everything I've got. I'm used to talking to people—with Carolyn—not picking through old records. I get home and my brain is mush, and I can barely decide what to have for dinner, let alone figure out our guest list."

"You're reading way too much into this."

"Someone from Camp Hell ended up at The Clinic. He hired Patrick Barley—who made it all the way to the FPMP without anyone being any the wiser. I'm just supposed to compartmentalize that and go on with my life like everything's fine?"

Here's the thing about Jacob. He'd been under the illusion that anything could possibly be fine a hell of a lot longer than I ever had. "You'll find Kamal," I said.

"Don't be so sure. It's as if he just disappeared."

I tried to put the stack of catalogs I was holding on the coffee table, but the paper was glossy, and they slid to the floor with a papery sigh. I ignored them and turned my whole body toward Jacob, propping my elbow over the back of the sofa. "I get it. Kamal freaks you out. He freaks *me* out too. But we both know how it is when someone wants to disappear. If they're really determined to fall off the map, it can be done. If you're overwhelmed, tackle one thing at a time. Don't even think about the wedding."

"So you're saying...you don't want to get married."

I batted a table-topper catalog out of his hand and shoved him back against the arm of the couch. "Look, mister. I would marry you in a big church ceremony in front of everyone we know. I'd do it shotgun-style with the justice of the peace and a random witness off the street. I'd tie the knot at a destination wedding on a fancy beach, or a low-key picnic in the park, or any other venue we could imagine. I'd even write my own vows if push came to shove—though we both know I'd just find something online and try to pass it off as my own. Heck, I'd take you downtown and marry you tomorrow, if that's what you wanted. But I'd rather not have the pall of Camp Hell and Dr. Kamal hanging over us while I'm sticking my ring on your finger, so in that case, I'm willing to wait until your investigation plays out."

Or until he decided that Kamal was essentially a ghost...and not the sort I could strike up a conversation with, either.

CHAPTER 3

MY PEP TALK WITH Jacob must have done the trick. He fell asleep fast, and greeted me the next morning with a vigorous session of rise and shine. We were so into it that we left a few minutes later than usual and ended up at The Clinic well after they officially opened...which was probably the only reason we stumbled across a familiar car in the parking lot—a car I'd always been particularly careful not to smudge.

A pristine Impala.

At first, it didn't really surprise me to find Bob Zigler at The Clinic. He'd been seeing some kind of headshrinker there ever since the unfortunate incident in the zombie basement. I hadn't seen Zig in a while, so instead of just leaving Jacob to his paperwork and heading downtown to HQ, I decided to stop in.

It wasn't that I missed Zigler. Frankly, we'd never been buddies, just co-workers. But it always seemed like maybe I should've said something or done something to help him cope with all the shit he'd seen on my watch. And maybe it was better late than never.

Once we signed in at the desk, it wasn't hard to figure out where all the action was. As medical facilities go, The Clinic is pretty quiet. There are no screaming children in the lobby. No screaming GSWs or mental health crises, either. Just workaday psychics having their blood tests or picking up their antipsyactives. No one kicks up a fuss unless someone's fighting for the last slice of pound cake.

But not today.

A big red button lit up on the phone and it let out a horrible squawk. "What's that?" I asked.

Troy looked flustered. "Our emergency number." The line went solid as someone picked it up elsewhere in the building, and then an urgent voice sounded over the PA. "Code Blue. Repeat—Code Blue."

Since Jacob and I are trained to run *toward* emergencies, not away from them, we hurried through the building. By the time we closed in on the emergency bay, judging by the screams, the Code Blue was already there.

"They're everywhere! Get 'em off me! Get 'em *off me!*"

Doctors who normally found time to gossip with me around the coffee pot were now rushing past us for the hall the screams were coming from. I recognized that ward. I'd woken up there once myself, back when Roger Burke had dosed me with experimental psyactives until I puked all over myself and blacked out.

In retrospect, I was probably lucky it had happened in public so he couldn't get away with chopping me up and flushing me down the toilet to cover his tracks.

Since we were official FPMP agents (and we had the sense to stay out of the way) no one stopped us. I spotted Zigler when we approached the room. That mustache of his is hard to miss. But then he shifted to one side and revealed another familiar face I hadn't seen in ages.

Carolyn.

They were together. I read it immediately in their stance,

in the tactical way they flanked the guy they were interviewing...in the way Zig was doing the talking while Carolyn did the heavy lifting without the subject being any the wiser. The guy currently under the microscope was your basic bureaucrat—an administrator whose presence wasn't actually needed in a medical emergency. While the nameplate on his office door read *Dr. Gary P. Bertelli*, I don't think he was the kind of doctor you'd see to get your appendix out. As he yielded to Zigler's questions, his body language projected, *I'm fine, you're fine, and everything's under control.*

But given the blood-chilling screams ringing through the hall, I didn't trust his body language any farther than I could throw it.

The PsyCops currently chatting with him had likely come to the same conclusion. Since her subtle nods wouldn't be cluing in Zig on anything he didn't already know, Carolyn peeled off and headed our way.

I gave an inward cringe on Jacob's behalf.

It was coming up on a year ago that he'd pissed her off by leaving the Twelfth Precinct, and in that amount of time, he must've offered a good half-dozen olive branches. Eventually, he got sick of being shot down and stopped trying.

Carolyn didn't bother with a greeting—but she didn't lay into him either, so that was mildly encouraging. "Are the two of you here in an official capacity, or for medical reasons?"

"FPMP business," Jacob said. He cut his eyes toward the screaming. "What's going on?"

"Kick, that's what. Are you investigating it too?"

In lieu of an answer, Jacob looked meaningfully at the swinging door as yet another doctor barreled through. Maybe, in a normal human, she would've sensed the falsehood of that single glance. But not a True Stiff like Jacob.

She said, "Then we should pool our resources. Even

though you're the last person I want to see." Ouch. "Kick isn't just dangerous, it's lethal—and it's hitting the streets like a bomb. First we heard of it was a week ago, and now it's all over the city. Low-level Psychs are overdosing left and right. We need to do something about it. Now."

A tendril of unease crept across the back of my neck. And then the cacophony in the ER got louder as it was punctuated by additional raised voices, including a doctor shouting over the general din, "She's coding!"

I realized with sudden, striking certainty that I should probably get the hell out of there...and that making tracks wouldn't be any use. If a dying Psych this close shot out a spirit body hell-bent on finding a new skin suit, there was no way I could outrun it. Not when it could go right through the walls like a round from an AR-15. So I did my best to set my chakras spinning, shotgun a bunch of white light, and brace for impact.

Adrenaline's a powerful drug, and if there was a scale that could measure my psychic ability with any amount of accuracy, my mediumship would've shot off the chart. A temporary spike—but one that caused a flash of giddy lightheadedness to my physical body. I swayed, but just a little, and no one noticed. They were all too focused on the emergency bay.

I made a decision. Since I'd never get away in time, I'd better see what I was up against.

I shouldered through the swinging doors and flattened myself out of the way the best I could. While one medic was doing chest compressions, another shot something into the patient's IV. I was taken aback by the twenty-something woman on the table. She looked so *normal*. Aside from being intubated and hooked up to a bunch of monitors, I mean. She was a tiny thing in wooly tights and a purple corduroy jumper...which had been unceremoniously hacked open at the top to stick electrodes to her chest. Her body heaved with the chest compressions while the monitors flatlined and droned their death-knell beep. But her hands were what got me. Not because of her purple sparkle nail polish...but how they were twitching in a way that had nothing to do with the CPR.

If I hadn't been rife with panic-induced vigilance, I might not have caught the moment her spirit popped out of her body. It was subtle. Like when you see a dark speck some-where in your periphery and don't know if it's an eyeball floater or a gnat until you try to get a better look.

I focused on the ghost...and wished I hadn't.

It wasn't *moving* right.

The thing jerked and stuttered like a creepy-crawlie in a Ja-panese horror flick or a club kid doing a horrible new dance. But before I could backpedal and redirect my mojo to my pro-tective shell, there was a bright blip of incandescence—the source of the white light, which twanged a sick resonance through my third eye. Not that it was *bad*, only way too much to handle, and me just a little too close. Like electrical out-lets—great for plugging in hairdryers...but not forks.

I felt the source hum like a high-tension line, not with my physical nerve endings, but my extrasensory awareness. The ghost shambled toward me and I staggered out into the hall. I scrambled to get out of range. But then, with a startling etheric burst, it disappeared, leaving a vacuum in its wake that made everything flex painfully until I released my white-knuckled grip on my shielding. The girl in purple—her spirit—gone, too, in a soupy burst of afterimages that fluttered away while my second sight recovered. I relaxed, and an uneasy equilib-rium settled in.

Psychically, anyhow.

Physically, the doctors were still yelling stuff at each other, pounding on her chest and pumping her full of chemicals while all the machines and monitors kept right on shrilling. They were still laboring under the assumption that The Clinic had never known the touch of death.

One of the PAs—a mom-ish lady named Gina who was the queen of bizarre non-sequiturs—took notice of me peering into the room and said, "Vic! You shouldn't be over here." I didn't resist when she dragged me toward the nurse's station, where suddenly everyone took notice of me.

I'll say one thing about Zigler—he was always good at running interference. He asked Bertelli a very urgent question to monopolize the administrator's attention while Carolyn and Jacob hustled me off to the nearest empty exam room. Carolyn's eyes bored into me when she asked, "What did you see?"

I hate describing my psychic experience to other people. Even when I minimize—which I typically do, just to be safe—it's obvious most people really don't want to know. But Carolyn was in a different category. Tough as nails and psychic, to boot. Plus, her talent would prevent her from asking unless she really did want to know. I said, "There's not a lot to tell you. The victim wasn't aware of me. Tough to really get a bead on her. She was kind of flickery and jerky and...she didn't stick around."

"Well, that's just great," Carolyn snapped. "Those dead pedestrians will stand around in the intersections forever, but the one that has evidence we need just up and disappears."

In the ghosts' defense, the accident victims were mainly repeaters, and any evidence I found on them would be fairly incidental.

Jacob was none too keen on being left to deal with Carolyn on his own, but he was even less eager to report to Laura Kim. While the two of them regarded each other with a great deal of professional respect, I doubted the Director would ever really get over him accusing her of murder—even if it technically *had* been her finger on the trigger. I got Laura on the phone and filled her in on the situation at The Clinic. There was a small, tense pause in which I suspect she was wondering whether or not I was possessed, but luckily I'd thrown around enough federal agent jargon that she believed I was actually me—without even seeing that although it wasn't quite 10AM, I'd already dribbled coffee on my shirt.

"This isn't the first report about Kick that's come across my desk," she told me, "but it's definitely the scariest. Tammi Pauls taught grammar school at a special magnet program for emerging Psychs. She was a good resource for the Program. I'd met her several times. A real sweetheart—lit up the room. And now...I can't help but feel like we failed her. We need to find out whatever we can about this drug. Where it comes from, what it does. The DEA recovered a few pills, but we need to find the source and cut it off before it spreads."

"Couldn't Darla get in touch with Tammi and find out where she scored?"

"Unfortunately, Agent Davis is on assignment." The words themselves weren't particularly alarming, but the implications were. The fact that Darla was completely uninterruptible made me worry that she could potentially disappear for good. "Vic, I'm reassigning you to The Clinic, but I don't want to create resistance there by sending in Carl—Dr. Bertelli has a tendency to be leery of the FPMP. But under no circumstances am I okay with you investigating potential spirit activity without backup. I hate to ask Agent Marks to double task with his ongoing investigation of Kamal—"

"I'm sure he'll jump at the chance. Anything to get a break from the wall of paperwork."

"Good. I'll pull together whatever documentation I can find and have it to you within the hour. I know street crimes aren't your specialty, so I really appreciate you stepping up to bat."

"I'll give it my best shot," I said. And I was profoundly glad that Laura Kim wasn't a human polygraph. Otherwise she'd probably hear me thinking that I had a lot more first-hand experience with street drugs than most ex-cops. "And another thing. We've got company. Chicago PD has PsyCops on the case."

I felt like a Benedict Arnold tattling on Zig and Carolyn, but no matter what I did or didn't report, word would get back to F-Pimp eventually. It always did. So I might as well try to work it to our advantage. "Listen, if the cops are already involved…maybe we should team up."

"Absolutely. I'll make the arrangements."

I stared at my phone for a second or two after Laura hung up. Guess I still wasn't used to my superiors agreeing with me.

On TV, when federal agents get involved in a police investigation, it invariably turns into a pissing contest of the highest magnitude. But in terms of police business, my real life wasn't much like TV. When I was a homicide detective, occasionally a fed would step in. My typical reaction wasn't mulish resentment, though—it was: *Great! I get to clock out on time tonight.*

One thing you can say for Laura Kim—she knows how to pull some strings. By the time I found my way back to the emergency room hallway, official pings were landing on everyone's phones informing us that until we stemmed off the budding Kick epidemic, we were one big, dysfunctional family again.

CHAPTER 4

THERE'D BEEN SOME CHANGES at the Chicago PD. From the few curt answers we were given, I gathered that with Jacob no longer at the Twelfth and their Sergeant assigning Carolyn to work with anyone and everyone who suspected their perp was lying, she decided enough was enough. Her contract stated she'd have a permanent Stiff, and when a Stiff wasn't forthcoming, she put in for a transfer. Warwick scooped her up for the Fifth, and Zigler opted to stick around after all.

Even with all our combined years of experience and resources, the four of us would have our work cut out for us, no doubt about it. Carolyn assessed the situation and said, "We'll need to interview the staff as soon as possible, while the incident is still fresh in their minds."

It was still chaos in the emergency bay, even though time of death for the girl in the purple glitter nail polish, Tammi Pauls, had officially been called. There'd be plenty of personnel to go around, that's for sure. Zigler pulled out his notepad and started divvying up the staff between us, but I interrupted him and said, "I'll take Gina."

Zig shrugged and moved her to my column.

Gina had always acted maternal around me, despite the fact that she couldn't have been more than a dozen years older than I was. While the dress code at the clinic was subdued and jewelry was kept to a minimum, Gina managed to skirt the unspoken rules by hanging her reading glasses around her neck from beaded, baubled chains so colorful and psychedelic they had the capacity to provoke a seizure.

A key part of the whole "carpool" plan had involved introducing me as Jacob's fiancé (who was only incidentally a federal agent.) While the staff hadn't exactly greeted the news with a spray of rainbow confetti, in their eyes, this nugget of personal information humanized both Jacob and me. And a small contingent—the ones eager to hear my opinion on their baking—all women, mostly older—was inexplicably smitten with us.

I've been called plenty of things in my life. "Adorable" had never been one of them. Until I'd started ingratiating myself to the backroom staff of The Clinic.

When I approached Gina at the computers, she met my eyes briefly and shook her head. Her cheaters danced on the ends of a bright beaded chain. "Poor Tammi," she said. "So young. What a shame. I'm glad I'm not the one who needs to notify her family."

I was just about to question Gina like a cop when I realized what a waste it would be for me to blow all the friend-cred I'd made. I shifted gears and pitched my voice gossipy instead. "I heard someone say it was *drugs*."

Gina leaned in and whispered, "They call it Kick—I guess it kicks up your psychic ability. Nasty stuff, and who knows what it's cut with. From what I've heard, the side-effects are really unpleasant. Nausea, cramping." Yeah, that about fit my own experience of pharmaceutical psyactives. "What I heard? The NPs who dabble with it don't try it again, but Psychs start looking for their next hit the second it wears off."

That last part was disturbing, to say the least. Because even though psyactive horse pills let me do neat parlor tricks like astral projecting while I was awake, at no time was I eager for another hit.

I found I didn't have to act scandalized and intrigued—I actually felt that way. But before I could see what else Gina'd heard about Kick, Dr. Bertelli snuck up in his expensive Italian loafers, and Gina quickly swung her attention back to the computer.

Smoothly, he said to me, "Agent? Mid North is truly grateful for any assistance your team might provide. But given the seriousness of the medical emergency and any residual issues, the Board of Directors insists we ask all non-medical personnel to vacate the premises for the day. I'm sure you understand."

He'd phrased it as a request, which was trickier than him actually pulling rank. Given that I knew Tammi's ghost had moved on, I figured it wasn't the time for me to challenge that request. Not yet, anyhow.

My colleagues must've come to the same conclusion. We gathered in the parking lot between the Impala and the Crown Vic and tried to figure out our next move. It was too cold—and too public—to reconnoiter outside in the parking lot. But my powerful resistance to reconnoitering at the Fifth Precinct surprised me.

"Why don't we go back to the cannery?" I suggested...and got three startled looks in return. But the more I thought about the Fifth, with the swaggering, smug cops I'd left behind, the less I wanted to darken its doorway. "There's no privacy at the Fifth, and the Program's all the way downtown." Not to mention the fact that mere cops wouldn't have the clearance to even get off the elevator in the Oversight Division where Jacob's office resided. And my office still held an embarrassing treadmill desk.

Carolyn nailed me with the entirety of her telepathic focus and said, "This isn't some sorry attempt to act like everything is smoothed over just because we're working a case together, is it?"

No, it was a burning desire to avoid the Fifth Precinct. "Not at all," I said with utter conviction.

Grudgingly, she said, "Fine. But only because it's closer—plus I hate the way that annoying Officer Raleigh is always smirking at us."

Once we were alone in the car—and out of Carolyn's range—Jacob said, "I hope you know what you're doing."

"What do you mean? The porn's all upstairs. We didn't leave out any incriminating lube, did we?"

He thought for a moment. "No, it's in the medicine cabinet. I'm talking about this whole partnership. Ever since your undercover assignment, you've been a really convincing liar."

"Gimme some credit here—I've always lied like a rug."

"But in a tone of voice that made it obvious you were just saying whatever someone wanted to hear to avoid the conversation. Lately, though, you're a lot better at inhabiting a role. I see you playing those women at The Clinic."

"I'm not—"

"Take it as a compliment. I didn't realize you had it in you to schmooze like that. But you can't block against Carolyn's talent like I can, so you'll be back to square one. I just don't want you to get discouraged."

I laid on the horn at someone dawdling at a left turn—probably more aggressively than I needed to—and said, "Don't worry about me, I've had plenty of practice at being discouraged by now."

And while I might not be a telepathic lie detector, I did

know Jacob pretty darn well. He wasn't worried about how I'd handle close quarters with Carolyn, he was worried about himself.

Carolyn and Zig were waiting for us when we pulled up by the cannery. We let them in, and I leapt over a fresh pile of catalogs and barged ahead while the others were still hanging up their coats. Nothing X-rated was lying around, but I did bury the lube behind all of Jacob's hair products to make sure no one mistook it for a hand sanitizer.

"I'll put on some coffee," Jacob said, while I moved to clear the dining room table. Normally, it was too big for just the two of us, which was why so much random paperwork piled up at the far end—but four investigators and their laptops would fit just fine. When I grabbed an armload of mail, a catalog slid out and landed at Carolyn's feet—one with two brides in white fairy princess dresses gazing adoringly into each other's eyes.

She scowled, then looked at the bundle in my arms—which touted champagne and photographers and rings—and realization dawned. "You're getting married."

That was the plan, anyhow, if we could ever negotiate all the details.

While I scrambled to figure out how to answer truthfully without hurting anyone's feelings, she turned to Jacob and said, "Were you going to invite me?"

True Stiffs are so rare, Jacob has only had the most general of FPMP Psych training. And when you blindside him, his shields tend to slip. He stammered out, "I—it's—we haven't—"

"We're not that far along in the process," I said.

"But were you *going to?*"

Of course, he clearly wanted to say. But then he reconsidered his words and admitted, "I don't know."

Carolyn squeezed her fists so tight her knuckles went white. "After everything we've been through, you just cut me out of your life—"

"I've tried reaching out!"

"You've tried giving me excuses. You've tried making me wrong. You've tried painting yourself like the good guy, and making me the bad guy for not following you into a new job that's so dangerous, the Director himself went into hiding. There's a reason you got the nickname Mr. Perfect—and, newsflash—it's not because it's true."

Things had escalated to yelling by now, and Carolyn was turning an unfortunate shade of red. Before Jacob could say anything in his own defense, she turned on her heel and stomped off toward the bathroom. Jacob looked to me. I held up my hands helplessly—I'm the last one you want to ask about mending fences. And then the guy no one was paying attention to piped in. Zig said, "The thing about most women is, when they walk off like that, they expect you to follow them. Ask me how I know."

Jacob blanched and hurried after her.

Zigler and I stared awkwardly at the hallway for a moment, and then he said, "I'll take that coffee."

We retreated into the kitchen where the sounds of Jacob trying to explain himself were somewhat muted. I dug out the artificial sweetener packets from the cupboard, put them down in front of Zig, and said, "Teaming up was a shitty idea."

"From what I gather, no one's been able to tolerate Carolyn as long as Agent Marks. All that truth...it's not easy to handle. No big surprise she feels lost without him."

"How about you? How's it going?"

Zigler gave a rueful smile that looked mostly like a twitch of his mustache. "First day out she told me my breath smelled. Now I go easy on the garlic, brush my teeth after lunch, and everyone's happy. It was just a shock to deal with someone who says exactly what she's thinking."

Whether she wanted to or not.

As Zigler and I both focused on avoiding the drama taking place at the other side of the cannery, I realized what a relief it was that Zig and I were both okay—with each other, at any rate. He still looked somewhat haunted by what he'd seen on my watch. But if anything, he was probably relieved I'd moved on so he could partner with a different Psych.

We settled in with our coffee and Zigler pulled out some notes. "Fortunately, Kick has only been spotted in and around Chicago. So far, at any rate. We need to put a stop to it before it spreads."

"I've gotta admit," I told him. "I'm out of my element here. Without a body or a murder scene to investigate, I hardly know where to begin."

Zig considered this. "I thought dead addicts had a lot to say."

He had a point. Addicts did seem to be prime *complainer* material. And though I wasn't sure you could compare a Psych OD'ing after a few doses of Kick to a longtime junkie—psychologically, at least—it might be a decent lead. I checked my F-Pimp inbox and, as promised, Laura Kim had stuffed it with all the info she currently had on Kick.

I could tell by the way Zigler was focusing over my shoulder that it was more than he'd had access to through the Chicago PD, but I didn't feel smug about it. Not after all the time I'd spent on the force hating that Con Dreyfuss and the FPMP were continually one step ahead of me. I had to admit, though, I didn't mind being the one with the good intel for a change.

Thanks to the presence of fentanyl in the heroin supply, an unfortunate number of users OD faster than emergency responders can whip out the Narcan. The average statistic is about two overdoses a day. In the past week, it had doubled—

and the new folks weren't testing positive for opiates.

Narcan might avert a potentially fatal heroin overdose, but it did nothing at all for Kick.

"Three of the non-opioid ODs are at LaSalle General," Zigler noted.

And we were well acquainted with LaSalle—we'd spent a good week exorcising the joint once I rousted a horrifying fire ghost from the basement. I called up current info on the hospital, and discovered I just might have a promising lead after all. "One of us needs to go tell Jacob and Carolyn to wrap things up," I said. "It's time to pay Dr. Gillmore a visit."

CHAPTER 5

Dr. Gillmore looked the same as usual. Same rumpled lab coat. Same no-nonsense natural hair. Same weary expression. When we showed up at LaSalle General, we found her scrubbing blood off her hands. Probably a bad time. Then again, it was always a bad time to interrupt her, so I opted to wait. Eventually, she turned off the faucet, grabbed a big wad of paper towels, and said, "Whose doctor-patient privilege are you disregarding today, Detective?"

"Actually...it's Agent now."

She gave me a 'yeah, sure' look, then motioned for me to hand over the goods. "And I'm just supposed to believe you? Show me."

I handed over my F-Pimp license, to which she said, "Hmph. At least this one's laminated. Okay, I'll bite. What brings you to LaSalle?"

"We're trying to get a handle on Kick. What can you tell me?"

"From what I've seen—generally, mind you—it's hallucinogenic, with nasty side effects. Headache, nausea, severe cramping, but the biggest danger is a nasty combination of a spike in blood pressure and seizure."

"That's fatal?"

"Can be. If it causes an intracerebral hemorrhagic stroke."

"Which might or might not have happened to some of your recent ER patients."

She gave a shrug which could have meant anything, but I took for a yes.

"This week it's three patients—what if next week it's thirty? We need to find the source."

"Which is your job. Not mine."

We were on the same side, and Gillmore was a sharp woman. But there was only so much of her obstinacy I could take.

"Look," I said. "I get it that you need to stand up for your patients. But you should be more worried about the ones who haven't come through that door yet, not the ones who've already bought it."

"According to hospital policy on patient privacy—"

"I already have their names, I just want to know which emergency bays they died in."

Gillmore narrowed her eyes and said, "Let me see that new license again."

I half-suspected she'd go throw it out the window. But if she did, HQ would just print another one, so I handed it over. She turned and strode off, leaving me to wonder if I was supposed to follow, or what. I glanced around. The ER nurses who'd been watching us face off quickly got busy doing something else. I glanced down at the sink. Pinkish spatters clung to the basin where some unfortunate person's blood hadn't quite rinsed away. I'd seen my share of blood spatter through the years. Even so, I was staring at it, noting the position, the pattern, the density, when Gillmore returned.

She handed my ID back to me with great annoyance.

"Three, four and eight."

"There. Was that so hard?"

I turned to get out of her hair, figuring that she was eager to see the tail end of me, so I was surprised when she had something more to say. "Just because that badge is as good as a subpoena, don't let it go to your head. Someday, it might be you under the microscope, dealing with whatever precedents you set."

I gave a humorless laugh. "You have no idea." When I glanced back, I saw she was at the sink again, rinsing away the spatter. I said, "The patient who belongs to that blood—don't worry, no names—are they okay?"

"Sure. Now that I sewed their finger back on."

"Didn't they need a specialist for that?"

"It was just the tip."

Was that...a joke? Damn it. My life would be so much easier if I could hate her.

I approached the emergency bays with no little trepidation, funneling white light for all I was worth. The image of Tammi Pauls in her purple corduroy jumper was fresh in my mind. I could still picture the flickering twitch of her ghost, and the freakish way it exited the physical plane. And the thought of someone hitching a ride out of LaSalle inside my body made me wrap the light around myself tight.

Jacob, Carolyn and Zigler were talking with some orderlies over by the desk, and I swung by and grabbed Jacob. Not only was he most likely to notice if I suddenly didn't sound like myself anymore, but he was impervious to possession.

As we headed for the first emergency bay, he asked, "If a Psych dies—let's say a telepath—do they die with their telepathy intact?"

"I dunno. Some ghosts focus in on a single, obsessive thought, and some wake up to expanded horizons. Maybe those are the Psychs."

As little as I knew for sure about ghosts, I did know a thing or two about LaSalle. In the weeks I spent scrubbing terrified ghosts and repeaters from a long-ago fire, I'd learned that in terms of physical traffic, it was feast or famine in the ER. It was either packed to the gills from a ten-car pileup or an outbreak of food poisoning, or it was quiet enough to hear crickets chirping. Fortunately, we'd hit them in a slow patch, and we were able to get in and out of the three bays in a reasonable amount of time.

Un-fortunately...there were no ghosts sticking around to tell me where they'd scored. I did encounter one disgruntled ghost wandering down the hall with a blood-soaked throw pillow clutched to his belly, calling out, "Who do I gotta blow to get some help around here?" He didn't know anything about Kick. And when he called me a useless piece of shit for telling him he was dead, I threw salt at him till he moved along.

The staff weren't too freaked out—they remembered me from the exorcism. They just slid me some cautious looks and called the janitor to sweep up after I was done. As Jacob watched me brush off a few stubborn grains clinging to my hands, our former PsyCop partners joined up with us. And Zig had an evidence bag in his hands.

It was like that end-of-the-meal moment at a restaurant where I didn't know whether to try and pick up the check or throw twenty bucks on the table and call it good. Someone would need to process the amber plastic pill bottle in that baggie. And if we were all working for the Chicago PD, I don't suppose it would've mattered one way or the other. Not unless our respective precincts had some sort of unspoken rivalry.

All four of us stared at the pill bottle, waiting to see who'd eventually make the call. "We all have access to the same federal database," I said.

Jacob added, "But the Program has more technicians available to process the prints."

Zig handed over the bag. Carolyn scowled and said, "Did you seriously think I'd challenge you on which agency claimed the evidence?" Luckily, she didn't wait for either of us to shoot ourselves in the foot over that one. "Psychs are dying. We need answers. That's my top priority."

It was a palpable relief to climb into the car and head downtown to drop off the bottle.

"She hates me," Jacob said.

Poor guy was patently unused to people treating him like a pariah. "Did she *say* that?"

Jacob shifted his jaw mulishly and gazed out the passenger window.

So, no.

"If she hated you, she wouldn't be upset about you not giving her a preliminary heads-up on the wedding. Give her time. She'll come around."

After all, she'd handed over the evidence without complaint, hadn't she? Unless you counted the complaint about us doubting her, anyhow.

When I ran the pill bottle up to the F-Pimp forensics department—and when I compared the facility to what we'd had back at the Fifth—it was obvious we'd made the right call. The evidence guy at the Fifth was no slouch, don't get me wrong. But the FPMP had something the Fifth didn't: federal funding. There wouldn't just be a tech lifting prints. There'd be an entire team...one equipped with all the latest and greatest toys.

Eileen, the tech who'd greeted me, was a sturdy, middle-aged woman with a P-4 designation on her official F-Pimp badge. I wondered how much of her precog ability played into her work—if she was ever tempted to just say, "Eh, don't bother," and lob something straight in the trash. But precogs aren't as omniscient as you'd think. Even if their flashes of insight are accurate, they usually only make sense in hindsight.

"You might as well stick around," she told me. "Director Kim said this is our top priority, and with the latest improvements, the federal database can turn up results surprisingly fast." The team subjected the bottle to some specialized colored light sources and snapped a bunch of photos. "We're in luck, these are good, clean prints. We've got the decedent's prints on file, so we'll eliminate those. And we'll run what's left through the criminal module—it's a smaller database than the general archive, so it's faster to search. And since we're looking for a drug dealer, chances are good they're on record."

I watched with interest as a massive print filled a monitor, along with a bunch of data I had no idea how to interpret. But I also kept one eye on the techs, and I saw the moment their eager anticipation ebbed.

"No hits," Eileen told me. "But don't worry. We still have more modules to search."

Did she realize she was subtly herding me toward the door now? Or was her precog sense subconsciously telling her not to bother wasting any more of my time? I might not be able to see the future. Even so, something told me our pill bottle wasn't such a hot lead after all.

I swung by my office to refill my sacred salt, brought Carl up to speed, then went to grab Jacob from the Oversight Division. Unlike me, he's got a private office. I used to envy that privacy, especially whenever I realized Carl was watching me accuse my computer of hiding my files with that look of disgusted resignation he does so well. But Jacob is a social creature. And if you leave him alone in a room with a problem, he tends to stop working and start brooding. He claims he's thinking. But I can spot his brood-face a mile away.

I got Jacob up and out of his seat and hauled him off to

start canvassing the victims' family and friends, searching for any crossover we might find. Common friends, acquaintances, routines. I don't know what it says about us that interviewing a weeping mother or a shell-shocked boyfriend was in our comfort zone. I guess it was better than glowering at the walls.

Unfortunately, we came up dry. Carolyn and Zigler too. And while I was as invested as the next guy in getting a lethal Psych-targeted drug off the street, I realized the bigger reason I wanted to crack this was for Jacob. If he and Carolyn could have this win, it would go a long way toward smoothing over whatever resentment and hurt was between them.

The wedding catalogs were piled in the recycle bin and our dining room table was now brimming with lists and notes. We sat, long after Carolyn and Zig had called it quits for the day, silently cradling our half-eaten takeout and staring at our notes.

"We've got nothing," Jacob said with disgust.

Not only was it past our bedtime, but he handled discouragement worse than most people, having so little experience with it.

"We've only just started the case."

"We're supposed to be elite psychic investigators—the best of the best—and what've we done? Interviewed some useless neighbors and dug up a fingerprint with no match. Tell me how a bunch of NPs right out of the police academy would do anything different?"

There was no comforting him when he was in a mood like this, and I tried not to take it personally. True, I was one of the highest-level mediums on record. Even so, psychically, I'm a one-trick pony. And it wasn't my fault if there were no useful ghosts to see.

At least...not the *victims'* ghosts. But maybe there was another living-challenged witness who could shed a little light on our investigation. "Heads up," I said, and tossed Jacob the car keys.

He raised an eyebrow.

"Maybe we haven't gotten anything we can use from the victims—*yet*—but I can think of someone who's always taken a very particular interest in the neighborhood drug trade. With any luck, maybe she can tell us something."

CHAPTER 6

Pulling up outside my old courtyard building was a major blast from the past. Back when I lived there, I would have said I was content. That the sounds of other people's TVs and the smells of their cooking didn't bother me. That I was perfectly fine with microwave dinners and waking up alone. Seeing the place now, I realized how numb I'd been. And how far I'd come.

Jacob, too. He always figured himself for a boring old NP, and here he was, some important so-and-so at the FPMP—and psychic Teflon, to boot. Still, his anti-talent was nowhere near as flashy as he might have liked, and as I powered up on white light, I wondered how hard he would take it if I told him to stay in the car. His presence had never seemed to make any difference before. And given how much I wanted to talk to this particular witness, it wouldn't surprise me if—

"Hey, white boy!"

Well, damn. I gave Jacob's forearm a quick squeeze, turned toward the sidewalk—even though I couldn't see her, as usual, and didn't know exactly where she was, the sidewalk was the best bet. "Hey, Jackie... Long time no see—"

"Twenty dollar. Twenty dollar and I'll do you *and* him. Suck you both off. You want a little pussy, that's thirty."

"Jackie, it's me." Did she even know my name? No idea.

"Twenty dollar—blow both of you. You know that's better than you'll get anywhere else around here. You know I'll suck you good."

I rolled down my window and leaned my whole head out. "Jackie—*it's me.*"

"Fine. Ten dollar, but only because you're a repeat customer."

"What the—? No, I'm not. I used to live here, remember?"

"You wanna go upstairs? Twenty dollar for pussy, both of you. And you don't need to wear no rubber."

I shoved open the car door and hopped out onto the sidewalk. I stood with my legs planted wide and my arms spread so she could look at me in all my tall, gangly, black-suited glory. "I am not here to solicit you. I'm here to talk. That's all."

"All right, all right…. You're one of those? I can talk you through it, I can get you off. But we should go up to your place and get off the street. There's law sniffin' around."

"I *am* the law!"

Silence.

"Jackie?" I turned in a circle—as if it would help me get a bead on her when she was completely freaking invisible. "Jackie!"

I had no idea ghosts had such lousy memories. We met umpteen times over the years, though. Shouldn't that count for something?

I got back in the car and did up my seatbelt with a disgruntled jerk.

Jacob was watching me sympathetically. "No luck?"

"Useless." I was still pulling down the white light—not that it did me any good. "I couldn't see her—that's nothing new, I usually can't. I mean, one time I did. It was easier when I could see her. At least I could read her body language and tell whether she was listening to me or not. Have some clue as to whether I was getting through to her." I thought back to that time I'd had a really solid visual of her with the shank that killed her sticking through her chest…and remembered that sighting only happened courtesy of an experimental psyactive Roger Burke had been slipping into my Starbucks.

A little devil on my shoulder whispered, *Maybe with a little Kick, you could see her now.*

I shuddered and pushed that thought far, far away.

We took the long way home, zig-zagging through Ravenswood to see if there were any other ghosts around who might care to spy on their dealers. We couldn't pay them off. Despite what Jackie seemed to think, ghosts had no use for cash. But maybe the satisfaction of knowing they'd stuck it to a dealer would be a decent incentive. Even though we hit every major intersection, every known OD hotspot, we found nothing but an alleycat fight club and a heart attack repeater.

It figured.

The only time I ever stumbled across ghosts was when I'd rather be dealing with anything else.

CHAPTER 7

I'D LONG AGO RESIGNED myself to having a one-note talent, because at least it could shed light on some deaths.

Except when it didn't.

The next morning, we hashed out our plan of attack. My best chance at grabbing the next drug casualty before the ghost headed off to the Great Beyond would be corralling the ghost just after it ejected. Zigler and Carolyn would keep an eye on LaSalle while Jacob and I scoped out The Clinic. That way, while Jacob kept plugging through old records for Dr. Kamal, I could question staff members who were so inured to Psychs that I didn't freak them out by simply existing.

On the surface, the mood at The Clinic was somber. They'd lost their first patient yesterday. I've learned this much from living with Jacob—when you're unaccustomed to failure, it hits pretty hard. As the day wore on, people opened up and started talking. A few words here and there at first. Then more. In whispers, glancing around to make sure Dr. Bertelli wasn't eavesdropping. And finally, full-blown retellings of exactly what they were doing when the girl in purple coded.

I listened, and I responded with my most sympathetic

nods. But eventually I realized everyone was just processing their shock and guilt aloud, and no one knew any more about the victim than I did. No one could do anything more than spew gossip and conjecture about Kick, either.

Then again, the pharmacist hadn't weighed in with her opinion yet.

I headed downstairs and over to the pharmacy, and found Erin Welch running off prescription labels. If she'd been working at your typical chain drugstore, she'd have helpers doing her grunt work. But she served such a small and specialized clientele, it was only her, doing everything from counseling the patients to sticking the stickers.

Erin glanced up from her work. Her glasses were so thick, they made her eyes look beady even when she wasn't squinting...although she may very well have been giving me the stink-eye for interrupting her, regardless. She tucked her limp hair behind her ear, and said, "This isn't a dispensary. Your Aura-cel's ready, but I can't just hand it over. Policy is very strict on this. You really need to check in with Mr. Malone."

"Who?"

"Troy Malone." When she saw the name rang zero bells, she added, "At the front desk. Where you sign for your meds."

"Oh. Right. Yeah, I'll do that. Say, listen—what can you tell me about Kick?"

Like most introverted workaholics, she was happiest when you left her to her job, so she seemed relieved I wasn't just there to try to be social. She called up a report on her computer. Even from where I stood, it looked as dry as the jars of powder in the locked cabinets all around her. "Well, Kick affects the adrenal system," she said...and then launched into an explanation of the mechanics I had no hope whatsoever of comprehending. After a litany of phrases that meant nothing, ratios that could have been anything, and terms I couldn't pronounce, she added, "There was a psyactive called Palazamine that was never approved by the USDA. According to mass spectrometry, Kick is most likely a combination of Palazamine with amphetamines and a few synthetic compounds that don't appear on the controlled substances schedule."

"So...it's a Frankendrug."

Erin was not impressed with my summary.

I said, "If Palazamine was never marketed, where would someone go about getting their hands on it?"

"If I were to guess? India, maybe China. Government oversight can be lax overseas, not to mention the counterfeiting. Drugs that are banned here could very well be legal there. It's not as if psychic ability is strictly an American phenomenon."

I was suddenly very aware of the fact that people out in the real world didn't walk around labeled with a psychic rank and level, not like they did back at the FPMP. "What about you?" I asked. "Have you been tested?"

"Everyone here has been tested." Yeah, a fat lot of good that did with Patrick Barley...though given that he was a True Stiff, I could hardly ding the evaluators for marking him as an NP. "Don't tell me the FPMP doesn't have a mile-long dossier on everyone here."

If anyone would've asked me if I'd acclimated to my role at F-Pimp, I would've laughed in their face—or at least turned away and camouflaged a chuckle with a dry cough. But given how surprised I was over being resented for my inside information really gave me pause. "I'm sure the Program's got...records. But I don't. Not me, personally."

"I tested average in everything. Twice."

"We're on the same side, you know. I'm just trying to get a handle on a drug that's been killing Psychs. That's all."

Erin accepted my explanation with a somewhat-mollified

shrug, then printed out the most recent bulletins from her pharmaceutical feed regarding Kick. I folded the papers into my pocket and, to both our relief, left her to her work.

I shouldn't have been surprised to encounter hostility as an FPMP agent. Heck, usually I was the one who felt violated. No one likes to be checked up on. I get it. Still, I was pretty sure Erin wouldn't be baking me brownies anytime soon.

Or if she did, they'd be full of Ex-Lax.

I spent the bulk of the day at HQ with a pharmaceutical consultant trying to explain an unfathomable table of numbers to me, then swung by the surveillance department to see what they could tell me about Erin's movements. According to the experts, she ran a tight ship, the company she kept was benign, and the shadiest place she visited was the public library.

And she truly had scored a big fat "average" in every psychic ability. Twice.

As an FPMP investigator, the amount of information I had on Erin Welch was staggering. The ease with which I could obtain it, even more so. And while I was 99% sure she was on the up and up, I wouldn't have minded running her through a polygraph, just to be sure.

Not really. I valued the relationships I'd fostered within The Clinic, and I suspected all that trust and goodwill could eventually uncover some important piece of info no video surveillance or wiretap would ever dredge up. A sure way to turn a workplace against you is to start hooking people up to lie detectors. Even the less social members of the crew, like Erin.

I was pondering this as I pulled up to The Clinic, spotted the Impala, and remembered Carolyn was on my team. I found her and Zigler combing through records with my buddy Gina, who glanced up and shot me an "oh God, please help" look I didn't need telepathic skills to pick up on. "Say, can I borrow you?" I asked Carolyn.

Gina looked very grateful. I suspected there might be some homemade snickerdoodles in my future.

"I need to clear the pharmacist," I explained.

Carolyn nodded. "Given that we're dealing with a pharmaceutical, and this particular place will have the most experience with psyactives, it seems like a logical choice to me. So, why do you seem so reticent?"

"I'm not," I said...and she shot me a look. I sighed and reconsidered sharing my real reason. "Back at the Fifth, no one wanted to deal with me. I could clear a room just by crossing the threshold...and then there's all the *Spook Squad* comments from the peanut gallery. I guess I got a little too spoiled by the camaraderie here, and if I'm the one who finds someone on the team is part of the Kick pipeline, I'm back to being the odd man out."

I thought Carolyn would tell me to grow a pair and stop worrying about winning any popularity contests, but instead she just said, "Welcome to the club."

It was getting late, and we found Erin neck deep in her whatever rectification procedure she did at the end of every day. Apparently psychic pharmaceuticals are even more rife with paperwork and red tape than police work. She looked up from the report her printer was spitting out and said, "Can I help you?" in a tone that clearly conveyed, *And make it fast, I'm busy here.*

"I just needed to verify a few things, and then we'll be out of your hair." I tried for an encouraging smile. She gave me a blank look in return. "So, there's no Palazamine currently in stock, right?"

"Why would there be? I told you, it was never approved."

Carolyn gave me a subtle nod.

"What about in the testing phase? Don't clinical trials happen here?"

"Very rarely, and usually just for antipsyactives. The last psyactive trial that was run, I wasn't even working here yet. I was at the Drug Right on Lawrence."

That answer jibed with the mass of documentation I'd scanned back at HQ. Plus, Carolyn nodded again.

"Then you haven't handled any Palazamine recently?"

"Are you kidding me?" Erin jumped up from her desk, red-faced. I thought she was angry—until I realized there were tears glittering in her eyes behind the thick barrier of her prescription lenses. "You want my official statement? Here? Now? In front of *her*?" She swung an arm at Carolyn with such force I was worried she'd dislocate her own shoulder. Good thing for the barrier of the safety cage between us. "I've never so much as *seen* Palazamine. I've never seen Kick. I have no idea where you might find any. And I most certainly am not dealing it myself!"

Carolyn answered—thank God, because I had no idea how to respond. "A piece of advice, Ms. Welch. Most investigators will presume you're hiding something if you overreact like that...so be thankful the person you just blew up at is a telepath."

CHAPTER 8

I HADN'T REALLY CONSIDERED that most everyone at The Clinic had access to our files, and they'd know full well if I had Carolyn at my side, she was doing a lot more than just listening. Suddenly the idea of investigating the place that dispensed my Auracel and touched my urine samples took on a whole added layer of complexity.

"I thought that talk would go a little smoother," I admitted to Carolyn as we headed back upstairs.

"You can cross the pharmacist off your list now. Was it pleasant? Maybe not. But you got what you wanted. Sometimes, that's the best you can hope for."

We were just coming out of the stairwell when the sound system that usually piped in banal smooth jazz came to life with a startling beep. "Code Blue." Was that Gina? I'd never heard her sounding so official. "Repeat, Code Blue."

The Clinic bolted into action. Doors flew open up and down the hall. Half the staff ran toward the entrance, the other toward the emergency bay. It was the end of the day and a lot of them had on their winter coats and hats. A few ran back in from the parking lot. The doors with electronic security locks swung wide open. Within seconds, the whoop of an ambulance siren approached.

Paramedics shoved a gurney through the doors like they were in the final stretch of a soap box derby. The guy on the stretcher was some kind of construction worker, judging by all the reflective tape on his work clothes. Between the paramedics filling in the doctors and the doctors ordering around the PAs and the whole mob hurtling down the hallway as fast as humanly possible, it was a barely controlled chaos. But there was one shout I picked out from all the others. One of the staff exclaiming to her friend, "Oh my God, is that Reginald?"

White light. I opened my valve wide and sucked it down for all I was worth—and I wished I'd found the time to grab a yoga lesson, because if they were on a first-name basis with Reginald, he was a well-known Psych. I might not know what Reginald's talent was, or if it might make him more likely to be able to possess me. But I didn't want to find out the hard way.

The staff was administering activated charcoal now in an attempt to soak up whatever was in his stomach, and I'm guessing it was more than just his lunch.

I realized I'd been holding my breath and reminded myself to keep breathing. The full-of-mojo feeling washed over me with its cottony lightheadedness. Or maybe I'd held my breath longer than I realized. Either way, I was all hopped up and ready to ghost. Vaguely, I heard Dr. Bertelli nearby, trying to get rid of us investigators while Jacob steered him in the opposite direction. Bob Zigler was at my side, a familiar presence, sharp and observant—and I knew that he'd been paying attention to all the bazillion details I couldn't afford to take in. "Is it Kick?" I said softly.

He nodded. "Sounds that way."

"Is that guy gonna make it?"

"We'll see."

It was a tense half an hour that felt like it stretched well into the night. There was no known antidote for Kick. The team got as much out of Reginald's system as they could, and then pumped him full of IV drugs to stave off seizures and bring down his blood pressure, and then they waited.

He still wasn't conscious by the time they were through with him. But they stabilized him well enough to transfer him to intensive care at LaSalle, where they could keep him overnight.

Jacob and I took the first shift outside his room, with Carolyn and Zig promising to relieve us later. Eventually, the adrenaline rush of high alert wore off, and I eased up all the internal clenching. I can only hold the white light for so long. Maybe if I figured out some yoga, I could extend my holding power. But as it was, eventually I got wobbly and weird until I allowed the light to recede to normal levels.

Jacob stepped away as I was counting linoleum tiles in the floor, and came back a few minutes later with a wrapped sandwich. "I don't know how good it is," he said. "It might've been sitting around since lunch."

And with that, I realized my stomach was currently attempting to digest itself. I've always had to fend for myself, and having someone looking out for me was definitely nothing I took for granted. The longing to touch him welled up inside as he handed over my turkey and swiss on rye. Just a tiny brush of the fingers—anything more would be unprofessional—but I refrained. I wasn't clutching my white light, but its levels were still high. I didn't want it to jump over to him and leave me wide open to be hijacked the minute someone in the hospital died.

While I scarfed down my stale sandwich, I pulled out my phone and had a look at the files Laura sent me on Reginald.

He was a well-documented empath, high level three. That's pretty darn high, when you consider that Stefan could trigger a bowel eruption as a five. For some reason, I always presume empaths will land themselves in fields well-suited to their talents. Doctors and nurses. Therapists and counselors. Teachers and coaches. Even salesmen, like Crash. But Reginald had been working for the Department of Transportation, pouring sidewalks and patching potholes, since he dropped out of community college after the first semester. He was several years younger than me, so he'd escaped the "human guinea pig" phase of psychic discovery I'd suffered through. No, younger Psychs had a different path than my generation. They were often caught up in a net of optimism from a time where corporations left and right were sucking up anyone with talent.

Some Psychs thrived.

Lots of them didn't.

Reginald was not one of the success stories. He grew up in a rough neighborhood and never had any reason to learn impulse control. The emotional signals he picked up on were distractions at best, obstacles at worst. He was considered untrainable. Eventually, he found his groove working with his back and his hands among a crew who said what they meant and meant what they said, and went home alone each night covered in asphalt crumbs. The highlight of his day was Netflix and a six-pack.

I was pondering what my life might've been like if I'd ended up more like Reginald, when a nurse came out of his room looking wide-eyed and a little freaked out, and told Jacob, "He's awake."

Although Reginald's eyes were closed, the top half of his bed was elevated, and he was pulling on the straw of a hospital cup. He cracked open one eye, took a look at my suit, and said, "You here to arrest me?"

"Uh...no. Actually, it's so new, I don't think you've broken any laws."

The corner of his mouth quirked up. "Well, that's a relief. Even if my head is pounding and I feel like the devil just shit in my mouth." He opened both his eyes now, and looked from me to Jacob and back again. "I'll talk to you. Not him."

Jacob has a tendency to freak out empaths. He knows this. But he still takes it pretty personally. "I'll be right outside."

There's empathy...and then there's empathy. With all the dubious pills I've swallowed over the course of my life, all the things I've huffed and smoked and snorted, it could've been me in that bed. Easily could've been me.

There was nowhere comfortable to sit, just a rolling stool, but I perched on it so I wasn't looming over the guy. "Was this your first time?"

"Kick? Naw. First two, three times you do it, ain't nothing too bad, except the cramps."

I tried to wrap my head around the reason anyone would subject themselves to that experience more than once. "So, it must do what it claims to do. Psychically."

Reginald shrugged.

"There are other ways to get that hopped-up feeling." How hard would he roll his eyes at me if I suggested yoga? Maybe there was a better way I could phrase it.

But before I could make a fool out of myself, he said, "That's the thing. When I was tweaking?" He thumped his sternum for emphasis. "I hated it. Like someone skinned me alive, then fed me through a cement mixer. Angry. Jealous. Depressed. Scared. All of it flashing by, one thing after the other, so quick I didn't even know who it was connected to. Just me. Rolling in a bunch of shitty feelings till I came down."

We sat with that for a couple of seconds. "And then you did it again."

"I can't explain." My heart went out to the guy—it *so* could have been me—and for a change, it worked to my advantage to be an open book to the empath in the room. "Don't make a damn bit of sense, I know. But as soon as the Kick wears off...I am *jonesing* for another hit."

CHAPTER 9

By the time we headed home from LaSalle, it was pretty late. The streets were peaceful, with few cars and even fewer repeaters. But the bars were still open. In particular, a bar I used to frequent every couple of weeks, and not because I was interested in happy hour, either. My happy hour started back at home with my little red pills.

It had been a while since I'd slept the sleep of the blissfully sedated. It took Con Dreyfuss flinging drugs at me in a panic room under the railyard to make me realize I couldn't afford an addiction. Not if it gave Big Brother another potential weakness to exploit. Was my ex-boyfriend's pot dealer still holding court in the same sticky naugahyde booth?

Guess we'd soon find out.

"Pull in here," I told Jacob. He was puzzled, but he did what I asked.

According to Reginald, he'd scored the Kick at a party from "some white guy" nobody knew. He refused to tell me anything more about the party, but it gave me the idea to see what my old contacts might know.

I glanced down at myself. I wasn't exactly a fashion plate,

but I suspected there'd be subtle cues that I'd leveled up. My sleeves fit me now, for instance, and my haircut didn't scare small children. And the types of people who frequented this bar wouldn't take kindly to my success.

I loosened my tie and pulled it askew, then ran a hand through my hair. Hopefully it was dark enough inside that my quick rumple would do the trick. "You'll need to wait in the car," I told Jacob.

He gave me a look.

"I know, I know. You never get to have any fun. But trust me...if they see us together, I'll get nothing but some stale popcorn and a bunch of dirty looks."

When I walked through the door, the smell hit me first. Fake butter from the popcorn machine, cigarettes and BO from the customers, and stale beer from the pores of the wood. I should have been disgusted. But some small part of me perked up at the anticipation of a really freaking wonderful night's sleep. I ignored it and headed toward the back corner.

There was a big-screen TV mounted on the wall—that was new. My old dealer sat with a half-eaten personal pizza at his elbow and a half-drained beer between his hands, staring blankly at a dull sports recap on ESPN. I wondered if the TV had been hung where it was specifically so he could see it from his favorite booth. I suspected it had.

I paused beside him in my usual spot. It took him an extra heartbeat to acknowledge me, but then I saw it. The tiniest of nods. Just like always.

Someone told me the guy's name at one point, though once it slipped my mind, I made no effort to re-learn it. Seemed safer that way. To see him walking down the street, most people's first thought wouldn't be "drug dealer." He looked more like the type of guy who'd fix your computer—

and insult your choice of anti-virus programs while he was charging you an arm and a leg to do it. He was pale and hirsute. A hefty guy who kept the table shoved off-center for easy booth access. It irked him that I could slip into the seat across from him without sucking in my gut.

"It's been a while," he said unenthusiastically. "No joy for you here. I stopped selling Reds a long time ago—they're hard to find and there's no market for them. It'll take at least a week to get more. And not at the old prices, either."

"I'm not interested in Reds," I lied.

Wait. No lie. I wasn't interested. At all.

"I heard about something called Kick—"

The dealer cut me off with a scoff. "Have you been under a rock? That shit'll *mess* you *up*. One hit of Kick and you'll *wish* you'd only been snorting bath salts and chewing off people's faces. Unless you're psychic...and then, supposedly, it'll blow your mind." He had himself a good chuckle. "You're not suddenly convinced you're psychic, are you?"

His reaction nearly threw me, but I recovered. Convincingly, I hoped. "I was just curious about all the hype."

"On Kick? You see stuff." He waved a hand vaguely. "Lots of drugs'll make you see stuff. Save yourself a fuck-ton of trouble and drop a hit of acid instead. It won't leave you cramped up like a ten-pound rat in a five-pound bag. Now, if it's psychedelics you're looking for, Special K might be more up your alley, since you like to keep things mellow. I don't have any on hand, but I could certainly get my hands on it...for a price."

Normally, I wouldn't challenge him—his ego didn't take kindly to being challenged—but since I didn't need to worry too much about ending up on his shit list anymore, I decided to turn the thumbscrews on the Kick. After all, if I managed to score, maybe we'd find some prints we could actually use.

"Horse tranquilizers aren't really my style. I'm only in the market for Kick. I heard you couldn't score—just thought I'd check. For old time's sake."

He narrowed his eyes. "You don't find Kick. The Kick finds you."

How long had he been waiting to deliver *that* line?

Jacob didn't mention the stink of the gin mill on me, but he didn't need to. I was well aware of the way a trip to see that smug dealer lingered in my hair and clothes and car well into the next day, plus my throat kept catching as if the stink of the bar had lodged behind my tonsils. I hung my winter coat inside the basement stairwell, not willing to contaminate our closet, then closed the door behind it. Maybe the brick foundation would help suck out some of the bar-stench.

I paused to glare at the closed door.

I was not interested in Seconal.

Didn't need it. Because I practiced good "sleep hygiene" these days—a joke of a term if ever I heard one—which meant no more coffee after three, no succumbing to random naps, and no lit screens in the bedroom. And if I were to wake up ridiculously early after four and a half hours' sleep, well...no doubt I'd find plenty of work in my inbox to keep me busy until the rest of the world woke up.

I hit the shower and turned up the water as high as I could stand it. Other people say they feel their muscles relax under a hot shower. I never did. Maybe mine didn't have an unclenched setting.

Falling asleep wasn't normally my problem—staying asleep was—but the way my mind was racing, it was obvious tonight was going to be a smorgasbord of sleeplessness. I could've just rubbed one out in the shower stall. But I don't get off anywhere near as hard or as well when I do it alone.

Jacob was already in bed with the lights out when I joined

him, steamy hot from the shower, totally naked, and hell-bent on distraction. I burrowed under the covers and fit myself against Jacob's side, sliding a hand under the stretched-out tee he wears to bed. When I toyed with the treasure trail, he made an inquisitive, half-asleep sound. I raked his belly gently (and low) to let him know it could be more than just a passing grope, if he was up for it.

He was.

He shifted to slide an arm beneath my neck, and rolled himself on his side to face me. We kissed our minty, toothpaste-flavored nighttime kisses, him still groggy and me with something to prove, though exactly what that might be, I wasn't really sure. Together, we eased his sweatpants down. Gravity pulled our dicks toward the mattress, but even semi-soft, the weight of him felt right in my hand. His touch was just as familiar on me.

There's a cheap runner we bought for the upstairs hall to buffer the echoey sound of our footsteps, a temporary thing we'd laid down to determine if it was worth covering up the wood just for the sake of a little noise control. Give it a month, he'd said. And if we don't hate it, we'll shop for something more permanent.

That was a year ago. And our comings and goings had worn a distinct rut into the cheap acrylic fibers.

That's how it was, jerking each other off. We didn't need to reinvent the wheel to get where we were going. I still got off on the way his breath hitched. On his facial hair ruffling my chin and the way his thighs trembled when he was on the brink of coming.

He surprised me by ducking under the covers and sucking me off in my last few precious seconds—and holding down my hips to do it hard, way past my big finale, to the point of too much. But he only rode that squirmy, painful pleasure for a moment. Then he reared up beneath the tent of our sheets and comforter...and spilled on my belly.

As I groped for a cum-rag in my nightstand—the thermal long-johns I always regretted not wearing to outdoor winter exorcisms would have to do—Jacob propped himself on his elbow and said, "I would've gotten over it, you know. Not that I'm complaining about the apology."

"Gotten over what?"

"Sitting on the sidelines."

"I wasn't sidelining you."

"I get it. Believe me, at my last job, there were so many times I wanted to tell Carolyn to sit it out—let me come at the subject with honey, not psychic vinegar. But the precinct wasn't paying me to get people to open up. I was just supposed to trap them in a lie. Vic, people like you more than you real-ize. You have a certain something. Not everyone's gonna re-spond to it...but a lot of people do." By "a lot," he meant the occasional mom-type hoping to fatten me up. Even so, I couldn't entirely disagree. "You have your interrogation style, I have mine."

That's for sure. I was like a housefly battering itself against a closed window, making random observations while I tried not to put my foot in my mouth. Unsuccessfully at that, if my talk with Erin was anything to go by. Jacob was more like a hornet, circling hypnotically until he could glide in for the sting.

"I'm going to look harder at Bertelli," he decided. And with that, he conked out so fast I half-expected to find a tranq dart protruding from his sleeping body.

I pulled on a T-shirt and boxers and settled in against him, and proceeded to stare at the tin ceiling tiles long into the wee hours, waiting for sleep to come.

CHAPTER 10

For as many years as I had been coming to The Clinic, and all the poking around I'd been doing lately, it surprised me to discover I'd never been inside the director's office. First thing I noticed, it had windows. Reinforced glass block windows that you couldn't really see through, but real windows nonetheless. By contrast, the exam rooms took the phrase "window dressing" to the extreme. There was trim, and there were curtains, but there was no window underneath...so the glass block in Bertelli's office was a vast improvement. And I don't think the view would've been anything too spectacular anyhow, just a bunch of high-fenced Lincolnwood backyards.

Despite the fact that there was actual daylight present, I disliked the office right away. Not because it reminded me of getting called down to see the principal—which it kind of did—but because of all the clutter. Oh, it was arranged artfully enough and wasn't even too dusty, but there was just too much stuff. Artsy-fartsy sculptures on the credenza. Piles of books everywhere. And on the walls, a mosaic of crap, all in frames. Photos and news clippings and, of course, the ubiquitous diplomas. Was I jealous of those? Not really. I just found it pretentious to see them so arrogantly displayed.

Jacob settled into a chair, smooth as can be. "Thank you for taking the time from your busy schedule," he said. Of course, what I heard was, "You couldn't avoid us forever." But that was probably just me.

"Always happy to assist in any way I can," Bertelli claimed.

"Our first reports about Kick started coming in about a week ago. What can you tell me about your day last Monday?"

"I'd have to check our schedule," he said. Nothing about patient confidentiality, I noted, not like Dr. Gillmore would've said. Then again, he was probably just curating the information without announcing it to us first.

"Not The Clinic," Jacob clarified. "What can you tell me about your day?"

"I'll forward you my calendar," he said. Maybe too eagerly.

Jacob accepted the offer as if it were obviously his due. "That's very helpful, but what can you tell me about, aside from your appointments? Anything that struck you as unusual."

There was a pregnant pause, and then Bertelli said, "I'm not sure what it is you're hoping to find." No, he wasn't. Otherwise he would contrive to say something to extricate himself from it.

"Just establishing a timeline on the staff," Jacob said smoothly. "It's procedure."

A lot of nothing was asked and answered. What a conversation—those two were out-smoothing each other so hard, it was a wonder they didn't come out of it spit-polished and gleaming. Bertelli insisted he was deeply concerned and eager to be of assistance. Jacob reassured him all the questions were perfectly routine. But nobody was buying any of it.

I had nothing to add to the questioning. But I did have the sneaking suspicion that our invitations to Bertelli's office would be few and far between, so while Jacob politely grilled the guy, I pulled in white light and had a look around for anything a physical pair of eyes might miss. I must've been secretly hoping I'd find something lurking there among all the neatly arranged clutter. But, no. There was nothing but a bunch of stilted photos. Bertelli shaking hands with the mayor. Bertelli receiving some kind of award. Bertelli beaming as the ribbon was cut on an expansion of The Clinic. Everyone looked pretty pleased...everyone but the wrinkled up guy holding the scissors.

Sweat prickled my armpits and the small of my back before I even registered what I was seeing.

"Who's that?" I asked.

Bertelli rounded the desk and joined me at the wall that was an homage to himself. "That? My predecessor, Dr. Kamal."

"Friend of yours?"

"There wasn't really a lot of overlap between us. His background was in a more experimental area of pharmacology. Initially, this facility was set up to distribute antipsyactives on a case-by-case basis, and to provide the statistics needed for FDA approval. I was hired at the expansion, when we became a full-service psychic medical facility. Shortly after that, Dr. Kamal moved on to a new challenge."

"What 'new challenge' would that be?"

Bertelli smiled at me like I was horribly thick. "We didn't keep in touch."

He dismissed us—and Jacob allowed it, but only because Bertelli was giving us nothing more than fuck-all.

As we headed back toward the break room, Jacob bent his head toward mine and murmured, "You went a little pale when you spotted Kamal. Recognizing him—isn't that a good thing?"

Maybe. If it were something useful I recalled, and not a one-way ticket to a panic attack. "Intellectually, I knew Kamal was at Camp Hell—but this is the first time I've found a face to put to the name...or maybe vice-versa. Either way, I just now realized exactly how well-acquainted we were...and let's just say there were reasons I conveniently 'forgot.'"

A blur of experimentation tried to push to the surface and I shoved it back down.

I paused and backed into the wall as an orderly wheeled by with a bunch of supplies. Once he was past, I said, "So, Kamal signed me in to Camp Hell. And then he was director here at The Clinic when Heliotrope's doors closed two years later. And if we can believe Bertelli, at that time, this place was a glorified pill dispensary." Back then, I hadn't really given it much thought. I was so unaccustomed to having any amount of personal liberty—and so busy pretending to be cop material—I never realized The Clinic wasn't particularly interested in my well-being. They were just making sure Auracel didn't kill me.

Once we were in the privacy of Jacob's makeshift office, he took me by the upper arms and said, "Listen to me. You're safe. I've got your back. And wherever Kamal ended up, he's not here. Not now."

And the past is just the past. I took a few breaths to calm the impending freakout and told my memories I'd deal with them later. I didn't think they'd actually listen, mind you. But I knew how the movie ended, and the tall, skinny kid with the bad attitude does make it through to the credits. Besides, wherever Kamal was these days, he'd gone so far underground, it wasn't as if he'd pose any threat to me now.

Jacob dug back into his files with renewed vigor, but since I'd be no help in that arena, I set off for the break room to see if the coffee looked fresh—though to be honest, even if it had burned down to a syrup, I'd probably choke down a cup. It was before my arbitrary and useless cutoff point, after all, so I'd better take advantage of it. The break room was empty except for Gina, whose cheaters hung on a string of alarmingly pink plastic beads today.

"Is it true?" she asked dramatically. "Did you follow Reginald to the hospital?"

"I did." As I said so, I wondered exactly how much information I should give. I wasn't bound by doctor/client privilege, after all. But I'd also need to be sure not to leak anything sensitive about the investigation…all while making sure my contacts didn't get frustrated with me. But no pressure. "He woke up."

"Oh, thank God." Gina collapsed into an uncomfortable plastic chair. "I was worried sick about him. He's a real character, you know? Always joking around with the staff. He would make up songs about us and sing them. Right on the spot."

She was clearly hurting, so I said, "I can't really speak for him medically. But he seemed lucid."

"Thank God," she repeated. We sat together, gazing at the crumb-scattered table for a few seconds. And then Gina said, "Just when I thought the kinks with psychical meds were all worked out, something awful like this comes along. And now the clouds are gathering."

"Wait, what?"

Gina gave a nervous titter. "Ignore me—you know how it is, the mouth engages before the brain's in gear. Kick just has us all on edge."

CHAPTER 11

It's pretty morbid to think I was basically lingering around The Clinic waiting for someone to OD—but that's what it amounted to. Thankfully, or not, no one did. I gathered Jacob from his mass of paperwork and the two of us headed home. The sun was still out, if only for another half-hour, so I drove. I was in the general vicinity of LaSalle when I realized that while The Clinic hadn't seen any overdoses, that didn't mean we were in the clear.

When we visit the hospital, we get to use the staff parking—a perk of being a big shot federal agent. Also the reason we encountered Dr. Gillmore crouching behind the fender of a small silver Prius.

"Someone dinged my car," she said in disgust as we approached. There was a scuff of red paint on the back bumper. "If I call the cops, what would they do?"

"Take a report," I said. "Eventually. It's more of an insurance matter."

"This is why we can't have nice things. So, what can I do for you today?"

"Actually, we came to check on Reginald."

"Reginald is out of my hands." She must've seen the panic in my eyes, because she was quick to add, "We discharged him this morning. He went home."

Thank God.

"Speaking generally," I said, "why do you think it is that anyone would be eager to try another hit of Kick? I've experienced the sort of cramps you get from a psyactive, and they're brutal." I met Jacob's eyes. He nodded, remembering his own ride on the horse pills to the land of painful hamstrings. "Add the killer headache and the potential for dropping dead...I just don't get it."

Gillmore shook her head. "You're the psychic, not me. Why would you want to mess with your talent? Is more always better?"

"Not necessarily." While it would certainly be convenient to have 20/20 vision all the time where ghosts were concerned, I couldn't say I dug the sensation of my subtle bodies falling out. It was like putting on yesterday's pants, heading outside, and only then realizing you had a pair of used underwear dragging along at the hem. "But judging by what Reginald told me, he wasn't actually trying to increase his ability. It was more like an urge. You know—an itch you can't help but scratch."

Jacob said, "Is there some kind of test that can be run to explain what's going on? A scale of addictiveness?"

Gillmore shook her head. "Empirically? No. It's not like rating Scoville units, where they can pull the capsaicin out of a chili pepper and tell you how hot it is. Addiction is measured by the diagnosis of observed and self-reported behavioral symptoms."

Going by what Reginald told me, then...Kick was disturbingly addictive if he hated every minute he was on it and then immediately jonesed for more.

Three more patients had come through the LaSalle ER, unconscious, with blood pressure through the roof, while Jacob and I were at The Clinic that day. "And tremors," Gillmore added. "Every one of them had tremors."

"Like DTs?" I asked.

"No. Alcohol withdrawal—that's a shiver. What I saw in the ER today was more like..." she jerked her arm as if she'd just noticed a spider crawling across her hand. "More like a twitch."

"Maybe from the cramps," I ventured.

"Maybe? We need answers, Agent. I suggest you figure out what's going on before anyone else dies."

Yeah. That was the idea. "What I really need is to get a handle on people after their first or second dose. Not when they're at death's door. Is there any way to divert people like that to the psychic clinic in Lincolnwood?"

"It's not that simple. There are systems in place. But I'll try."

It was probably for the best that Gillmore was on her way home. That way she didn't have to watch Jacob commandeer the personal info on the three ODs so we could retrace their steps and try to figure out where they'd scored. From the passenger seat of the Crown Vic, he fed all the info to the Surveillance Department to get the team working on their timelines. Hooray for smartphones. And Surveillance Departments.

Meanwhile, I worked on getting us home. I was perfectly capable of driving at night...I just hated doing it. But I didn't want to sit around doing nothing while Jacob ironed things out with HQ, so I sucked down white light and turned down a less trafficked side street. It wasn't as brightly lit as the main drag, and it was peppered with stop signs, but I'd be less likely to be spooked by any repeaters.

A double-parked car had me regretting my decision until I spotted a nearby alley. Residential alleyways in Chicago all look pretty much the same...unless they're yours, in which case you tend to recognize the graffiti.

Somehow, I'd ended up by my old apartment again. Unless there were multiple spots in the city where really poor spellers had tagged a sagging garage with the epithet "fuker." Which might actually be the name of a metal band, if you threw in a random umlaut.

I stopped behind my old building and stared at it from the back. There was currently a light on in the apartment where I used to live. Were the walls still painted landlord white, or was whoever lived there now the ambitious sort of person who'd try to jazz up their apartment with things like artwork and paint?

As I was staring up at the lit window, faintly, I heard, "Hey, white boy. Where you been at?"

I rolled down the window—in retrospect, this made zero sense, I know—and said, "The answer to a blowjob is still no."

Jacob's head snapped up at that. Lucky for me he'd been texting HQ and not calling.

"All right, I feel you. You got that big fine man and all. Mmm hm—he sure is tasty. I was just being friendly cause we neighbors and all. No crime to be friendly, is it?"

"Hold on...you recognize me now?"

"I wasn't sure without that ugly car of yours till I got up close and seen it was you. But, yeah. Why wouldn't I?"

Because the other night she'd taken me for a stranger trolling for a twenty-dollar whore. Judging by her tone of voice, though, she'd be insulted if I pressed the matter. "Say, Jackie...I was wondering if you heard anything about a drug called Kick."

"You mean Special K?"

Why was everybody so keen on Special K lately? "No, that's a horse tranquilizer. Kick is more like...acid."

"Never heard of it. You wanna get high, how 'bout some

Mary Jane?" She proceeded to name a good two dozen pot dealers, even though I insisted I wasn't in the market for weed. Guess she was just worried about me going home empty-handed.

She promised to keep an eye out for Kick, we said our goodbyes, and I pulled out of the alley. I was well aware that Jacob was watching me…but it was full dark now, and I was more worried about misreading a spectral car crash repeater. Eventually he said, "That sounded pretty congenial."

"It was."

"But the other night, you told me she was hardly more helpful than a repeater."

I'd called her a few more choice words afterwards, too, as I ranted to Jacob over dinner. We turned on to our street, which peters out into a scrap of unused land surrounded by a chain link fence, and I caught a glimpse of the moon between a gap in the trees. It was a partial moon. Waxing or waning? I wasn't sure. But maybe its phase had something to do with it. Astrology, astronomy…. How should I know what it was that made the dead act the way they did?

As we lay in bed that night—Jacob snoring, me staring at the ceiling—my thoughts kept circling back to something Jennifer Chance told me once, after she killed herself. That everything felt foggy and strange, and she was a slave to her urges and compulsions.

Hell, I could say that for the majority of my thirties. In fact, even now that I'd crossed the big 4-0…I was still struggling with the yen I thought I'd left behind ages ago.

I'd be lying to myself if I pretended sleep was in my immediate future. I was so keyed up I'd been jiggling my foot beneath the covers. Good thing Jacob sleeps like a sedated log. Otherwise he'd ride me about the twitching blanket, for sure.

Thinking about ghosts was clearly not lulling me to sleep—

not that it ever did—so I figured I'd try some reading. There was always more research waiting for me than I could ever hope to digest, and it periodically left me nodding off in the recliner. That tactic lasted maybe ten minutes. After which I discovered that not only did I have no clue whatsoever about a passage I'd just read a half-dozen times, but that I'd violated my no-screens-in-bed rule, and was now more wide awake than ever.

And also, that my foot-jiggling had intensified to the point that Jacob actually grumbled and rolled away from me.

If I couldn't read away my restlessness, I reasoned, maybe I could walk it off. I deepened the furrow in the cheap hallway runner for a few minutes, but that was useless. Plus there was a loud squeak right by the bedroom door I couldn't seem to step over or around. I did a few laps around the living room and even considered hitting the home gym. But even though I knew the cannery's basement wasn't haunted, I still got the heebie-jeebies when I thought about being down there alone at midnight.

I pulled on yesterday's pants and my slightly beery winter coat. Not because I thought a drive would be relaxing. Just that it seemed better than waking up Jacob and having us both be useless come morning. The roads were empty. I meandered through the neighborhood and wound up at the drug store, in search of some over-the-counter solution to my insomnia. But when I got to the door, it didn't magically whisk open for me. I checked the hours. It closed at ten.

I could've sworn the joint was open twenty-four hours…but that would explain the dim lighting and mostly-empty parking lot—and what those other cars were doing there, I couldn't even begin to guess. But as I turned away from the door, I experienced a twinge of something that felt suspiciously like relief.

I opted not to analyze it too closely, since I was obviously overtired and stressed.

Before I knew it, I was parked outside the dive bar. I wanted to believe I was hoping to shake down more information about Kick...but I knew damn well it was that yen for Seconal at the helm. My guy wasn't even holding. I knew that...and apparently, it didn't matter. Being inside that bar—the sights, the sounds, and particularly the smells—had woken a disturbingly familiar urge in me that I'd figured was long dead.

But what if it had only been buried?

Well, shit.

CHAPTER 12

I KICKED UP SOME gravel peeling out of the gin mill parking lot. I told myself I'd rather sit awake all night than wind up hooked on Reds again. And I ignored the fact that if I thought I actually could score, I might not've been able to resist walking through the doors of that goddamn bar.

On the way back to the cannery, I passed my old apartment building again. I pulled over in front of a fire hydrant I'd blocked on numerous occasions, itched absently at the side of my neck, and stared into the courtyard. This wasn't my life anymore, I reminded myself. I didn't get a faceful of murders every day, come home to a shitty apartment and drug myself to sleep. Not anymore.

And yet, the routine felt not only familiar...but comfortable.

I'm sure the notion of comfort was nothing more than an illusion. Not only did that life suck—I couldn't go back. The apartment had a new resident. The Fifth had a new PsyCop. And my dealer had no Seconal.

Unless my recent visit had prompted him to procure a few pills. Just in case I changed my mind.

I was gazing up at my old window when I heard Jackie calling me. "Hey! White boy!"

I rolled down the window. Again, despite the fact that there were no actual sound waves traveling through glass. I was eager to talk to her. Everyone was buzzing about Kick lately. Maybe she'd have a lead for me. A name. Something important for me to research that would put me to sleep. "Any news?" I asked.

"Sure, baby. Here's the headline: twenty dollar'll get you some real fine pussy."

I did a double-take—which was useless, since I couldn't see her—and said, "It's me. Vic." Actually, I wasn't so sure she'd ever registered my name. "Remember? Just a few hours ago, you said you'd find out about Kick for me."

"Kick, huh? The rough stuff cost extra—"

"Jackie, damn it. It's me." I sucked down white light, thinking that if I could just see her, meet her ghostly eyes and make some kind of connection, I could pull her out of that ugly rut she was in. I leaned out the window so the streetlight shone on my face and said, "Come on, it's not like I'm that easy to forget."

"What do you care? There's no return customer discount. Whatchoo think, I got a punch-card—buy nine pussy, get the tenth one free?"

I was sorely tempted to send her and her vagina packing to the other side for good. In fact, if I had my sacred salt on me, I might have flung a handful in her general direction. I'd left my salt back at the cannery, though. I was running on fumes, and whatever white light I pulled down was leaking right back out. In the end, I thought better of sitting there arguing with a dead hooker while my reserves were running low. If she took it in her mind to do more than just proposition me, I could very well wake up to find myself splayed on a stained mattress somewhere with a compromised virtue, a pocket full of twenties, and no memory of how I'd gotten there.

I skedaddled back home, closed the cannery door behind me, and leaned back against its solidity. Even though it was nearly a month since the cannery was psychically fumigated, our constant bolstering of the vibe had a cumulative effect. I felt calmer, mostly.

Except for the nagging thought that a certain red pill would really augment that calm feeling in the best possible way.

Eventually, Jacob got up to pee and realized I wasn't in bed beside him. He found me parked at the dining room table, basking in the lambent glow of research on my laptop. "Are you up really early…or really late?"

I glanced at the time in the corner of the screen. Nearly four. Ugh. "What do you suppose makes people crave things?" I asked him. "Is it neurotransmitters? Dopamine?"

"To some extent."

"Then why are there dead junkies out there jonesing for their next hit? What is it that keeps pulling Jackie back to her favorite street corner even after her brain and its reward centers are long gone?" And why was I wanting Seconal—to the point of distraction—long after the physical addiction was old history?

Jacob was too groggy for any kind of theoretical debate. He coaxed me back to bed and folded himself around me…and even though I would've thought I'd have a hard time nodding off that way, given my mental state and the fact that his forearm was seriously impeding my diaphragm, eventually I did drift off.

Two hours' sleep was not nearly enough.

Since I was clearly out of it, Jacob shoved a travel mug of strong coffee into my hands, piled me into the car, readjusted all the mirrors, and drove us to The Clinic. He nearly ended up wearing that mug of coffee when I plowed into the back of him at the entrance.

"New policy," the guy at the desk—Troy?—told us. "Dr. Bertelli wants everyone to sign in now."

He pushed a clipboard through the slot in the window where he normally handed over my drugs, but thankfully spared us a recap of last night's *Clairvoyage* marathon. Jacob signed and dated. I scrawled my name underneath. Under "Purpose of Visit," he'd written *INVESTIGATION* in neat block letters. I put a pair of tic marks below it to indicate the same. It was all I could do to stop myself from jotting down, *What the hell do you think I'm here for?*

Barely nine and I already needed a nap.

I slid back the sign-in sheet. Instead of buzzing the door open, Troy produced two more clipboards and pushed them through. "Liability waivers," he said.

I squinted. The print was ridiculously small. And the urge to nod off at the mere sight of it was profound.

"We're here on an official FPMP investigation," Jacob said. "We're not signing anything."

"Sorry—I'm just the messenger."

Short of breaking down the door, the only thing to do was check in with HQ and see how they wanted us to proceed. Jacob took a snapshot of the documents and sent them to Laura. We cooled our heels in the waiting room while she ran it all through the legal department, and eventually came back with instructions to sign. We headed to the empty conference room commandeered by Jacob and his research. Carolyn and Zigler joined us a little while later. "What's with the new hoops we've gotta jump through?" Zig wondered.

"Maybe Bertelli's hiding something," Jacob said. "Or maybe he's just being cautious. Either way, let's make the most of our time here in case he somehow manages to get us all blocked from The Clinic."

Zigler said, "Maybe someone here has connected a few dots now that they've had time to sleep on it."

Jacob agreed. "We'll split up and re-canvas the staff."

The mood in the trenches was understandably subdued. A group of clinicians who normally dealt with things like routine bloodwork and Auracel-induced nausea had a death on their hands. Counting the folks who'd died at LaSalle, more than one. These weren't just random deaths, either, but patients they knew by name and had seen on a regular basis, many of them for years. There was no easy banter at The Clinic now, no homemade peanut butter cookies in the break room. Everyone was grim. And focused. And scared.

Everyone has their own way of coping with trauma. Some folks get loud and panicky and start yelling at their coworkers. Some make completely inappropriate jokes that piss everyone off. Some fall back on their training, function like a well-oiled machine, then go home and cry into a couch cushion.

Some tell you what they watched on TV last night.

Troy Malone—The Assassin's front desk replacement— had a front row seat to a drama way more intense than any primetime show. No doubt he was in his glory. "Say, listen," I said. "I wonder if you've got time for a few questions."

"Absolutely. Maybe some detail I saw could be the key to the whole investigation. Like on *Cold Case: PsyCop Edition*, when that clairvoyant detective has the crazy dreams, the ones where they do those closeup shots of a random jumble of stuff, and then his Stiff weaves them all together to figure out what happened—"

"Sure. Like that." I did my best to steer the conversation away from basic cable's latest, greatest Psych drama and toward something I might actually use. Because I couldn't discount the fact that this guy had access to all the medications of the psychic population of the greater Chicagoland area. If anyone was in a good position to skim psychic pharmaceuticals, it was him.

Except there were no psyactives being distributed, not anymore. Just Auracel and Neurozamine—antipsyactives. "Actually," Troy said, "you've got a scrip ready. If you want it."

"Might as well, while I'm here. So, how many prescriptions would you say you hand out on any given day?"

"Well, it's heavier after the first and the fifteenth—that's payday for a lot of people, and copays can run pretty high. On an average day, maybe ten or twelve. Mostly right after we open or right before close. Or lunch hour. Lunch can get pretty busy, so I have to take my break late, after one. I eat a protein bar at ten so I don't get lightheaded. Which reminds me—did you see the *Dr. Precog* episode where the new lab assistant diagnosed a type-1 diabetic with nothing but a candy bar wrapper?"

"Probably not—I'll have to catch it sometime." Right after I finished detailing the mildewed grout in my downstairs bathroom with a toothbrush. "Thanks."

I tossed my bag in the recycle and pocketed the amber plastic bottle inside, thanked Troy for his time, and headed down to the pharmacy to see how long it had been since any of The Clinic's patients received a psyactive in their pill bottle—because maybe I could blame the whole thing on Patrick. Though the FPMP had his prints on file, so probably not. Erin was busy pushing little pills around a scale with a rounded metal spatula. She reassured me that no psyactives were currently being prescribed, and any clinical trials had been well before her time.

Did she seem nervous? Yes. But lots of people got flustered around investigators for no good reason at all. Plus, she'd passed Carolyn's innate lie detector test. I was about to go on a little fishing expedition anyway when the announcement system startled us both with a beep. "Code Blue! Repeat, Code Blue!"

CHAPTER 13

When I turned on my heel to high-tail it upstairs, Erin chose that particular moment to let her true feelings be known.

"Where do you think you're going?" she called out over the urgent 'Code Blue' announcement. "Are you a medical professional? Were you going to scrub in? Christ, all you FPMP assholes swaggering around like you own the place—how will you feel when someone *dies* because you got in the way of their actual medical treatment?"

Wow. Now, *that* was something to unpack later. But not until I got a look at the latest emergency.

The pharmacy was tucked well away in the most secure corner of the basement, and I'm not exactly quick on my feet. I jogged to the stairwell and up a flight of grated metal stairs, already winded. I was just swinging around the midpoint landing when I saw him.

It was just a flicker at first. A trick of the light. And me, running up that metal staircase with so much visual information it was hard to tell what was what...until I ended up skidding to a halt on the landing as something stepped through the door.

And not by opening it first, either. A flicker. A jerk. And I realized, with a sinking feeling, I recognized the guy. Reginald had found another hit of Kick. He was back at The Clinic. And I'm guessing if he was transferred to LaSalle this time, it wouldn't be to the intensive care unit, but the morgue.

"Reginald!" I said—without realizing that, hey, my white light level was practically nil. Blame it on distraction, blame it on lack of sleep. It was a dumb move. And as the flickering ghost of the dead Psych locked eyes with me, I realized just how dumb it was.

White light. I pulled, but the connection felt sloppy and ragged. My physical senses aren't the only ones that suffer when I'm running on fumes. But one thing I can say for fear—it'll wake you up. Fast. As the ghost turned and walked toward me, step by flickering step, I felt my white balloon strengthen as I pumped all my energy into my protective shield. "Reginald, what can you tell me about the Kick? Where'd you get it? Who'd you get it from?"

Reginald was halfway to the landing now, close enough for me to get a good look at his face between flickers. But the expression was enough to chill me to the bone. His eyes were wide, pained...but almost unseeing. And it wasn't just the fact that he was coming toward me that spooked me, but the way he was moving. All wrong. As if an apprentice puppeteer was running the show—and they were woefully unrehearsed. I scrambled down the stairs backwards and somehow managed not to land in a heap at the bottom. Reginald's ghost kept right on coming.

My hand reached toward my weapon, brushed the shape of the holster, then delved into the pocket where I kept my sacred salt. No time to fiddle open the baggie. I bit into it, tore the plastic with my teeth. Salt sprayed everywhere. I spat. It was edible, right? Probably. And it wouldn't much matter if I found myself possessed.

Whatever salt hadn't spilled down the front of me, I dumped into my palm and diverted a stream of white light toward it. "Reginald—c'mon, man, don't let what happened to you be for nothing. Tell me—where'd you get the Kick?"

But Reginald wasn't home. He just kept lumbering toward me with an expression that kept flickering between wide-eyed pain and a thousand-yard stare.

I backed into the fire door at the foot of the stairwell and said, "Reginald Green—you're dead. Got it? You're dead. So you might as well tell me—Jesus Christ." I flung the salt. No doubt, the security camera in the corner would just show a tall, skinny, out-of-breath guy throwing a handful of salt at nothing. But to my inner eye, at least, the salt picked up the white light I was grappling with like a giant cloud of heavy metal pouring from a smoke machine at a Füker concert. And then it parted to reveal Reginald's ghost. His face was twisted in a rictus of agony and he twitched like he was struggling against an invisible net. The sight of it only added fuel to my fire—the certainty that he was coming for me, and if he forced himself under my skin I was utterly screwed—which must've activated my emergency switch.

Something shifted inside me and the white light thundered down. The whole stairwell lit up to my second sight as I channeled the white light down from the heavens, in through my third eye, and out in a defensive wall of *don't-you-dare-even-try-it*. The white light rolled through the stairwell like a shockwave. Reginald lit up like he was surrounded by etheric clouds. He wasn't shoved toward the veil, like the other ghosts I've exorcised. It was more like he came apart. It was fast—split-second fast—but hunks of him flew upward, leaving a smoky shell of a ghost body that collapsed in on itself, and was gone.

I stood there for several rapid heartbeats while my pulse thundered in my ears, watching the whiteness sparkle and fade. Was I alone? I thought so. I *hoped* so. Gradually, while the sound of my own heartbeat was replaced by a digital ringing sound, I was vaguely aware that the "Code Blue" had stopped. I turned around, sat on the stairs, and dropped my head between my knees. It gave off a sick throb, the type of startling, intense headache I only experience when I flex my psychic muscles way too hard.

Was my telltale knife of pain in the same region of the cortex that psyactives were designed to tickle?

My phone was ringing. Had been for a while now. I focused on deep, steadying breaths as I tried not to freak over the thought of rupturing something important *in my brain.*

How crazy would it be if, after everything I'd done over the course of my life—all the murderers I'd inconvenienced, all the dubious pills I'd swallowed, all the ghosts I'd underestimated—the thing that ultimately killed me was the act of trying too hard?

Up on the main floor, a door opened. Jacob called, "Vic?"

"Down here," I answered to my knees.

The metal stairs vibrated as he hurried down to where I sat. He paused, took me in, and said, "You already know what just happened, don't you?"

"How'd you guess?"

"You're covered in salt."

I raised my head gingerly. Jacob was scoping out the area—not that he'd actually see any ghosts, even if one happened to linger behind. He's all about due diligence, though, so it doesn't stop him from checking. "Are you okay?"

"Peachy." I gave the back of my neck a good squeeze to try and alleviate the throbbing in my skull. It didn't help.

"Vic...look at me."

I glanced up. "Maybe I should go home and grab a quick nap."

Jacob looked the way he looks when he's really concerned about something but trying to come off as casual. "Maybe you should see someone."

"I just overdid it, that's all. Once I've had some sleep—"

"There's a burst blood vessel in your left eye."

Oh hell. I didn't like the sound of that.

Luckily, we just so happened to be inside a highly specialized medical facility created specifically for Psychs. Against Jacob's wishes, I headed up to the top of the stairs on my own volition—yeah, I felt like shit, but I could still walk. The team was all clustered in the emergency bay with Reginald's body, but when Jacob grabbed a doctor and pointed me out, someone announced, "Code yellow!" and I found my ass in a wheelchair cruising down the hall, *stat*. I wasn't necessarily keen on all my new "friends" knowing I'd just seen a ghost, particularly the ghost of one of their favorite patients, but given that they knew my whole medical and psychic history, there was really no way to hedge.

Most people need to go to big hospitals or specialized imaging centers to get MRIs, but The Clinic had their very own claustrophobia tubes. I was no stranger to the procedure. In Camp Hell, we used to joke that they scanned our brains every time we took a dump. I'm not actually afraid of enclosed spaces, and it's never bothered me to lie there and listen to some music while the magnets did their thing, just as long as I got to pick the album.

I knew the rigmarole. If I'd had a piercing—or a wedding band—I would've needed to remove it. I knew better than to remark on that to Jacob just now. I went behind the curtain, changed into the scrubs they gave me, shoved my feet into the paper slippers, and let the orderlies help me over to the tube.

The doctor in charge of my "code yellow" was an older woman, kind of stern and not really one for break room gossip, but her air of competence was encouraging. As they IV'd contrast dye into my arm, she explained it was critical to do the functional MRI as soon after my "psychic event" as possible, so as to map the effect of increased psychic stressors on my brain.

I'm familiar with the tube—and I'm familiar with all the braces and harnesses that're meant to "help" you hold still. I gave them a hard pass. What if another Psych bit the dust while I was strapped into a machine?

I was pretty emphatic about my refusal. Let's just say if that particular doctor were to bring in some banana bread tomorrow, it's unlikely I'd be offered a slice.

There wouldn't be much of a view with me lying flat on my back in a magnetic tube, but I didn't take the eye mask they offered me. Not with the potential of another "psychic event" happening while I was in the machine. I'd accepted the headphones, though, but only so the folks in the control room could talk to me. I followed all the instructions as the machine powered up, and soon enough, they were feeding me into the singing, pinging tube. What I didn't expect was Jacob's voice to follow.

"Everything's going to be okay," he told me reasonably. "Are you comfortable?"

"I'm fine."

"If you're feeling sweaty, they can up the AC."

For a change, no, I wasn't sweating. "Jacob, I'm fine."

"I'm right here. And everyone on the team is a top expert in their field. You're in good hands."

"Yeah, I know."

"Agent Marks?" said the doctor in the background. "We can't start the scan until Agent Bayne stops talking. His head needs to be completely still."

"I can stay here. Talk you through it."

Jacob may have been acting calm, but I knew it was just a front. "It's okay," I told him as reassuringly as I could. "Seriously. This isn't my first magnetic rodeo—and if you really want to help me, you'll go to the break room and commandeer the salt shaker."

"Got it." I think Jacob was relieved to have something to do. "And, Vic...."

"I'll see you in a few," I said, before he embarrassed himself by getting all choked up. "Just...whatever you do, don't forget the salt."

I'd elicited promises that they'd inform me immediately if any "Code Blues" came in while I was tubing. Even so, as the scanning commenced, I narrowed my eyes to the smallest slits, as close as they could be to "closed" while still letting me keep an eye out for a potential ghostly hijacker. I performed admirably well, I thought. Though it did occur to me that most people who couldn't handle the restraints would've at least been offered a sedative. Not that I wanted one. I just thought I should've had the option to refuse.

Scratch that. I did want one. But I wanted it curled up in my bed in my favorite sweatpants and an old T-shirt, not laying on a plastic slab in too-short scrubs and a pair of paper slippers.

By the time the scan was finally done, the urge to move around was excruciating, particularly my hands and feet, and my neck itched like crazy. I shuddered as they pulled me from the tube. Was this what it felt like when susceptible folks watched those whispery paper-folding videos? Unlikely. I could hardly see anyone going out of their way to experience the wiggle-willies. Not on purpose.

I'm told regular people need to wait for their test results. I had the top psychic brain expert in the Midwest watching as the images unfolded. By the time I was dressed, the medical team was ready to give me their verdict.

The brain guy was about my age—way too young to be a doctor, if you ask me—and his people-skills were negligible. But The Clinic didn't keep him around to be anyone's buddy.

"Bayne, Victor," he announced as I took a seat in the consultation room. "What a rare opportunity to record the vascular changes in a level-5 mediumship subject so soon after an extrasensory event. So. Let's have a look." He called up a slide. Yep. Looked like a brain to me. "There was significant activation involving the right parahippocampal gyrus, as you'd expect."

Sure. Totally.

"Under the influence of all known pharmacological psyactives, the left inferior frontal gyrus would also be affected. But in this case, activation of that region was within normal range."

"I'm not on psyactives."

The brain doctor clicked forward a few frames and began pointing out another indecipherable blob on the screen. "Now, if you take a look at the hippocampus—"

"Hold on. Did you *think* I was on psyactives?"

"I don't postulate until I see the empirical evidence," he said with some annoyance.

He totally thought I was on psyactives. Specifically, on Kick.

The world's brainiest slideshow played as he droned on about this or that structure with a bunch of terminology that meant absolutely nothing to me. Meanwhile, I fumed over the notion that he'd seriously thought I was under the influence of the very drug I was trying to stop from killing anyone else.

As much as I get annoyed with airy-fairy New Age types with their utterly groundless magical thinking, I find they're right just as often as the scientists and doctors with their bone-dry terminology and data. The fact that I was utterly lost didn't register. He was scowling at the pictures of my headmeats when I prompted him with the question, "What about my eye? Is it okay?"

It took the brain guy a few startled blinks to switch gears. "The subconjunctival hemorrhage was due to a small, temporary spike in blood pressure."

"That sounds bad."

"Nothing to worry about. The bleeds can be caused by something as unremarkable as straining to move your bowels."

Great. Yet another distracting mental image to subdue the next time I faced off with a ghost.

CHAPTER 14

I WAS PERFECTLY FINE to press on, but the team at The Clinic insisted I call it quits for the night. In fact, they strongly suggested I take the next day off too while I was at it. But, let's get real. Unless I was suffering from something more than a funky eyeball, that wasn't gonna happen.

Before they let me go, Erin met me in the consult room with a white paper bag containing several amber plastic pill bottles. She seemed sheepish, and vaguely, I remembered her telling me off before the whole code rainbow fiasco went down. She went through a whole raft of meds with me. Lubricating drops for my big red eye. Mild beta blockers to keep my blood pressure normal. Even pain meds for my head, though the headache had long ago subsided to a dull throb. I was tempted to ask for something to help me sleep—*that's what my doctors were there for, weren't they? To help me*—but if I had to endure another lecture on quitting caffeine entirely, it would cause another blood pressure spike for sure.

"Do you have any questions?" she asked, like she'd rather be talking to anyone but me.

"Don't worry," I told her. "I didn't end up in the MRI tube

because you were yelling at me. Believe it or not, I'm used to that kind of thing."

She cringed. "I was out of line. I know someone's gotta keep an eye out for all our patients. But the FPMP can just be so...." She trailed off and shrugged, but she really didn't need to explain herself. I knew what she meant. And I had no great fondness for spies myself.

Jacob knocked off early too—with Laura Kim's blessing, since she was highly invested in making sure nothing put her star medium out of commission for good.

When Jacob drove us home, there was no disguising the fact that he was incredibly freaking worried. He held onto the steering wheel with the grip of death, and asked me at least a half dozen variations of, "Are you okay? Do you need anything?" before we even hit the first traffic light.

"I just need to lie down," I said. "I'll be fine." As long as I didn't push myself, anyhow. I half suspected the comment about straining on the can was a subconscious attempt on the brain doctor's part to make a dig. I'd been challenging him, and rock stars in their respective fields don't like being challenged. And yet, there was a ring of truth to what he was saying. When I popped my eyeball's blood vessel, I really had been straining. But not in any effort to void my bowels.

If trying too hard meant stroking out, worst case scenario, then I'd need to dial it back. But what else was I supposed to do when a fresh ghost came shambling directly toward me?

A text landed in as we pulled up in front of the cannery. Crash. *What time do you want your smudging?*

I showed it to Jacob. He said, "It's that time already?"

"Must be getting use to the smell, if the lack thereof isn't noticeable anymore."

"We should take a rain check. You really need to take it easy tonight."

Can't say I actually did much of anything while Crash and Red re-stinkified my house. "No, it's fine." I gave my white paper bag a wave. "If my headache gets any worse, they gave me pills for that."

Since we were home early, our friends opted to head right over. It still seemed weird to see Crash during business hours, but apparently the day-to-day workings of their store could now happen without them being physically present.

It was also weird how fast they could get here when they didn't have to rely on the Damen Avenue bus. Before I'd even settled my new amber bottles among all the other ones in our medicine cabinet, they were knocking on the door. I wasn't entirely sure I was fit for company, but at least they knew enough not to ring the doorbell. That thing could wake the dead.

Crash was looking unabashedly outrageous in a long army duster no one had any business wearing outside a World War II action film, but Red was twice as striking in a black vinyl biker jacket painted top to bottom in rainbow colored mandalas. Red hung his coat on a peg. Crash threw his duster on the floor. "So," Crash said. "I'll bite. Why are you two home so early?"

"I got sent home from the nurse's office." I pointed out my eye and Crash gave a low whistle, then proceeded to grill me until I told them all about the blood pressure and the MRI. I summed up the whole thing with, "No straining allowed. So don't provoke me."

"Me? I'm the picture of innocence. But is the smoke gonna bother you?"

Maybe. But a herky-jerky ghost sneaking into my house while I slept would bother me a hell of a lot more. "I can handle a little smoke. Besides, that's what fans are for."

They carried their exorcism gear in a bedazzled knapsack

that looked like it should be holding glow sticks, a fifth of vodka, and a few hits of whatever the cool kids were snorting, smoking or swallowing these days. "Say, have you guys heard anything more about Kick?"

"Just some rumblings about whether or not some anti-Psych hate group developed it to cull the city's population of empaths and telepaths." Crash was about to shove aside the papers on the dining room table to dump his gear in its usual place, but when he realized it was more than just the typical barrage of junk mail, he swung the bag onto a chair instead. "Hey, now. Is this extra-super top-secret spy stuff I shouldn't be looking at?" Most people, at that point, might back away. He bent over the table and peered more closely.

I didn't stop him—I was still digesting that hate group thing he'd said in passing—but Crash said a lot of things in passing, and he didn't really mean the majority of them. Red, however, adhered way more strictly to the Right Speech tenet of the Eightfold Path, and he didn't utter a word unless he damn well meant it. I turned to him instead. "Do you really think this is some kind of targeted attack on Psychs?"

"I suppose it's a possibility—but would it make sense to target the drug population in general if what you're really after is the few with abilities?"

Maybe not. Unless the drug population in general contained a higher proportion of Psychs trying to erase a bunch of baffling extrasensory junk that only caused them distress.

Jacob made his go-to Crash and Red dinner—pasta with veggie sauce, grated cheese on the side. Mere vegetarianism wasn't strict enough for Red, and apparently vegans can't eat much of anything, but we could all get behind a big mass of rotini. It's always been weird to imagine Jacob dating Crash, but now that Red was in the picture, maybe I could see it. We all have our types, and maybe Crash thrived best against a backdrop of self-righteousness.

While Jacob worked in the kitchen, our guests systematically blessed every square inch of the cannery. I usually stayed out of their hair by shifting to different parts of the house while they chanted and smudged, but tonight it seemed like more effort than I was willing to put out. Instead, I planted myself in the big recliner, fully intending to catch up with all the reading HQ kept dumping into my inbox. But the guys were pretty distracting.

I looked on as they moved through my place. Once you dug down past the superficial stuff—the ballsy hair, the in-your-face fashion sense—they were total opposites. But together, they were less like oil and water and more like yin and yang…or maybe that was just the impression I got from all of Red's punk-meets-boho jewelry and tattoos. Crash forged ahead, following his gut. Red hung back, guided by his mind. Between the two of them, no corner of the cannery was left unsmoked.

They finished just as the boiling pasta hit the strainer, right on time for an early dinner. I pulled a couple of chairs into the living room so we could eat around the coffee table without disturbing our notes. Crash moved a wedding ring catalog out of his way. I was beyond relieved he'd been in a relationship himself, back when we dropped our engagement bombshell—but even so, he still treated me to a catty smirk as he dumped the stack of glossy paper unceremoniously on the floor.

"Have you two given any more thought to the yoga?" I asked, hoping to stave off any prickly questions about our wedding. "I'm probably unteachable."

Red joined us from the kitchen with flatware in one hand and a handful of paper napkins in the other. "Of course, you're teachable. You'll need to be willing to learn—and to be gentle with yourself if results don't happen overnight."

Jacob set plates heaping with pasta in front of our guests, then fetched ours. Crash dumped half the can of parmesan on top of his mound, and stirred until the red sauce went stringy and pink. "For most people, 'yoga success' might be a sturdier headstand—or, if they're being real about it, firmer buns. But riddle me this, Mr. F-Pimp. What exactly are you hoping to achieve?"

"Well, it's obvious," I said. But judging by the way the other three were staring at me, maybe it wasn't. "I want to be stronger."

That answer wasn't good enough for Crash. "But how so? Take today, for instance. You saw a freaking ghost, literally saw it. You exploded it with white light when it got too close for comfort. What more do you want?"

"I have no idea—but maybe if I'd been more on my game, I could've convinced him to tell me where he got the Kick."

Red considered his own ability. "A telepath picks up on what's already there. We can't plant thoughts in other people's minds. Maybe that's all anyone can hope to do. And maybe that's for the best."

I decided not to mention that I knew an empath who could make people shit themselves. That would only muddy the waters.

Once we finished our food and I suggested we get going on the yoga portion of the evening, Red said, "I only practice asanas on an empty stomach." Oh, sure, now he tells me. "But even if we hadn't just eaten, I wouldn't guide you through any poses tonight. I'm no psychic neurologist, but if you've got a severe headache and your blood pressure is up, I can't in any good conscience encourage you to hold your head below your heart. What I can do is show you some techniques to make you more aware of your breath."

Why did New Agey types have to be so insufferable?

"Maybe next time. I'm done for the day—I'm just gonna go lie down."

And I was sure to swing by my medicine cabinet first.

CHAPTER 15

Jacob never throws pills away. We have four types of antacid. We have antibiotics that expired before we moved in together. We have cold remedies out the yin-yang. We have a multivitamin that revisits my taste buds every time I burp.

And then there's my prescriptions.

The pain meds I was set up with by The Clinic weren't half bad. Mostly Tylenol, but laced with enough opioids to knock me out good. I slept so soundly that I didn't wake up until Jacob gave me a shove that rolled me onto my face. "What?" I said into my pillow.

"Quit elbowing me."

"Well, you're no fun." I pried an eye open and noted it was almost light out, then checked the time. I couldn't even recall the last time I'd slept past six o'clock—and I'd turned in early, too. I shoved myself into a sitting position and tried to think past the brain fog. Was this what well-rested was supposed to feel like? Maybe my body just didn't know what to make of a full night's sleep. Plus, my arm was numb, the shoulder I'd been lying on hurt, my legs felt antsy, and I had a wicked kink in my neck.

And yet, beneath all that, the bone-deep satisfaction I felt from being unconscious for eight-plus hours was impossible to deny.

A blast from the shower cleared the sleep fog from my brain—the gray matter I'd so recently viewed. How anyone ever mapped the regions to their various functions, I'll never know. Or maybe I just preferred not to think too hard about it, given that bone saws and electrodes were probably involved. How close had I come to being vivisected, back in Camp Hell? I hadn't actually heard of it happening to any of us...but I wouldn't have put it past the regime in charge, either.

Especially with Dr. Kamal on the team.

I waited for a useful memory to emerge, something that would aid our investigation, but got only a queasy sense of something lurking just beyond my current awareness. Anxiety spiked. Probably blood pressure, too. I was supposed to take the beta blockers soon. But it seemed more logical to treat the cause than the symptom, though...didn't it?

And what if the beta blocker stopped my blood from rushing to the part of my brain that kept dead people out of my body?

Jacob was powering through some evil breakfast shake in the kitchen when I went to grab my coffee. I said, "There's something I want to check before I head over to The Clinic. Can you grab a ride with Carolyn and Zig?"

"Sure," he said...by which he meant *I'll call an Uber*, but I didn't think it was worth mentioning.

I pulled up at LaSalle General beside Dr. Gillmore's scuffed silver Prius and waited. Lucky for me, by the time my morning briefings were read and I could see the bottom of my travel mug, she finished up her night shift and was heading toward her car. I expected her to look annoyed with me for stalking her, but she didn't. She just seemed incredibly tired.

I rounded the Crown Vic while she leaned against the car and crossed her arms. "We lost another one to Kick last night," she said wearily. "Telepath level two. No known substance abuse issues. According to her records, she wasn't even a social drinker."

"I'm sorry," I said reflexively, and then added, "It can't be easy."

She beeped open her car and motioned for me to join her. The inside felt cramped compared to the expansiveness of Jacob's gas-guzzler. With the press of a button, she started the ignition, then cranked the heater all the way up. The engine died. Gillmore didn't seem particularly alarmed.

"Is that normal?"

"Yeah, it's a hybrid thing. Took some getting used to, though. My last car stalled out at traffic lights, which felt pretty much the same as this engine switching from gas to battery power." She fiddled with the blower settings. I waited until she was ready. After a few seconds, she figured out how to broach the topic she was wanting to talk about. "You asked me whether addiction could be measured. You'd think so, wouldn't you? But since you showed me how useless that psychic evaluation was, I've been digging into the reading. Lots of folks believe we're made up of more than just the physical body."

"Subtle bodies," I said, more or less to myself.

"You're familiar with the theory, then."

"You could say that."

"No way to measure, quantify or record an etheric form."

Unless you can actually see them. "They're real, all right."

"Not surprising. Now, what if illness exists in more than one plane, across multiple bodies? Maybe you can treat the physical body with drugs. But what about the etheric body?"

Not to mention the astral...and whatever else was tucked

inside everyone like a ghostly set of Russian dolls.

Gillmore looked at me meaningfully. "What if addiction is more than just mental and physical?"

I shivered, and not entirely from the cold—seriously, her "hybrid" took forever to warm up.

My lack of response gave her the impression I needed more convincing. "It would explain faith healing. Positive thinking. Law of Attraction."

It would explain habit demons, too.

Everybody asking me lately why I might want to strengthen my ability—here was a prime example. Those creepy etheric barnacles were really freaking hard to see. Con Dreyfuss had a whole school of them tethered to his ragged fingernails, and I didn't even know it until a GhosTV shed light on them. I shivered again, so hard that Gillmore turned up the ineffective heat another few degrees.

Dreyfuss must've been exposed to all kinds of freaky psychic shit in his line of work. Not to mention the fact that he had talent. "Your homeless woman," I said carefully. "The one you won't let me follow up on...."

"You think her alcohol addiction's more than physical."

"It's...a theory."

Gillmore scowled at her heater vent. "I don't doubt you're sincere. But I made an oath to give all my patients the dignity they deserve. Whether or not they have a traditional home and job and health insurance. Whether or not they're struggling with addiction."

"But what if I could help them with that struggle?"

She held up a hand. "I'll track her down and try again to get her to reach out. And I'll pray she does."

I supposed that was the best I could do—at least for now. If that didn't pan out, I'd have to keep wearing Gillmore down. "Listen, I know you're not technically on the clock, but...." I gave her a rundown of my adventures in magnetic tubes yesterday and then listed my new medication. "Is it possible that it's all a matter of how much blood is getting shoved into the psychic part of my brain? And if that's the case, will a beta blocker leave me standing around with my thumb up my ass waiting for some jenky ghost to slip under my skin?"

The air blowing out of the vent turned warmish.

"I don't even know where to begin." Gillmore turned around a few ideas in her mind. "Antipsyactives work on ligands and vasopressin uptake, and probably more processes than we even understand. But more importantly, correlation and causation are not the same thing. You don't know if blood pressure causes psychic phenomena or if it's the other way around—or if it's neither, and some undefined third variable is causing both. Logically speaking, if spikes in blood pressure cause extrasensory experiences, people would be tripping on birth control pills and some researcher somewhere would have figured it out by now. My guess? Certain compounds affect both physical and nonphysical bodies, and where those overlap, that's the sweet spot."

Sure. A spot where you're cramped in a ball, jonesing for your next hit, and eventually wind up dead.

I thanked Dr. Gillmore, left her in her lukewarm hybrid, and headed up to The Clinic.

CHAPTER 16

I'M NO PHARMACOLOGIST, BUT it wouldn't surprise me if the drugs that affected the extrasensory parts of the brain affected more than just the physical blob of gray matter sloshing around in a person's cranium. Did all the alternative things I'd tried in the past—from herbs to incense to cheap, perfumey hoodoo charms—have the same potential? If they did, additional trial-and-error was required. Because their effects were so subtle I could chalk them up to wishful thinking.

And what about yoga? Did the practice affect the subtle bodies, or did bending into a Triangle Pose just send all my blood rushing into my head? Or was it a little bit of both?

I was pondering this as I pulled into The Clinic's parking lot...and found Carolyn pacing back and forth in front of the door. I didn't need to be an empath to read her body language, arms crossed, shoulders hitched up.

She was royally pissed.

"Nice of you to join us," she told me.

"I was interviewing the ER doc in charge down at LaSalle," I said. "One who's got a front-row seat on this whole Kick epidemic. Thanks for asking."

"I'm sorry. I'm just aggravated. Bertelli's suddenly convinced we're a liability issue. The Clinic's attorneys made some calls that have Sergeant Warwick scrambling for subpoenas."

"Is that where Zigler is? Waiting on the paperwork?"

Carolyn gave a curt nod. "You might as well get in there so Jacob's got some backup."

She didn't mention that we feds were apparently above whatever rules kept her and Zigler out, but the way she glared at me, she didn't have to. I could've pointed out that we were all on the same team and it was a good thing some of us weren't hamstrung. But she'd already told me she was aggravated. No need to wave it under her nose that both she and Zig could've sidestepped Bertelli's machinations if they'd thrown in their lot with the FPMP.

Then again, you never know. Even though Warwick occasionally answered to F-Pimp, he wasn't nearly as easy to spook as Laura Kim. And maybe it was best not to traipse around with all our eggs in the same basket.

I ponied up to Troy's window, and he hefted a massive sheaf of paperwork onto the ledge for me to sign. I considered reading them, but zoned out before I got to the end of the first paragraph. "Did Jacob sign this?"

Troy assured me he had, and that was good enough for me.

By the time I got to the bottom of the sheaf, I'd received a rundown on the entire spring primetime lineup, and my already-loose signature had become a meaningless squiggle.

Starting off the day by signing waivers until my hand hurt was bad enough—especially to a tedious retelling of some lame psychic crime drama—but to add insult to injury, once I was through the door, I nearly collided with Dr. Bertelli.

"Agent Bayne," he said grandly. "What a relief to know you're still working with us. Recent events have been so tragic—losing not just one of our longtime clients, but two—I'm thankful the investigation remains a top priority with the FPMP."

That's what he said. With his mouth. But he was standing so that I couldn't walk toward the urgent care part of the building without shoving him out of the way. I was fairly sure the ghosts of the two dead Psychs hadn't somehow come back, but I didn't want to just presume. After all, Jackie's demeanor shifted inexplicably—sometimes she had a sense of who I was and what history we shared, while other times she didn't know me from Adam. Maybe the Kick victims would have a similar kind of reset. And it would be a shame if I wasn't there to question them if they showed up again.

I said, "You know who else would be helpful? The PsyCops from the Fifth Precinct."

Bertelli pretended to be contrite. "Such a shame. All the legal red tape. Rest assured, I'm doing everything I can." To let Carolyn and Zigler back in? Or to toss Jacob and me out alongside them? "In the meantime, to satisfy our legal team, I'll just have to ask you to follow a simple new protocol."

"And what would that be?"

"With all the liability issues that have come to light, certain areas are, understandably, off limits to anyone but staff." He indicated the floor with a sweep of his hand. It was a typical medical floor made of rubbery gray linoleum tiles with flecks of lighter and darker gray. But now it was decked out with strips of tape—garish safety tape covered in red and white diagonal stripes. "I'd really appreciate your cooperation, Agent. These are trying times...for all of us. Now, if you'll excuse me, my inbox has blown up and I've really got to get back to my office."

I watched him turn and walk away on the opposite side of the tape. Once he turned the corner, I glanced down and gave the tape an experimental tap with my toe. Nothing happened. Then again, it's not as if the tape would know whether I actually worked at The Clinic or was just visiting. Any discomfort I had with it was purely psychological.

The summer I was nine, I briefly shared a bedroom with an eleven-year-old foster kid, Charles. To say the two of us never got along was an understatement. Charles dumped grape juice on my favorite Simpsons T-shirt, peeled the stickers off my knockoff Rubik's cube, and stuck his grubby fingers in my dessert whenever Mama Brill or Harold weren't looking. Usually, I gave Charles a wide berth. That year, though, one of our foster parents' adult sons was between apartments, and Charles found himself displaced.

He ended up in my room.

It was the world's most passive-aggressive summer. We wound up with our every last toy "accidentally" broken, though how you can accidentally tear all the hair off a plastic troll, I'll never know. In desperation, Mama Brill attempted to mark off our respective territories by running a strip of masking tape down the center of the room and forbidding either of us to cross it.

The main thing we learned that summer was how far each of us could spit.

We also learned that Harold wasn't above doling out a good spanking.

Corporal punishment has fallen out of favor these days, but in my case, it had clearly done its job. As much as I would've loved to step over the boundaries just for the sake of being contrary, I felt a visceral aversion to crossing that red-and-white striped line.

I decided I should at least get an idea of how far my approved area extended. I turned and followed the tape. It rounded a corner and then ended within sight of some exam room doors, though I was at an angle where I couldn't quite see through any of the doors, and at a distance where I'd really have to yell to get someone's attention.

I backtracked and followed my safe zone into the stairwell. Second floor admin...off limits. Break room...off limits. Even the janitor's closet was off limits. When it was all said and done, the only thing I could access was the stairwell, a bathroom, the boiler room, and the conference room Jacob was using as an impromptu office.

I found him there, flipping through a file and snapping pictures on his phone. Watching him in action never gets old. It's not just the movie star cheekbones and the ridiculously broad shoulders, either. It's the calculating intelligence behind his eyes. He glanced up and said, "Bertelli's doing everything he can to get us thrown out of here."

I'd figured as much. He'd been far too affable about that stupid tape. "So what's the plan?"

"Right now, I'm documenting the oldest records I can find. Maybe some of the earliest patients can tell us something about Dr. Kamal."

That group of patients...did it include me? The thought must've registered on my face. Jacob met my eyes and gave me a slight nod. I returned it.

He said, "I've got this under control. You should probably focus on re-canvasing the staff to see if there's any new news about Kick."

"Not sure how far I'm gonna get with all the, uh...." I trailed off before I got to "tape on the floor" when he glanced up from his work and raised an eyebrow at me as if to say, *seriously?* "Never mind. You've clearly got your work cut out for you. I'll leave you to it."

I headed out of the conference room. Of course, Jacob wouldn't be intimidated by a few strips of tape. But he was him and I was me. And striding across the lines in the sand (or the lines tacked down to the linoleum) just wasn't my style. I relied more on stubbornness, stealth, and passive-aggressive displays to do what needed to be done. I was tracing the perimeter of my taped-off boundaries again when the bathroom door swung open and Erin the pharmacist nearly walked right into me. "Agent Bayne," she said with some surprise. "How are you feeling today? Beta blockers can take some getting used to."

Right. The beta blockers. The ones I'd conveniently forgotten to take, probably because I was worried they'd affect my ability to block a potential possession. "No problem. I'm fine."

She peered at me hard. What if she'd lied about being an NP and was actually a telepath? Or what if beta blockers had some kind of telltale sign that only a pharmacist could see? I looked back at her, stony faced, and forced myself to hold her gaze.

"You'd tell me if you had any problems, right? Even after yesterday."

"Sure. I told you, we're good. And everything's fine."

Her shoulders un-hitched in relief. "Thank God. Because Dr. Bertelli was so worried about you, he made me rotate fresh stock on all your meds, then stood over me and literally cataloged every move I made while I filled your prescription. I think he was even counting the pills to make sure I didn't screw up."

No doubt he didn't want the FPMP's favorite medium to die on his watch. Just imagine the liability. But if Bertelli was so concerned about my physical wellbeing, maybe I could turn it to my advantage. "I mean...everything's *basically* fine. A little dizziness is par for the course, right?"

Erin went pale and took me by the arm. Not in a show of companionship, either, but in the way the Police Academy had taught me to escort exuberant drunks off the street before someone mowed them down. "We should probably have that looked at. Just to be safe."

Well. That was one way to get past the red tape.

CHAPTER 17

THE MEDICAL TEAM SWOOPED in and hooked me up to some machines—heart rate, oxygen, temperature, and of course, blood pressure. Only somewhat elevated. Given how much I hated medical facilities, thanks to all the experimentation I'd endured, somewhat elevated was as good as I could hope for.

Once the heavy hitters were convinced I was in no danger of collapse—the hyperspecialized physicians with a half-dozen medical titles per person—they left me in the capable hands of a physician's assistant to unhook me from all the stuff. My break room buddy, Gina.

"Well, look who it is," she said...but when I expected her to blame me for the two deaths that darkened The Clinic's doorstep, she added, "Such a relief to have you here, what with everything going on."

Well, that was going to take some getting used to.

"Say, Gina, you've been here a while, haven't you?"

She took a few pumps of hand sanitizer from a wall mounted unit beside the door, scrubbed the jelly through her fingers, and said, "Eight years now? No, nine."

"The precursor to Kick...where do you suppose people are finding it?"

"It's really above my pay grade—"

I pitched my voice low and conspiratorial. Not only did she know something...but I'd bet she was willing to share, given enough stroking. "Come on. You must've heard *something* around the water cooler."

"I'm sure it's just idle gossip."

"Isn't that the best kind?"

She quelled a tiny smile. "Well, back when Palazamine was taken off the market, where did it go? Normally, when you're left with extra prescription pills, there are takeback programs in place in hospitals and police departments."

Sure. The Fifth Precinct had a box in the lobby that some knucklehead would attempt to break into on a weekly basis.

"But when Dr. Morganstern managed to get Palazamine re-called—"

"Hold on. Dr. Morganstern was involved in Palazamine?"

"Of course. Dr. Morganstern was one of the top psycho-pharmacological clinicians in the country. Such a shame."

"Yeah," I said noncommittally. Because Morganstern had been offed by Roger Burke simply to install crazy Dr. Chance in Morganstern's place. He'd been murdered to get to me. Calling it a shame was the understatement of the century.

"If he wasn't working on that super secret project in Japan, maybe he would have some ideas for you."

Wait a minute. Was *Japan* some kind of euphemism?

While I was figuring out how to ask, Gina said, "He was such a character.... Sure, he came off a little dry, a little clinical, but that's just because he was so brilliant. What the patients didn't get to see was that he could really have a sense of humor about himself. Every Christmas we all chipped in for a new sweater vest, all the PAs and nurses. We found some real doozies. And he actually wore them."

"So...Japan."

"None of us were surprised. He was such a pioneer in the field. Just a shame he left so suddenly we didn't have a chance to say goodbye. We always joked about getting him a giant cookie when he retired—you know, the cheap grocery store kind with all the sickening frosting?" She sighed. "He was a good sport. He would've gone along with the gag. Let's hope he's reveling in all the sushi he can eat."

Was there sushi in the afterlife? For his sake, I hoped so.

Gina glanced down at my chart and said, "You know, I keep forgetting you're a federal agent—you're so down-to-earth—but if anyone can track down Dr. Morganstern, it's you."

Me? Not exactly—not since I'd seen his spirit cross the veil.

But I did know someone who could make a long-distance call on my behalf.

It was hard not to act too excited—after all, Gina might want another blood pressure reading—but I kept it low-key until she finished telling me about her granddaughter's tap dance recital and left me alone in the exam room. My phone was out of my pocket before the door had even swung shut. Unfortunately, my call went right to voicemail.

"You've reached Special Agent Darla Davis of FPMP Indianapolis. I'm currently on assignment until further notice and will not be checking my voicemail. If this is an emergency, please hang up and dial—"

I hung up and wondered, briefly, what kind of emergency, exactly, was likely to land in Dead Darla's lap. Maybe if I'd listened to the whole thing, I'd discover the message was left specifically for my benefit. Luckily, Darla and I both answered to the same boss...and when it came to ghosts, Laura Kim didn't screw around.

I called Laura, who told me, "Unfortunately, Agent Davis is

on assignment."

"Yeah. Her voicemail said."

"I can put in a request...."

To who?

I almost asked—but maybe I didn't want to know. In matters of Psych, the Director of FPMP Midwest Division ranked pretty high. But no matter how high up the food chain you got, there was always someone above you. FPMP National. The Pentagon. The White House. I was suddenly really grateful that whatever ghost business was going on out there, Darla had been sent off to deal with it, not me. Still. Dr. Morganstern's input might crack the whole Kick fiasco wide open. "If it doesn't compromise Darla, I could really use her help."

"I'll do my best. But in the meantime, Vic...please. Figure this out. Before anyone else dies."

I didn't miss working homicide, that's for sure. But I had to admit, there was a lot less pressure when the victim was already dead. "Say, Laura...do you find it odd that the staff at The Clinic still think Dr. Morganstern is in Japan?"

She sighed. "That was Constantine's doing."

Sometimes I almost convinced myself that the FPMP wasn't all that bad—but then I'd be reminded how fast and loose they played with the truth. "What about his family?"

I must have taken a tone, because Laura sounded defensive when she said, "A body was never recovered, so they're not going to have much closure anyway. Jennifer Chance and Roger Burke were the ones to concoct the Japan story, and we opted to run with it. Right now, as far as everyone's concerned, Dr. Morganstern is on a top-secret development team in Okinawa that precludes contact with anyone...and a nice paycheck is hitting his wife's bank account every other week."

"You could've achieved the same thing with a life insurance settlement."

"Maybe so. But do you really want everyone at The Clinic to know their beloved colleague was murdered solely to gain access to you?"

No. Damn it.

As much as I dreaded it—now, even more so—I really wanted to talk to Morganstern, though I wasn't sure if I'd be able to reach past the veil. Because I'd never tried, or because my talent simply didn't work that way? I dunno. But I had to try something.

I had a feeling I couldn't talk Red into helping me yoga. He'd been pretty clear yesterday about me taking some recovery time after my eye bleed and stabbing headache before he'd be willing to walk me through even the most basic of postures. But who needs Red when you've got the internet?

I headed back to the cannery to make a fool of myself in the privacy of my own home.

In my opinion, YouTube was made for reruns of old TV shows and bootleg copies of stunningly bad B-movies. Seeing what passed for fashion in the 70's never got old. But I never realized how much yoga instruction could be found there until I looked. I had so many options, it was hard to determine exactly which YouTuber was right for me. You'd think I would jump at the chance to ogle so many shirtless men. Too bad they all annoyed the ever-loving crap out of me.

From the young and hip to the old and sinewy, each one was smugger than the last. And every one of them wielded their expression of self-satisfied serenity like a weapon.

By the time a cab deposited Jacob on the cannery's doorstep, I'd resorted to geriatric "chair yoga"—the only thing that didn't send a bolt of pain down my sciatic nerve or make my hamstrings twang like piano wire. He pulled up a second dining room chair in front of the TV set and joined me in twisting around to face the kitchen.

"Is your back bothering you?"

"No. I mean, yeah…but that's not why I'm twisting around like a chair-bound pretzel." I focused on my white light, my chakras, my chi, but it was no use. If the chair yoga was helping, it was so subtle I couldn't feel it. I un-twisted myself, grabbed the clicker and lowered the TV's volume so we could talk over it. "Did you know everyone thinks Dr. Morganstern is in Japan?" I gave a bitter laugh. "He'd know what to do—or at least he'd point me in the right direction. But now that I need to make a long-distance call to the other side, Darla's gone dark. Can I do it myself? Who the hell knows. Laura must have a few more of those horse pills, but I don't want to take one—and even if I did, in all likelihood, all I'd accomplish is astral projecting."

Jacob twisted the other way so as not to end up lopsided. His back gave off an enviable crack. "Are you sure about that? When the waking projection happened back at PsyTrain, the psyactive wasn't the only thing in play. You also had a GhosTV tuned to the astral setting."

I hadn't really thought about it that way.

He glanced down at the floorboards, as if he couldn't resist thinking about the console that was still in our basement.

I sighed. "Look, I know you've been dying to encourage me to master that thing, and I can only imagine how much self control it's taken for you to keep yourself from bringing it up. But if that contraption didn't terrify me before, the knowledge that the personality of Jennifer Chance still exists somewhere out there—with its obsession completely intact—has got me totally spooked. She *is* out there. We both heard her talk through Darla's mouth. What if I turn the dial and it sucks her ghost right back through the veil?"

CHAPTER 18

JACOB NARROWED HIS EYES, as if he wanted to reassure me that hauling a ghost back in through the exit door was impossible. But he couldn't. Not with any degree of certainty.

"Maybe I do need to let a bunch of blood rush to my head and spike a major headache," I said. "That's how I paused the old repeaters in Dreyfuss's office. That's how the ghosts claim I really light up."

Jacob grabbed the seat of his chair and hopped it sideways until it was directly beside mine. "You'll figure this out." He threw a leg over one of mine and hooked his heel around my calf, squeezing gently. "You have the raw ability. We both know how strong you are. But you're writing the playbook as you go. Literally. So it's bound to get frustrating."

"Playbook? This isn't a game. People are dying."

Jacob looked hard at the side of my face until I met his eyes. Firmly, he said, "And it's not your fault."

Of course it wasn't.

"And neither was what happened to Dr. Morganstern."

I opened my mouth to tell him that much was pretty fucking obvious...until I realized what had driven me to even attempt something as asinine as chair yoga.

Guilt.

Oh, I knew it was Roger Burke who'd done the deed, but it wouldn't have happened if he hadn't been trying to rope me into their crazy scheme. If you took me out of the equation, the most powerful known medium in Chicago would've been Richie. And he'd been safe in the loving embrace of the FPMP.

Dr. Gillmore might claim that correlation was not causation. Even so, in a roundabout way, Morganstern's death really was my fault. Not because of something I did, or something I failed to do. But the mere fact of my existence.

I didn't need to say it, either. Jacob knew me. He could see the guilt was eating at me. He swung out of his chair and went down on one knee at my feet. His big, strong hands ranged up and down my thighs, as if he could chafe the shitty feelings away. "Vic, look at me. You were drugged and kidnapped. You and Morganstern were both victims. No one would see it any other way."

For the most part. Except for a tiny, niggling voice that insisted if I hadn't been in the picture, Morganstern would still be alive. I could handle a stranger thinking something like that. But, disturbing as it was, now that I'd shared some baklava with the break room gang at The Clinic, I felt alarmingly distressed over the thought of them all hating me once they realized *Japan* was just a euphemism for *dead*.

It was a conversation I wasn't particularly keen on having, but when I stood up to go do something else—anything else— my pesky sciatic nerve announced that even in a chair, it found yoga to be a real pain in the ass. I winced, and Jacob noticed.

Because that guy notices everything.

He stood up and held out a hand. "Here, lie down."

Well, at least the yoga mat I'd hauled up from the basement

was good for something. I'm not really one for back rubs—they felt decadent and a little selfish—but Jacob is well acquainted with my physiology by now. And I was likely to feel better once I let him have his way.

I stripped down to my underwear and assumed the position, face down. He straddled my thighs and dug his thumbs into my back. The TV blathered on in the background as the perky girl on the folding chair did a few more stretches, then implored her audience to come back again tomorrow. "Like all journeys, the journey to a healthful habit begins with a single step."

The same could be said of all habits, not just the "healthful" ones. After all, how many Psychs tried a single hit of Kick and found themselves traveling on the journey to addiction?

Jacob's thumb found a bright point of pain and I groaned. "Too much?" he asked.

"A little."

He eased up, but only marginally, and kept on pressing the sore spot. Eventually, either my nervous system fatigued itself so I no longer felt the pain so acutely, or some buried trigger point eased up.

On the TV, the next video had begun playing while I was riding out the torture. I recognized the yoga guy's voice—I'd dubbed him "Mr. Dramatic," because every damn phrase he uttered was delivered like it was life or death. Which was a shame, because his shtick, "Vibrational Yoga," had seemed so promising. At least until he opened his mouth.

Our chakra system is like an energetic recording device that harbors our emotional and physical traumas. These energetic imprints can alter the proper flow of chi.

I sighed into the yoga mat, which Jacob took as an invitation to press harder. "You're gonna leave a bruise," I said, though not very forcefully.

Jacob shifted his tactic to running his palms up either side of my spine from my ass to my shoulders and back again.

"There," I said, as he hit another knot in my lower back. "Little higher. Yeah."

The Muladhara, or root chakra, is located at the base of the spine. It's associated with our primal needs: food, shelter...sex.

Thumb-pressure eased up...followed by the hot, wet swipe of a tongue down my spine.

Something perked up—probably not my root chakra. Funny thing. I wouldn't have thought I'd be in the mood since I'm no masochist, and I'd been busy flagellating myself over Dr. Morganstern's murder. But actions really do speak louder than words, and Jacob's tongue trailing down my back was stunningly distracting.

He paused at the waistband of my boxers to gauge my interest, and I answered by shoving them halfway down. He rumbled his approval and pulled them the rest of the way off, then got back to what he was doing before...and working his way even lower.

It's vital to keep the Muladhara in balance. It's the basis and foundation of the rest of the chakra system. Improper flow can manifest as spaciness, anxiety, loss of appetite, and a general feeling of ungroundedness.

By the time Jacob spread my ass, I was rock hard. I have no idea how people in long-term relationships get bored in bed. The longer we were together, the better Jacob got at making me whimper and squirm. All my awareness surged down to one particular point in my body—and this time, it wasn't my sciatic nerve.

He made a leisurely sweep of his tongue, and I let out a shuddering breath. Jacob got off on getting me off, and when he was in the mood to prove something, there wasn't much I could do but settle in and enjoy the ride. He knew how to work that tongue of his, that's for sure. But it wasn't only that. It was the hot, wet tickle of his breath, the rasp of his goatee between my cheeks, the occasional broken fragment of a word. I wouldn't come from rimming alone...but by the time he got to my dick, I'd be ready to explode.

And as you bring your awareness to your root chakra, feel the solidity of the ground beneath you and imagine the earth's energy traveling up into your body.

That solidity was starting to get painful. The yoga mat was a hell of a lot less padded than, say, a mattress. And a very sensitive part of my physiology was starting to feel squashed. I tried to roll over, but Jacob held me down and delved in, deep and nasty...and maybe I could tolerate the tongue-lashing for just a little while longer. Because whatever he was doing down there might not be enough to bring me off, but it felt indescribably good in its own special way.

His tongue danced over some nerve ending just right, and my breath caught.

With each breath, give yourself over to the support of the earth and lift through the crown chakra at the top of the head.

Finally, when I thought I might freaking implode, Jacob pushed up from the cleft of my ass, triumphant, and flipped me onto my back. He pawed a half-empty lube from a drawer in the coffee table, then shoved down his slacks, knelt between my rubbery legs and dragged me into position. There was probably some kind of yoga name for it. Shoulder blades pressed into the mat. Legs splayed. Hips angled up toward the ceiling.

Breathe in...breathe out....

New Age music was playing behind Mr. Dramatic, and it felt like my heartbeat had synchronized itself to the rhythm of the tablas and bells. Jacob felt it too. Once he eased himself in and found his angle, he started serving it up in perfect rhythm. Where normally he might've upped the pace, he held steady. And a weird plateau stole over me that felt spinny and a little strange. Part of me wanted to do something to hasten things along. A deliberate clench. A cant of the hips. A few grunted, awkward words of encouragement. But part of me was game to see exactly how long this eerily deliberate pounding might last.

...and as your root chakra comes into balance, open your eyes, take a deep and cleansing breath, and rejoin your day, grounded and aligned.

The music faded into an earnest entreaty to donate money to Mr. Dramatic's Patreon page, but I hardly heard it. Jacob pulled me against him and rolled onto his back so I was straddling him—me butt-naked and him still dressed, with his pants around his thighs. Yet another yoga started up—a very granola woman who spoke way too softly—but at least it was easy to ignore her. I focused on the stiff length of cock up my ass and angled myself so it hit me inside right where I liked it. All that ass-eating and slow-fucking left me with a hair-trigger orgasm, just like I knew it would. And when I shot my load, not only did I hit my peak hands-free, but it was accompanied by an embarrassing moan of release. That hardly ever happened. The hands-free, I mean. One of Jacob's favorite pastimes is forcing all kinds of unfortunate sounds out of me.

I hadn't really been paying any attention to how it was for Jacob, but fortunately, I hadn't needed to. He'd been just as hot and bothered, just as ready to peak as I was, and the self-satisfaction of wresting my control away from me had been enough to drag him along for the ride.

Once we were both sated, I held my position for just a moment and took a good look at him. Flushed and satisfied. And I was glad. Because if I could play a part in making someone feel that content, maybe I wasn't half as inept as I always made myself out to be.

"That was really hot," he said, and I made a noise of agreement. "How's my suit?"

Miraculously, though his shirt and tie had been amply spooged, his jacket was unscathed. I'd need to do a careful dismount to preserve the trousers, though.

Eventually, as we dug into the leftover pasta—with chicken sausage sliced over the top, now that there were no vegetarians around to offend—I realized Jacob had somehow managed to bang my guilty ruminations right out of me. I didn't reach too hard to remember exactly why I'd felt so acutely low about Dr. Morganstern, since I didn't want to hop back onto the treadmill of "it's all my fault." I'd have the rest of my life to stew over my role in his death. Right now, I needed my head in the game.

After we ate, Jacob went up to his office to take stock of the files he'd gathered at The Clinic. Meanwhile, I cleaned up the kitchen. As I did, I frankly wasn't thinking about much of anything beyond the feel of the soap suds on my hands and the mild funk wafting off the sponge.

And that was just fine by me.

I slept well that night—shocking, I know. Thing is, I'm so accustomed to waking up ages before I need to, I was startled by the sound of Jacob's alarm. Luckily, I'd showered the night before. I barely had time to shave, throw on a suit and knock back a cup of coffee. So it wasn't until we pulled up by The Clinic that I realized I had a new text waiting for me—and that text was from Dr. Gillmore.

Angelica Barth, room 221, Lakeshore Center.

I wondered if maybe she'd accidentally texted me instead of one of her colleagues...until I looked up Lakeshore Center and saw it was a vaguely-named drug and alcohol rehab.

"There's someone I need to see," I told Jacob. Because in my well-rested clarity, I was sure that if I could understand addiction, I'd have a way better shot at dealing with Kick.

CHAPTER 19

The Lakeshore Center was an unmarked cinderblock building that looked more like a juvie detention hall than an inpatient rehab. Once the sour guy at the front desk determined I wasn't there to check myself in, he informed me that there was no visitation allowed.

A call to Laura Kim got that straightened out in ten minutes flat.

The inside of the facility was even more off-putting than the outside. The activities room was inactive and the old set in the TV room was busted. In the residential hall, I did my best to focus on finding room 221 and ignoring the sound of people sobbing behind closed doors. It was only two patients currently crying—not like the whole place was in tears—but two was more than enough to make an impression.

There were safety glass windows in all the doors. It was reminiscent of my Thorazine years. But memories of my time in the cuckoo's nest didn't trigger any panic. That particular time in my life was lousy, sure. No personal liberty and a social circle that left a lot to be desired. But no one there locked me in a room with a dead body to gauge the effectiveness of a new antipsyactive like they did at Camp Hell.

I kept my eyes on my feet to avoid the curious looks I glimpsed in my peripheral vision. When I did look up, it was only long enough to find the door to room 221. I rapped on the doorjamb and someone answered. "Come in." Her voice sounded like she'd smoked a pack a day for the past hundred or so years. "It's not like I can stop you."

Probably not. Folks unfortunate enough to wind up in "facilities" didn't generally get doors that locked. Not from the inside, at least. I let myself in.

It was a double room with only one patient inside. The woman from LaSalle General, I guess, though I couldn't say I really recognized her. Back when I'd seen her being wheeled into the ER, I'd been focused mainly on the black blob of smoke trailing along, I didn't get a good look at her.

Thankfully, the blob wasn't with us today.

Hopefully.

The woman it had been following was Caucasian and very tan, thin and wiry, with steel gray hair cut short and combed straight back, and deep furrows in her forehead and around her eyes. According to what the paramedics told me that day, she was an alcoholic who'd been living on the streets. Double whammy in terms of premature aging. She looked to be in her seventies, but was probably more like fifty.

"Victor Bayne." I deliberately left out my job title on the gut instinct that I'd only sound like I was posturing.

My vagueness sparked a bit of interest. She narrowed her eyes and introduced herself...first name only. "Angelica."

"Thanks for meeting with me."

She indicated her room with a sweep of her hand. Two institutional twin beds, a table that contained a warped checker set and a half-eaten muffin, and a few tattered paperbacks on the windowsill. No computer. No TV. "It's a real strain on my packed schedule, but I suppose I can manage to fit you in. Doctor? No, you don't strike me as a doctor—what with that bloody eye. Social worker. That's what you are."

Better than a used car salesman, but I didn't confirm or deny it. "I'm in the middle of an investigation I think you might be able to shed a little light on."

"Whatever it was, I didn't do it," she said glibly.

"I never said you did."

"I didn't see it, either."

"Uh huh."

"In fact, whatever it is you're after, I'm sure I've never even heard of it—so it looks like you've come all this way for nothing. Tough luck, Victor Bayne, whatever you are, and whoever you work for. Don't let the door smack you on the ass on your way out."

Apparently, I'd mistaken hostility for interest, not that I expected a grand welcome. In fact, I would've been suspicious of any homeless person who seemed too eager to help an authority figure. While most street people I'd met would've obviously preferred to not have to sleep on ventilation grates or eat from the trash, they also tended to be fiercely independent and leery of authority.

"Listen," I said. "I'm not trying to get you to rat anyone out. I'm not accusing you of doing anything illegal. And I frankly doubt you know any specifics on my current case. I was hoping to get your opinion."

"Opinions are like assholes. Everyone's got one and they're all full of shit."

I ignored the bravado. "How long has it been since your last drink?"

"Thirty-two days." She cut her eyes to an Alcoholic's Anonymous one-month token on the checkerboard. "And all I got was this stupid chip."

Well, what did she expect—champagne? "Is it any easier now than it was when you first came in?"

"My first few days were a walk in the park—they were treating my DTs with barbiturates. After that, though...." She focused on the backs of her sun-browned hands. "It sucked. It continues to suck. And I imagine the suckiness will still be there by the time the treatment program's run its course and I'm back out there begging for pocket change to buy myself an airplane bottle of vodka. And now that I've admitted as much, I suppose I'm not eligible for any housing assistance."

I could've denied being a social worker, but I was too busy scanning the area for habit demons to correct her presumption. Not only had I completely neglected to do a thorough visual sweep, but I hadn't bothered powering up my third eye on my way to her room, either. If this was how careless I'd become by sleeping in, I'd take my normal insomnia any day.

I opened up to the white light—or I tried to—but it felt like getting laid through two condoms. (Let's just say *that* guy didn't get a second date.)

Once I realized how thick and stunted everything felt, my adrenaline spiked. I had an inkling of the psychic mojo floating around in the ether, but it filled the tank in dribs and drabs, not the steady stream I'd come to expect.

"So, did you get what you came for?" Angelica asked bitterly.

I scanned the area around her, searching even harder for habit demons. But if some scary black blob was listening in on our conversation, I couldn't see it.

Though that didn't mean it wasn't there.

I wrapped my meager white light around myself and said, "I'm sure you know a few addicts. Do you think they're born or made?"

"I can't see that it makes any difference where you start.

What matters is where you end up."

There was probably more she could tell me, but I was itching to get out of rehab and shore up my defenses. It wasn't exactly the first time I'd realized my white light was running on fumes—but given the fact that I knew I was walking into a potential habit demon scenario, my timing was lousy, to say the least.

I thanked Angelica for her time, received a sniff of disgust in return, and peeled out into the hall. Anticlimactic—but what had I expected? A big fanfare and a pat on the back? I'd better not hold my breath. Not until I actually did her any good.

As I made my way back to the car, I shot a quick text to Crash: *Are you awake? I need to see you.*

In just a few seconds, he replied that he was heading to the store and I could meet him there.

I sucked down white light all the way to Curious Curios. At first, it was like trying to drink through one of those narrow plastic coffee stirrers instead of an actual straw. But by the time I got there, the constriction eased, and my white-lightness felt almost normal again.

I tromped through the rooms of dusty junk until I found the guys in their brightly-colored haven of bohemian shabby-chic glory. Red stood on an ottoman replacing a burned-out twinkle light, while Crash was busy scraping the brass coating off a candlestick that was old, though not quite old enough. The smell of copal hung faintly in the air and some kind of psychedelic improvisation piped through a hidden speaker. I felt my internal rhythms start to synch up with the percussion and said, "Turn the music off."

Crash quirked an eyebrow, hit something on his phone, and the music stopped. It must've been tempting to ride me for being so bossy, but he could read me well enough to know

I wasn't just being a jerk for jerkiness' sake. Instead, he said, "You're wound up tighter than a goth girl's corset—what gives?"

"Evidently, I've managed to yoga wrong."

Red hopped down off his perch. Unlike Crash, he doesn't take advantage of the myriad pot-shots I leave myself open to. With great concern, he said, "Did you hurt yourself?"

"Physically? No. I'm fine." I prodded my forehead in the vicinity of my third eye. "But psychically? I must've flipped some kind of switch and left it in the off-position all night. I'm slow and groggy, and I'm having a hell of a time filling up my tank."

"Vic needs to power up his mediumship," Crash explained to Red. "Like a video game avatar."

"Not literally," I said.

"Close enough. So this feeling you had—relaxed and psychically stunted—isn't that the effect you're actually trying to achieve with Auracel?"

I opened my mouth to argue with Crash...then closed it. Because if I looked at it that way, he might have a point.

Red said, "We should take advantage of the opportunity to analyze which poses might have an antipsyactive effect. If we do that, then maybe we can reverse-engineer some asanas to help you target the states you're hoping to achieve. Can you remember which poses you did, in what order?"

Great. Now I'd have to admit to doing *chair* yoga. Where even the instructor was nearly twice my age.

"I can probably find the video," I mumbled, and thumbed in the search term *chair yoga* on my phone instead of speaking it like I'd normally do.

Either Red was really good at maintaining a straight face, or he'd already figured I was on the verge of a senior discount at the local diner, so the chair yoga came as no big shock. He scrubbed through the video and took stock of all the poses. He pulled out an elaborately carved and painted dining room chair to do a few poses himself to get a feel for them. His brow furrowed ever so attractively. Puzzled, he said, "I'm glad you didn't do any inverted poses, especially after the headache and blood pressure scare. But I'm having a hard time seeing why this particular flow would activate your chakras."

"You don't get it. They're not activated—they're stuck."

"That's not how asanas work." He held out a hand. His palm was covered in faded henna swirls. Because that's what hot young guys like him and Crash did in their spare time. Painted designs on each other. Like they're not distracting enough as it is. "If you let me have a look, maybe I can get a feel for what's going on."

Since he already saw how lame the video was, I figured it wouldn't be much worse for him to get a psychic replay of me twisting my way through the postures. He wasn't a very high-level telepath...and even more importantly, I hadn't made a fool out of myself by falling out of the chair.

There are jacked up telepaths who can suck the thoughts right out of your head, but Red's not one of those. He needs to be touching you, and he needs to be concentrating hard. And even then, it's hit or miss. But Red's a smart guy, and even the tiny glimpses he gets—the flashes of insight—can help him come up with some pretty good ideas.

Crash draped himself across the top of an antique buffet and looked on with great interest. He's not nearly as snarky about psychic talent now that he knows his failing grade in empathy was only Constantine's way of keeping him off the radar.

Red enfolded my hand in his and said, "Now, think back to the asanas. Really picture yourself there, as if it's happening now. Is there any one in particular where your energy levels shift while you're holding the pose?"

"Not really. I was just desperate to talk to someone beyond the veil. I know it's possible, I've seen it done. So I was trying to tap that ability without bursting anything inside my head I might need later."

Crash said, "That doesn't sound like anything you've ever been capable of doing."

But Red gave a mild shrug and said, "But what if that's just because you've never tried? Put yourself through the poses again now, if it helps."

Right. Because just admitting to the chair yoga and picturing it while a telepath held my hand wasn't nearly mortifying enough. "No, I can remember. First I did all the breathing. Then I focused on my posture. And then I did some twisting...."

That's when Jacob had come home....

And nailed my ass to the yoga mat.

CHAPTER 20

I CLAMPED DOWN ON that mental image—the one of Jacob banging me—faster than a kid shoving a dirty magazine beneath his mattress, but I was already too late. Red's eyes twinkled, and the corner of his mouth quirked up in a smile. I jerked my hand away.

"What?" Crash said as he felt the energy shift. "Did you pop a boner during yoga? Big deal. Newsflash—it happens to all of us."

My embarrassment was shouting at me to walk out of there and not look back. And maybe change my phone number for good measure, and move out of state, while I was at it.

"I think we're on to something," Red said. "There's a reason why so many mystical traditions promote abstinence."

"Ohhh," Crash said knowingly. "I get it. You didn't just pitch a tent—you put down a sleeping bag and busted your nut all over it. Look, I'm not saying old-school magickal belief systems are necessarily right—there's a reason most of those practices went out the window when the Ganzfeld reports came out—but at least the practitioners were aware that their energetic bodies existed. If it turns out sex dissipates this 'white light' you're always talking about, then you might have to start curtailing certain...activities. Sucks to be you."

"Fine. But I haven't got time to wait for my usual equilibrium to come back. How do I force it back to normal?"

"There are plenty of ways to raise energy," Red told me. "Chanting. Drumming. Meditation. Visualization. It's just a matter of finding the way that suits you best."

Oh, please.

I left the two of them to doing whatever esoteric things they did to fill their days and headed back to The Clinic, but I was clenching the steering wheel so hard, my knuckles were white. I'd been hoping for answers...something that could just raise my white light back to its normal levels. I'd found a method. Several, in fact. Unfortunately, none of them were a magical pill. Which was pretty damn ironic, when the "magical pill" that raised psychic energy was the thing that started this whole carnival of fuckery to begin with.

Maybe a half-dose of Kick would help fill my tank.

It was just a passing thought—a thought that didn't even come with the sort of back-of-the-throat itch I associated with my yen for Seconal. Minor. Insignificant. So stupid that I dismissed it just as soon as it took shape.

And yet the mere notion left an indelible mark. I could tell myself it was a dumb idea, push it aside and resolve to forget it, but unfortunately, my mind didn't come with a delete key.

As I pulled up to The Clinic, I wondered how, exactly, I planned to explain my new theories to Jacob. I wasn't comfortable with him knowing I was off my psychic game, but I'd have to swallow my pride and tell him. To do anything else would just be shooting myself in the foot. But I really wasn't looking forward to that conversation. Abstaining from sex on the days in which I had to perform as a medium hardly seemed doable, since dealing with ghosts was literally my job, and I was on call 24-7.

Like we weren't already spinning our wheels about the wedding enough as it was. Jacob loves a good challenge as much as the next guy—probably more—but could he deal with some new abstinence protocol?

For that matter, could I?

The more I thought about sex being the potential problem, the more that theory began to fall apart. Jacob and I had a pretty active sex life, and it never stopped ghosts from pestering me before. I got laid all the time, but the chair yoga was new. So, obviously, if I was experiencing some kind of energetic shift, it had nothing to do with the sex, and everything to do with the yoga.

Good thing I got that settled before I said anything to Jacob. He had enough to worry about without needing to second-guess our sex life, too.

And as yoga went, the chair yoga was awfully mild. Hardly yoga at all, and more like a series of gentle back stretches. So it must've been the combination of the two—yoga followed by an orgasm—that did me in. Well, at least avoiding that combo in the future would be no problem.

I found the rest of my team in The Clinic's lobby. Zigler was at the receptionist window signing something, while Jacob and Carolyn were speaking to one another in low tones, looking very strategic. It was good to see the two of them together like that. I didn't want to jinx any tenuous new connection by taking too much note of it, so I joined Zig by the window.

Apparently our friends from the Fifth Precinct had their warrant. Finally. An office printer was busy spitting out papers. Troy slipped them through the window two or three sheets at a time so Zig could sign them just as fast as they came out of the machine. And Troy was busy spitting out a recap of some inane show he'd seen.

"...and the noises coming from the second-floor apartment? Everyone wrote it off to the plumbing, or the wind, or the old house settling. But then they got a medium in there—"

"Do you ever do anything but watch TV?" I snapped, realizing only belatedly that I'd actually said it out loud.

Troy blinked. "I like TV."

In my peripheral vision, I noticed Carolyn's head jerk up sharply—like she'd just smelled a lie. Jacob, right beside her, noticed too.

"Doesn't everyone?" Troy asked.

Jacob approached the window as if he had a sudden interest in watching people chase cold spots on TV. "What show was this?"

"Hidden Hauntings."

"Y'know, I'm always forgetting to set my DVR. So that's Tuesday nights?"

"I think so. Unless it's Monday. I usually stream it on demand."

Troy grabbed another few sheets from the printer. While his back was turned, Jacob glanced at Carolyn. She gave him a small nod. "We should try that," Jacob said. "But there's so many remotes to keep track of."

Not to mention the fact that the last time we tried to stream that new show with the guy we both like, I found myself snorting awake in the recliner three hours later, while Jacob had wandered off to read the latest work-related missive in his inbox, then fallen down a digital rabbit hole.

"You get used to it," Troy said. "You should really give it another shot. Binge the first three seasons—the fourth drops this summer. And then you'll be all caught up."

"The episode with the apartment—the one you were just telling us about—was that an old episode or a new one?"

"The current season."

"So, it was on last night?"

"I dunno. I must have streamed it."

"Because I want to make sure I catch the next episode."

Given that Jacob has experienced more ghost action than 99.9% of the population, he obviously had no interest in *Hidden Hauntings* and was poking around for an inconsistency in Troy's story. For someone who knows everything, he played the "I can't figure out how to stream things" role pretty darn convincingly...though why anyone would believe he wasn't good at absolutely everything was beyond me. Jacob was clearly a shark. I'm not sure what it said about me that I got off on the way he looked—predatory and sure—when he scented blood in the water. By the time he was done, Troy's story changed from having watched TV all night to having actually spent the majority of his time on the computer.

Probably browsing porn. You'd be surprised at how often this turned out to be the case, once we got a look at someone's search history.

But that wasn't the point. Jacob and Carolyn were working together to corner someone in a lie. What Troy had seen on TV last night might be insignificant. But watching the polygraph mojo flow between them again? It was a thing of beauty. Jacob missed Carolyn. I knew that for a fact. But I hadn't really stopped to think that beneath all the feelings of hurt and abandonment, she missed him, too.

Zig finished signing his last few papers while Troy jotted down a list of recommended watching. That's what Jacob got for acting so interested in the guy's nightly viewing.

We headed down to the commandeered meeting room to hash out our plan to divide and conquer. First step, re-canvas the staff before Bertelli managed to get us tossed out of The Clinic for good. Jacob must've expected me to head over to the break room where all my buddies were. He raised an eyebrow when I told him, "I'm gonna talk to the pharmacist."

"But Carolyn and I—"

"You think she wouldn't know exactly what the two of you were doing? She flipped out the last time I questioned her with Carolyn riding shotgun. Let me have another crack at her myself before she shuts down completely."

Given that there were a dozen other people to talk to, Jacob didn't put up much of a fuss—though I didn't doubt for a second that he'd find some reason to double-check my work. That was fine. He was better than me at grilling subjects.

I was just hoping for some off-the-record pharmaceutical advice.

I headed toward the pharmacy and was surprised to find Erin standing there in the middle of the hallway, arms crossed, looking annoyed. "I had a question about psyactives," I said. "Do you keep any on hand? Any at all?"

"None. We'd have to special order."

"What about herbal psyactives? Mugwort. Pennyroyal."

"We don't stock Western herbs. In fact, we tell our patients to steer clear. People think just because something is 'natural,' that means it's safe. But with herbal remedies, you don't know how fresh they are, or whether or not they're full of pesticides. The dosage is wildly inaccurate. Plus, there's the potential for interaction with whatever else you're taking. We do carry a few botanicals for our patients who prefer Eastern medicine, but only from a reputable source. And we have every single batch tested for purity and strength."

That was a lot more info than I expected, so I was surprised when she didn't ditch me by heading into the safety of the pharmacy. "So...did you lock yourself out?"

She rolled her eyes. "Audit."

"How does that work?"

"Around here? It's like a pop quiz—but for pharmacists."

"A random person shows up and counts your pills?"

"Not just anyone. Bertelli does it himself."

"Oh." Talk about stressful. "Does it happen a lot?"

"Lately? Seems like every other day...like I haven't got enough to worry about right now. If it gets around that patients at my workplace are ODing—even if it's not on our meds—that's the type of scandal that can end my career. I've got to be totally scrupulous. Above reproach. Or I can kiss my reputation goodbye."

My first thought was that Bertelli was gonna walk through that door any second now and catch me crossing the tape on the floor. I was excited about the thought of catching him skimming psyactives and kingpinning the biggest psychic drug scandal in the history of psyactives...until I realized it didn't make any sense. "So there are no psyactives here."

"None."

"And other than the Chinese medicine, no herbal remedies, either?"

"Only those few thoroughly vetted and highly regulated supplements." She gave me a sideways look and said, "You're gonna march right out that door and do the exact opposite of what I said and take some random herbs. I can tell."

I didn't bother denying it. "I've never had a reaction to mugwort before."

"Which is closely related to ragweed. Let's say you have a lurking allergy you're unaware of. And let's say the handful of twigs and weeds you manage to get hold of is stronger than normal. Better be ready for a trip to the emergency room, or at least have an epi pen handy."

Great.

Erin pulled a pad of sticky notes out of her pocket, jotted something down, and handed it over. I expected it to be the name of a reputable herbal medicine source, so it took me a second to register what she'd actually written. Not because I couldn't read it—she had some of the neatest handwriting I'd ever seen—but because I had no idea what it was supposed to mean. "Mood Blaster?"

"It's an app that combines binaural pulses and biofeedback."

That sounded scientific. "Okay. I'm listening."

"Recent studies have shown that light workers often get above-average results from biofeedback."

As much as I hated the term *light workers*, I had to admit...Erin's use of it made me think her research probably was pretty up-to-date. But before I could drill down with any more questions, the pharmacy door swung open, and Bertelli came out looking especially official, with an imperious look on his face and a tablet in his hands. He tapped in a few things, then said, "Keep up the good work, Erin." And then he glanced at the floor and said, "Agent Bayne? You signed an agreement stating you'd respect the red line."

"I was consulting with him," Erin said. "Not as an investigator. As a patient."

Legitimate reasons notwithstanding, Bertelli gave me a cool look and said, "Then I'll need to ask you both to step behind the red line. It would waste everyone's time to have to get our lawyers involved."

CHAPTER 21

If I were to retreat behind the caution tape on the floor, it wouldn't be out of respect for Bertelli's wishes. It was that the rest of my team was in their conference room and I didn't want to be the odd man out. According to Reginald, he'd scored from "some white guy." I found my team breaking down their lists of witnesses to figure out anyone who might have happened to see a random white guy selling drugs the night our victims had scored.

There were already more than enough chefs in the meeting room stirring the pot, so I left Jacob, Carolyn and Zigler to the strategizing, parked myself in the corner, and downloaded the Mood Blaster app...but, invariably, I picked the wrong one and ended up with some silly kids' game. I went back to the app store three more times to find the right one, in fact. Maybe Erin had spelled it wrong. Maybe I was reading it wrong. But, no. In that hyper-precise handwriting, the words Mood Blaster couldn't possibly have been anything else.

Eventually, I scrolled past the colorful cartoon spaceships and planets and read the description.

From Anger Asteroid to Serene Satellite, join Brainy as he blasts his way through Moodspace in his mind-powered spaceship!

What the ever-living heck?

I jabbed around, looking for a refund button—on principle, not because I cared about the $9.99—but I only succeeded in flipping to the last page of the description. The part aimed at parents.

Mood blaster employs the latest in brain research, including binaural tones and biofeedback, to entrain neuronal oscillations and achieve a desired state of mind. By learning to energize or calm themselves, children experience a greater sense of self-efficacy and control. Use stereo headphones for a full binaural experience. A fitness tracker with pulse monitor is required for the Biofeedback Blaster levels.

I glanced up at the rest of the team, who were busy divvying up the witnesses, then read through the app more carefully. Nothing about psychic ability—just mood. But I had to admit, regulating my own brain waves did seem to be what I was trying to achieve when I worked with the white light.

I didn't own a fitness tracker. It seemed redundant given that I probably had a chip under my skin from all the years I'd spent as a lab rat. But there was a set of earbuds in my coat pocket that always managed to snag me while I was looking for my gum. I pulled out the wad of wires, untangled it, plugged it in and fired up the app.

A smiling cartoon brain zipped up in a space ship. I might've pitched my phone against the wall, if not for the audio. Not the music—it was as hokey as you'd expect—but the sound beneath it. A rhythmic *whub-whub-whub*. I recognized it from the nighttime white noise app Jack Bly played to lull himself to sleep. And through headphones, the effect was ten times more pronounced.

The white light drained from me like someone had sucked it right out of my body. I flinched and tore out the earbuds before it emptied me out completely. Zigler glanced up, but he must've just chalked it up to my normal twitchiness. After a cursory glance, he went right back to what he was doing.

My first impulse was to delete the damn thing from my phone and forget it ever happened. But there was no denying that these brainwave sounds were powerful. What if there was a frequency that would help me fill up with white light instead of draining it away?

I angled myself so no one could see the spaceship-riding cartoon brain bobbing around my screen. I navigated to the menu and immediately glazed over when I tried to read the brainwave descriptions. Delta, Theta, Alpha, Beta...a big fraternity of the mind that I had no idea how to pledge.

Frustrated, I backtracked to the kiddy menu and looked at all the planets. Angry Asteroid was a snarling red ball. Mellow Moon was serene and blue. Giggling Galaxy. Calming Comet. I wasn't sure which state of being might fill my tank again, if any—so I turned the volume down low, plugged in the earbuds, and started poking through the screens.

The last thing I wanted was to feel any logier than I already did, so I started hunting and pecking toward the top of the list. Perky Planet had a big smile on its purple planetary face—okay, more like a manic grin—but it looked pretty alert. I tapped its icon and launched the game.

The music was peppier this time, but more importantly, the binaural sounds behind it were different. Higher in pitch. A more rapid pulse. Cautiously, I eased up the volume, leery about anything that might loosen my grasp on what little white light remained. But the Perky Planet music didn't make me drowsy.

In fact, it might have even perked me up.

My inner skeptic told me it was all in my head. But the same could be said about the psychic edge I was trying to achieve, so even if it was just a placebo, it didn't really matter.

Something on the screen was pulsing. I touched it, and my brain guy shot a laser beam at the spot, which made Perky Planet hop around. Did the music change? If so, it was subtle. Another spot. I shot it. And soon I realized where I was supposed to shoot without the tutorial pulses telling me where to stick my finger. Several minutes went by where I poked and prodded the purple planet creature while he got bigger and bulgier. There was no score—not a numeric score, at least— but it seemed like I was making progress. At least until the planet exploded in a fit of giggles, the binaural pulses faded, and the app bumped me back to the home screen.

"Vic?" Jacob said. "Are you interruptible?"

I glanced up and found all three of them staring at me. I thumbed the app shut, hoping no one got "toddler video game" from the way I was jabbing the screen. "Yeah. Sure."

"What do you think of splitting into teams and re-canvas-ing the last known areas Kick was found? Carolyn and I will check back with the witnesses the cops talked to, see if any of them 'remembered' new information, and you and Zigler try to find any witnesses a non-medium would have missed."

I was flooded with relief over the prospect of being paired up with Zigler again. Carolyn scared me, for obvious reasons, but you'd think I would jump at the chance to work side by side with Jacob. Personally, fine. But professionally? He could be a lot to handle.

Like...a *lot*.

Zigler flipped open his notepad and said, "The party where Reginald scored his drugs took place in a storage facil-ity on Lincoln. Start there?"

Contrary to popular belief, Jacob's ego isn't impenetrable, so I did my best not to sound too excited. "Sure. Oh, and guys? Don't lean too hard on the pharmacist while we're gone. I know she'd be the obvious one...but my gut's telling me she passed Carolyn's first test for a reason."

Climbing into the passenger seat of Zig's Impala felt like coming home...except the part where I had to fumble around for the seat latch and crank it back three clicks to keep my knees out of my ears. And thankfully, neither of us felt the need for idle chitchat.

All in all, my day was really looking up.

Lincoln Avenue is a diagonal artery that cuts through the Ravenswood neighborhood in a baffling mélange of old and new in a hodgepodge mixture of businesses and apartment buildings. The Lok-Tite storage facility, all forty thousand square feet of it, was on a particularly seedy block that developers hadn't quite managed to encroach on...yet.

While we waited for someone to let us in to the party space, we poked through the hallways. They were dark, thanks to the smashed-out lights no one had taken it upon themselves to replace. The perfect spot to turn tricks or deal drugs—if you didn't mind getting shot while you were trying to transact business.

I pulled down white light and felt that telltale headiness. Not the hard-edged, panicky suckdown that makes my head throb and my eyeballs bleed. Just the locked-and-loaded feeling of being psychically ready, should some dead guy try getting frisky. "Flashlight?" Zigler asked.

Awww. He remembered to check with me first. I scanned the dim hallway for ghostly movement, then gave him my approval. "Fire it up. That pile of trash drifted up against the wall is prime habitat for rodents."

As the flashlight flickered to life, a distant electronic whine resolved itself into a thread of feedback...that then thundered into a choppy series of power chords.

CHAPTER 22

ANOTHER RAVE? AT THIS hour? I checked my watch—not even noon.

Zigler and I found the stairs and headed up to the source of the music just as the song petered to a halt. There was a click of drumsticks counting down, a squeal of feedback, and then the same song started again. "A band rehearsing," Zigler yelled over the noise. "Probably cheaper to rent storage than actual rehearsal space."

Probably so. Because a real rehearsal space would've had some soundproofing.

The band wasn't too worried about disturbing the lockers full of furniture from people's deceased family members, all the stuff folks might not want to part with, but didn't have the mental energy to sort through. The door to the band's locker was propped open with a rickety box fan blowing in air.

Inside the eight-by-twelve space, three pimply twentysomethings were getting their metal on, shirtless, and most likely jobless. They all had short hair, but they swung their heads as if they had something meaningful to twirl. When Zigler pushed open the door, he caught the drummer's eye and the rhythm faltered. The guitarist screeched to a halt and yelled, "Dammit, Kyle!" But the bass player already realized they had company—and he was more concerned with trying to hide the conspicuous roach-filled ashtray.

When the guitarist finally noticed us, he announced, "We're not breaking any rules. This is *our* storage space. We pay rent. And there's nothing in the contract that says we *can't* jam here."

"Calm down, Metallica," I said. "We're not here about the noise."

The bass player edged the ashtray under a set list on the floor. I restrained myself from rolling my eyes.

Zigler flashed his badge, introduced himself, and said, "We're investigating a party that took place two weekends ago."

"The rave?" Defensive Guitar Guy said. "As if we'd have anything to do with that kind of techno-crap noise."

We both stared at him. His amplifier gave off a steady, low-pitched drone. Hopefully there was nothing binaural in the sound. I checked my white light. Seemed normal.

The drummer cleared his throat and piped in, "Stylistically, electronic trance has totally different roots from rock and metal."

Says the guy who can't hold a steady rhythm for more than thirty seconds. "So," I said, "were any of you here that night or not? Keep in mind that we have access to surveillance footage, and if we find out you're massaging the truth, we can stick you in an interrogation room a lot smaller than this until your memory jibes with the evidence."

Guy three said, "We didn't jam that day, but I swung by to re-string my bass. And then I stopped down for a beer."

"Dude," the guitarist muttered in disgust.

"What? They had a keg."

I focused on the bass player. He had the sallow look of

someone who'd get winded standing up from the couch. Either he was trying to grow a mustache, or he hadn't quite learned to shave. "Approximately what time were you here? Did anyone try to sell you drugs?"

He nudged the set list a few inches to the right.

"Not weed," I clarified. "No one gives a rat's ass about weed. I'm talking about Kick."

The guy didn't seem like he believed us—as if this whole thing were an elaborate attempt to bust him over a mostly-smoked blunt—but at least he didn't deny all knowledge of the drug in question. "No way would I even think about touching Kick. That shit'll mess you up."

The know-it-all drummer piped in. "Besides, unless you're psychic, you'd get a better high from some antihistamines and a shot of Jack."

I ignored him and said to the bassist, "But you were at the party. If you have any idea who was holding, where they scored...."

"No. No idea."

"Or we could bust you for the weed."

"What weed? There's no weed here." He reflexively backed up a step and kicked over the ashtray. The roach rolled out, along with a scattering of seeds. "That's not mine. It was here when I got here. Do you have a search warrant? Oh my god. My mother's gonna kill me."

"Sir?" Zigler prompted. "What can you tell us about the Kick?"

"I dunno—these suburban chicks were pooling their money to buy it. Like a dare. 'Cause everyone knows it's a really harsh buzz. But it was late and everything else had dried up. Plus, it's kind of a badge of honor to say you've done it at least once."

What the hell—would it be a badge of honor to step in front of a speeding bus, too? "Who was selling it? Did they say?"

"Some guy."

Deadpan, Zigler said, "Can you be more specific?"

"Some middle-aged guy. And, for real...that's all I know."

We took the band's contact info in case we had any follow up questions. They were practically shitting themselves over the thought that we'd darken their doorstep again. It might've been fun to ask them a few more random questions just to watch them squirm, but I got a text that the building manager was waiting for us downstairs where the rave had taken place, so we cut the band loose and headed down to meet him.

In the basement. Hooray.

As we jogged down a dark staircase covered in graffiti, Zigler said, "You've changed."

"Have I?"

"The way you jumped right in to question those kids. It was...different."

"Different bad?"

"Just different."

I wondered what was to blame for the shift—three months of intensive training at the FPMP, my fortieth birthday, or the fact that at some point in the future, I might actually get married. Any one of those things would leave a mark. Added together, it was no wonder Zig noticed something was up.

The manager was waiting at the foot of the stairwell. He was a sinewy Caucasian guy, late sixties-early seventies, who reeked of generic cigarettes—and his entire demeanor declared he was way too old for this shit. "Whatever happened here, I'm not responsible." We both gave him a bland look, and he said, "They signed waivers."

Zigler pulled out his notepad and told me, "I can take the statement while you have a look around."

Given that we were in *a basement*, I'd rather not. But I supposed if there were any ghosts around, I could hardly expect

Zig to find them. I opened up the top of my head and called down white light—and this time, I imagined I could hear the strobing sound of the Mood Blaster app while I did it. It was nothing at all like being on psyactives—I wasn't supercharged or anything—but I did feel normal. Normal for me, anyhow.

The lowest level of the storage facility was actually pretty similar to the cannery's basement, minus all of Jacob's exercise equipment, plus a lot of gang tags and other, more creative, X-rated graffiti. It spanned the whole building, with brick walls, concrete floors, and steel columns holding the weight of the structure. No doubt everything was crawling with asbestos.

As I noted with little pleasure that the corner spray-painted *Pee Here* had actually been used as a makeshift urinal, I nearly dropped my phone into a puddle of piss when a familiar voice said, "So I checked around, like you wanted."

I spun around. No visual. "Jackie?"

"About that Kick. Some white guy's pushing it."

I'm not sure what startled me more. That she actually remembered the last thing I asked her to find out, that it corroborated the statement of another witness, or that she even recognized me to begin with. I wondered how she'd even managed to find me, but diagonal streets are weird. It took me a second to realize I was actually within a couple blocks of my old apartment.

"That's all?" I said softly. "No other description?"

"Just an old white guy. Like you."

Nice.

"If you could get a description of him, that would be great. Height, hair color, that sort of thing."

"Sure. I can try."

At the presence of a ghost, my internal valve had automatically surged open. It might be tempting to get complacent around Jackie, given that she and I had a lot of history together. But that episode the other night, the one where she was stuck in prostitute mode, served as a stark reminder that she wasn't just some benign invisible friend. Not only was she unreliable. She was dead.

I didn't get a full-blown headache from expending my psychic resources into funneling down white light, but I did get a precursor—a sensitivity, like something was about to start hurting. The fact that I currently sported a bloody eyeball—no wonder that bass player seemed nervous—had me clamping down on a mental regulator valve. Jackie's threat level was moderately low. While I couldn't see her, I had known her for years, and she'd never tried any possession bullshit. Plus, her lucidity level was currently as high as I could expect.

Now that I looked at it that way, I couldn't help but wonder. "Say, Jackie, I'm curious. Why are you here?"

"You tell me to find out about Kick for you, then you wonder why I'm here?" She laughed. "You be trippin'!"

And with that, I felt a palpable shift of energy. "Jackie?" I whispered...though I suspected she was already gone.

I rejoined Zigler, who finished up with the manager, then double-checked to see if I had any questions for the guy, which I didn't. Back at the car, he said, "You saw something." A statement, not a question.

"Not exactly...."

Back when Zig and I worked together, I might've left it at that. But he was right. My time at the FPMP had changed me. "Actually, I don't usually see this particular ghost. I hear her." I relayed what Jackie said to Zigler while his eyes darted to the back seat. "She's not here. She wouldn't be able to resist putting her two cents in if she was."

"She's like an informant, then? An undead informant?"

"Not *undead*, that makes her sound like—" I almost said *a zombie*. But I know better than to joke about zombies with Zigler. "Just dead, I guess." No doubt he was already ruing the fact that he'd been paired up with me for the day, and not Carolyn.

Maybe if I could humanize Jackie somehow, it would make the fact that she was helping me out a little more palatable. "I'm wondering, since Jackie probably died in the Fifth Precinct, maybe you can dig up a little more information on her." The more I thought about it, the more I warmed up to the idea. I gave Zigler a description of her murder. In some cities, that and a first name might be enough to locate someone on the database. But this is Chicago. Homicide is the city's biggest amateur sport.

Zigler took down what I knew. Luckily I'd seen her that one time I was on psyactives when Roger Burke had been drugging my coffee, so I could give a physical description—because who's to say Jackie was even her real name? For that matter, it was possible the john who shanked her managed to toss her in a dumpster and walk away scot-free, so there might not be anything more than a disappearance on record, if that.

How depressing.

For old time's sake, we stopped for lunch at a taqueria on Western Ave where we'd hashed through a murder or two, back in the day. The salsa was worse than I remembered, but at least the guacamole was still decent. We didn't chat—we ate. It was the same rhythm we had as a PsyCop team, ingesting a big spread of food while we digested the facts we'd just put together. Unfortunately, there wasn't much to go on yet, since there happen to be more than a few middle-aged white guys in Chicago.

Once he'd plowed through the last of his burrito, Zigler apparently felt the need to sum up the morning. "Working with you is nothing like working with Carolyn."

"What do you mean?"

"She won't eat anywhere without a salad bar."

I texted Jacob to see if there was anywhere else he wanted me to stop, and he asked us to come back to The Clinic and help chitchat with the staff. I'd thought I was pretty satisfied after my enchilada plate—especially after all the chips I'd consumed—but I realized I wouldn't say no to a little break room dessert.

When we got there, I didn't see Bertelli lurking around, so I crossed the red line in a blatant violation of all the ridiculous papers I'd signed in search of some baked goods. Gina had mentioned rhubarb was in season, and I was interested to see how the nurses would use it to show off their baking prowess. Unfortunately, in that break room, you snooze, you lose. Whatever dessert had graced the communal table was long gone. But I did find a familiar pharmacist sitting there, with her elbows planted among the tantalizing crumbs and a sour look on her face. Probably not because she'd missed out on the goodies, either.

"What are you doing up here?" I asked. "It's not your usual break time."

"Audit."

But I'd been gone for several hours. "Do they usually last this long?"

"No, more like fifteen minutes, half an hour at the most. This is the second audit of the day. I have work to do, and this throws everything off. And I can't stay late past a certain time without wading through a bunch of red tape."

I glanced at the floor. Different kind of tape. But no less annoying.

"What's Bertelli's deal?"

Erin gave a humorless laugh. "Probably worried the whole

Kick epidemic will somehow bite him in the ass." She glanced up to see if I'd be shocked at her candor. When I wasn't, she went on. "It's not logical. I have no idea what he thinks he's going to find in my pharmacy. My numbers always add up. And the psyactive component of Kick has been out of production for years. I get it—we distribute Psych pharmaceuticals. We're the obvious place to look. But checking and re-checking the same stock isn't gonna make something appear that simply isn't there."

No, it wouldn't. And with everything going on, I doubted Bertelli could afford to waste his time on a fruitless task any more than Erin wanted to sit in the break room after the free goodies were all gone.

Which led me to wonder if Bertelli was doing more than just auditing.

CHAPTER 23

I TRACKED DOWN JACOB wrapping things up for the day in his commandeered meeting room. "Can we get a look at the pharmacy surveillance?" I asked him.

He flipped open his laptop. "Absolutely. Laura arranged for me to tap into that feed just as soon as they figured out a prescription psyactive was involved. What timeframe do you want to look at?"

"Right now. Can we watch it live?"

Jacob hit a few keys, and we were in. We pulled up a couple of chairs and bent over the screen. "The guy in the suit," Jacob said. "Bertelli?"

I was incredibly sure I'd spot something on the footage—something that would not only incriminate Bertelli, but wrap up the whole Kick investigation. What I saw...was Bertelli's back. No big surprise, given that he knew exactly where the cameras were, but frustrating nonetheless.

I sighed in frustration. Yeah, it was him, all right, fiddling around at the workroom counter while he completely blocked our view. "Obviously, he knows exactly what the camera can see."

Jacob stroked his goatee. "But what's he actually doing?"

"He's 'auditing' the pharmacy—a little too much for my liking. I was hoping to get some idea of what the so-called audit entailed. Maybe I can arrange to have a camera in the pharmacy he doesn't know about."

I watched Bertelli shuffling through the meds, and made note of their general location so I could pinpoint which ones he was interested in the next time I hit the pharmacy.

After a few minutes, I realized Jacob wasn't watching Bertelli's back. He was watching me. I turned to face him. "What?"

His expression was soft, and a smile tugged at the corner of his mouth. "At some point, you'll need to stop claiming the only thing you're good for is talking to dead people. You know that, right?"

I rolled my eyes. "Yeah, I'm a regular Sherlock Holmes."

Given how twitchy I felt about being the subject of FPMP surveillance, I didn't actually mind dealing with the guy in charge of that particular department. Agent Peter Garcia had been part of a four-person team that lost one member to a stairwell and another to a woodchipper. Jacob and I managed to hustle him off to a safehouse before anyone found a creative way to make sure he never planted another bug.

I put in a call to Garcia and told him what I wanted, and half an hour later, he shot me a text to meet him outside. I found an official-looking utility van in The Clinic's parking lot, with a couple of guys in coveralls tinkering with a cluster of wires that hung off the nearest telephone pole. They were so completely ordinary that even though I knew I was out there specifically to meet Garcia, I had to look twice before I recognized him.

I have no idea what it is that makes Garcia look like he's actually supposed to be wherever he is. I've seen him wearing everything from a power suit to a fast food uniform, but no matter what environment he's in, he somehow looks like he's been there all along.

I, on the other hand, knew I'd stick out like a sore thumb for talking to the "utility workers."

When I hesitated, Garcia pointed at the Crown Vic and barked out, "Hey, man, is that your car?"

I almost wanted to deny it—his natural machismo brought out the avoider in me. But I reminded myself that he was my colleague, not some random workman in a tool belt. "Yeah?"

"Your front tire is low." He cocked his head toward the car as if to show me, and I ambled over to join him by the car. He crouched by the wheel well and I followed suit. It effectively blocked our conversation from anyone lingering around The Clinic's lobby who might be tempted to lip read.

Something subtle shifted in Garcia's expression when it was just the two of us face to face, and he could be "himself"...however briefly. And if he even knew what being himself meant anymore. "I took a look at the surveillance area from the existing footage and came up with something that wouldn't be out of place." He reached into his coveralls and pulled out a round plastic air freshener. "Find your line of sight—the higher, the better—peel open the double-stick tab and stick it to the wall."

I gave it a sniff. "What's it supposed to be?"

"Lavender. Strong enough to seem real, but subtle enough that nobody's gonna freak out and toss it unless they're super sensitive to that kind of thing. If anyone rips it open, it'll just look like a normal air freshener inside. The important parts are hidden between two layers of plastic. Expect the battery to last about a week."

Did we have any air fresheners in the cannery? Only in the home gym, as far as I knew—it got pretty musty sometimes.

And those had been down there for months.

But who was I kidding? Those things would go right in the trash the second I got home.

I thanked Garcia, pocketed the air freshener, went back inside, and headed straight for the pharmacy. Bertelli was done "auditing" and Erin was hard at work trying to make up for whatever backlog his presence had caused. No doubt I could come up with some plausible FPMP reason for the air freshener other than "spy cam." I have no compunctions about lying to people if it means I'll get what I want. But something in my gut was telling me I'd be better off leveling with her.

Then again, my gut can be a phenomenally bad judge of character.

Erin caught me staring at her through the safety glass and snapped, "What is it?"

Maybe I was being way too trusting...but if she was trying to hide something from me, wouldn't she take greater pains to act nice?

I motioned for her to let me in. She'd been counting pills and would need to start all over, but the damage was already done. "Listen, something's not adding up." I held out the white plastic disc. The scent of fake lavender wafted up. "I'd like to place additional surveillance in the pharmacy."

"Are you kidding me? Like this job isn't stressful enough as it is. Swear to God, I've got an ulcer brewing. Bad enough I've got Bertelli breathing down my neck without finding you lurking nearby every time I turn around, and now you want to add your own crap to the mix?"

Erin might've had a few more choice words for me, but I wasn't the only one lurking nearby. At the sound of raised voices, the stairwell door swung wide and Bertelli came power-walking toward the pharmacy. "Is there a problem?" he demanded.

I cut my eyes to Erin. If she blew the whistle on me—if my gut was wrong about her—I could kiss my plans goodbye. Not only would I have procured the camera for nothing, but our chances at sneaking in any surveillance of our own would be lost. Erin looked from me to Bertelli and back again, and her eyes narrowed. *Please don't say anything*, I tried to convey with my eyes. *I really don't want to be wrong for confiding in you.*

I was no telepath, and Erin was a certified NP. And she really did seem to be working on an ulcer. But when Bertelli swept up to the pharmacy door, all self-important bureaucratic blunder, she said, "No problem here."

Bertelli puffed himself up self-importantly and said, "Even so, Agent Bayne has broken his agreement to stay within the designated areas for the final time."

What was he gonna do, arrest me? "I was just following up on a few questions—" I began, but Bertelli wasn't buying it.

"I've tried compromising with you people." He jabbed a finger toward the red tape in the hall. "I've tried to make reasonable concessions. But you're not holding up your end of the bargain. That's it—I've had it. I refuse to put the health and wellbeing of my patients at risk from non-medical personnel running wild through the building. If the four of you don't vacate the premises, I'll have no choice but to declare an emergency shutdown." He cut his eyes to Erin meaningfully. "Without pay."

Now he was playing dirty.

Not only would a shutdown seriously compromise our investigation, it would destroy all the connections I'd been working so hard to create—connections that extended beyond the investigation itself and into my role as a patient. Doctor's appointments were bad enough as it was. Just imagine knowing the whole staff hated me because I'd caused Bertelli to dock their pay.

I didn't need Carolyn reading him to tell me he was hiding something. He'd been hell bent on keeping us from finding something at The Clinic, and this whole "red tape" business was just an excuse to get rid of us. But he was serious about shutting down, that much was obvious, and I figured I'd better not press my luck. "Fine," I said. "I'm going."

But as I turned to stomp out the door, Erin sidestepped and blocked my exit. I braced myself for an especially nasty parting shot. "Aren't you forgetting something?" She thrust out her hand. "My air freshener."

And right under Bertelli's nose, she peeled off the tab and stuck my spy cam on the wall.

Jacob and I and the PsyCops from the Fifth Precinct packed up our stuff and headed out. Was the camera mounted high enough? Was it sticky enough to stay put? Had Erin stuck it in another blind spot?

Only time would tell.

As I climbed into the car, my phone rang, a special ringtone I set to make sure I never blew off the calls: Laura. Jacob recognized the sound. How strange that our boss was touching base with me on the investigation. Not him. I'm really not accustomed to being the point person unless there's a ghost in the room. But unless we could go back in time and have him un-accuse her of shooting Roger Burke, given the choice, Laura would rather talk to me.

She greeted me calmly and professionally with, "Dr. Bertelli is lawyering himself to the teeth. Care to speculate why?"

I thought back to the tirade I'd just been subjected to. "Uh-...concerned about putting the health and wellbeing of his patients at risk?"

Luckily, despite my dry delivery, Laura knew me well enough to hear when I was speaking in sarcasm. "Any idea what he's hiding?"

"Hard to say. He's been a little too interested in the pharmacy, even though they don't keep psyactives in stock."

"Maybe he's triple-checking, just to be sure."

"Maybe," I said, more to acknowledge it was potential theory than to agree with her. Hopefully the new spy cam would shed some light on the matter...if it wasn't randomly aimed at some spot on the ceiling, or maybe a trash can.

The FPMP prefers to fly under the radar, so the big stink that Bertelli was making didn't sit well with Laura. "I've been hoping Jacob could shed some light on who Patrick Barley is really working for, but right now, the drug investigation takes precedence. I've put feelers out to the other regional FPMP offices, people I know and trust, and Kick hasn't shown up on their radar yet. We need to put a stop to this whole thing before it spreads, or else we look like we don't know what we're doing. And that's something we really can't afford."

That sounded like a fancy way of saying she was worried FPMP National would march in and replace her. Since she knew the inner workings of F-Pimp better than me, if she was worried, then so was I. When I agreed to join the team, I'd done it because Laura had asked. The more I thought about working for some hardass ex-military type, the less I liked it. Laura might be just this side of neurotic, but she understood me. Probably *because* of the neuroses. If some macho, hidebound bureaucrat filled her shoes, I'd be screwed. If that wasn't bad enough, there was the mental image of the first Kick OD I'd seen—the girl in purple. And the way her ghost looked all fucked up. I shuddered and said, "We're on it."

Laura's professional veneer slipped. "I sure as hell hope so."

CHAPTER 24

THE NEXT DAY, WE trooped back over to The Clinic with the full expectation that we'd be met with some fresh new resistance. When Bertelli came out to meet us in the lobby, all smiles, I presumed it was because he'd found some bureaucratic loophole that would keep us out of there once and for all. So I was baffled when what he said was, "An emergency board meeting convened last night to address the recent developments. It's in our patients' best interest that we assist law enforcement in every way possible—and, as we always say, patients come first."

We all glanced at Carolyn to see what she made of that. She gave a subtle shrug, like it registered true-ish to her telepathy...and yet she still didn't quite believe it.

He had Troy buzz the team in, which was done with zero chatting. How I'd face the day without a recap of last night's lineup, I wasn't sure. The red tape on the floor was gone. Bertelli led us to an exam room that had been emptied of its medical gear and fitted with a meeting room table and chairs. "This will be your new office space. You're welcome to stay as long as you like—although I'm sure we're all hoping that this crisis can be resolved as soon as possible."

I would've considered the possibility that he'd actually had a change of heart, were it not for the shiny new keycard readers on the stairwell doors...which meant the basement level was now off limits. There was nothing down there but storage, maintenance, meeting rooms and pharmacy. And I'd bet my last paycheck he wasn't trying to keep us out of the janitor's closet.

Once Bertelli was gone, Jacob asked Carolyn, "What do you make of that?"

"Technically true. They do *say* their patients come first."

We all considered that, then Zigler asked her, "You're a patient here, right? Which means he has access to your files. I don't know exactly how detailed they would be...."

But I did. When I was on the force, I was given a psychiatric evaluation by The Clinic's top headshrinker every three months, so Carolyn must've been subjected to the same treatment.

And she couldn't lie.

I said, "We can presume Bertelli knows exactly how Carolyn's talent works. But I doubt it really makes any difference. Whether or not we had a telepath on the team, he'd still be just as slippery."

Our new office was actually a lot nicer than the stale meeting room we'd had before. Probably something to do with the stark white walls and piercingly bright exam room lights—always a comfort. As we broke out the laptops and file folders, Zigler plunked down next to me and said, "I got some potential hits on that old homicide you asked me about." Wow, that was quick. It's really a thing of beauty to see what someone who knows how to work a database can come up with. "I can send you the reports. Did you want crime scene photos?"

"Might as well." I didn't relish the thought of seeing them, but they might help me wrap my head around Jackie's behavior. "And, Zig? Thanks."

Jacob rolled out a list of associates for our victims and started to divvy it up between us. It would be a lot of ground to cover, so it was a good thing we had four investigators. I was just about to suggest I go do a quick reconnoiter of the break room when the PA system gave off a shrill beep. "Code Blue!" Gina sounded really stressed. When she repeated the words, I thought it was the same announcement, but then realized it was slightly different the second time around. "Code Blue Star!"

Star? That couldn't be good. We all exchanged a quick look and scrambled up out of our seats to hit the emergency bay.

While Bertelli himself had just welcomed us with open arms, we all knew we were really skating on thin ice. We split up and skirted around the perimeter, tucking ourselves away from all the action while keeping the best line of sight each of us could manage.

Medical personnel surged around me. The doctors called out a bunch of medical sounding jargon in which the word "Kick" stood out like a twitching sore thumb. The team readied everything they could possibly ready. Anticipation danced across the hair on the backs of my hands and I chafed gooseflesh from my forearms through my jacket. I was thinking more like an investigator than a psychic, I realized, and there was a lag between "Oh shit, this is happening" and "Oh shit, white light." I rued the fact that I hadn't mastered yoga since the last time I'd thought about it. And I well and truly related to whatever poor sap had decided to take the quick road to psychic enhancement. Hastily, I opened up the valve and drew down the mojo.

Even though we were prepared for an emergency arrival, when the paramedics came rushing in with a guy on a gurney, it still felt like an onslaught. "Patient started seizing en route." They handed a small paper card to the lucky doctor...which jangled my sense of déjà vu. "Detective Valdez. Forty-five years old. P3." P3? Precog. "Fourth Precinct."

I'm not sure why I had the moment of disconnect. Maybe it was that I hadn't carried an old-school paper card of my own lately. Or maybe it was that I thought a highly trained psychic would know better than to dabble in something so freaking dangerous. But it really hit home when, in a completely out-of-character moment of dismay, Carolyn cried out, "Oh my God. Oscar?" then darted forward and grabbed onto the gurney.

Kick's latest casualty...was a PsyCop.

CHAPTER 25

Valdez. Precog. PsyCop. I knew the guy from umpteen boring meetings. We'd sat through all the same dull presentations. We'd squabbled over the last cruller—in fact, I could even remember the last smartass remark I'd made to him as I plucked it from the tray: "Didn't you see it coming?" And just like that, the whole Kick epidemic went from "too close for comfort" to "one hundred percent personal."

Maybe it's a different Oscar Valdez, I thought lamely. One I don't actually know. But the fact that I was the tallest one in the room meant that I had a bird's-eye view of the proceedings, and despite all the frantic activity around him—the transfer from the gurney, the IVs and the oxygen mask—there was no mistaking it. The guy twitching on the bed? I knew him.

His head jerked back and forth while his palms and heels pattered against the thin mattress pad like he was keeping time to a particularly improvisational tune.

The doctors barked out orders and the team responded like a well-oiled machine. But despite the fact that they were pumping him full of drugs, the arrhythmic *beep-beep-beep* of his heart monitor fell into a telltale flatline drone. Someone dove in with chest compressions while the crash cart paddles amped up. The whole thing was urgent. Barely controlled chaos. Which was why my first thought was, "How is he still twitching if his heart's stopped?"

And then I realized it wasn't his physical body that was flopping around.

I sucked down white light for all I was worth. Half a second ago, I knew Oscar personally and felt scared *for* him. But he was dead now—and as strong a Psych as he was? Now I was scared *of* him. My head gave a little throb and a wave of light-headedness washed over me, but I ignored the physical symptoms. I've dealt with all that and worse. Besides, I really didn't think I was capable of overloading my own systems on the power of panic alone. Not without a GhosTV or an experimental psyactive.

Oscar sat up. Or, rather, his ghost did. It wasn't the transparency that gave him away—the ghost was pretty damn solid. It was the look on his face. A look of frozen horror.

I scrambled backward and banked off a rolling table. A plastic vomit-catcher clattered to the ground, but the sound was obscured by the shrilling of the monitors. Someone shouted "Clear!" and the electronic clap of the charge popped through the electronic cacophony. Oscar's ghost flickered transparent and a halo of *something* lit up all around him. Only for a fraction of a second. But in that brief glimpse, I knew the situation was seriously fucked.

The doctor called out orders, and his crew intubated him and shot the IVs full of drugs. But as the ghost swung its legs off the table and staggered toward the door, I had the sneaking suspicion that whatever they were doing was an exercise in futility.

As ER bays went, this one was a hell of a lot more spacious

than the curtained stalls over at LaSalle. Even so, I couldn't back up far enough as the ghost of Oscar lumbered past. He didn't brush up against me directly...at least, I didn't think so. But a squirmy resonance licked through my nerves as he passed by. Even though I wanted nothing more than to make tracks in the opposite direction, I was drawn to him. Not because of my reluctant hero complex—*if I can't stop him, nobody can*—but a visceral gut reaction to his proximity.

Carolyn and Zigler were fixated on Oscar's physical body while the team tried to revive him, but Jacob noticed me peeling out into the hall. The farther the ghost got from the body, the more it picked up steam. It didn't walk. It didn't run. It skittered along like a fucked-up bag of spiders. Me? With my whole self screaming at me to go the other way...I gave chase.

The ghost shuddered down the hall and rounded a corner. I swerved around a nurse and sprinted after it. And Jacob took off after me.

The branch the ghost was heading down led to the lobby and the stairwell. I figured it was heading for the exit—that's what I would do—but it passed the turnoff and kept lurching forward, toward the stairs. Good thing for those new keycard readers, I thought, before I realized it could obviously go right through the door. Or could it? Just as I wondered, the door flung open and Erin rushed out with an armload full of IV bags. My own heartbeat skipped as I realized she was right in the path of the ghost. At the last minute, thank God, it staggered around her.

"Wait!" I called out, and reached toward the door...just as the ghost lurched through and it slammed shut behind him.

Erin backed against the wall to get out of my way. But it wasn't a clear path I needed. It was access. "Open this door," I barked out. She juggled IVs, terrified. Jacob caught up with us and took the bags that were sliding from her grasp. She pulled out a keycard on a bungee cord and slid it through the reader. Nothing. Too fast. It was new, and she didn't have a feel for it yet. Again. It slipped from her hands. She grabbed at the cord. It took her three grabs to catch it. Another swipe—facing the wrong way now.

I was just about to snap at her to pull it together when finally, *finally*, the card reader clicked green. I barreled through the door, desperately sucking white light. The stairwell was empty. I pounded down the metal stairs. This was where I went face to face with Reginald's ghost, I realized. This was where I salted him and he flew all apart.

No keycard reader at the bottom. I tore open the basement door and flung myself through it, fully aware that the ghost might be standing right there just waiting for me to bungle out into the open. But it was walking with such screwed-up purpose, I didn't think so.

At least, I hoped not.

I burst out into the main hallway. There's not a lot going on in the basement level of The Clinic. Meeting rooms. Restroom. Janitorial. Pharmacy.

Everything seemed to revolve around the pharmacy. Unless he was making a beeline for the circuit breakers, the pharmacy was where the ghost of Oscar Valdez was heading.

I rounded a corner. Oscar, or what was left of him, shambled toward the pharmacy. Erin was still on the stairs, I knew that, so he wasn't heading toward her. But something about the urgency that ghost was displaying triggered the cop in me to follow. I scrambled after it, drinking down white light. And just as I thought I would lose my target to a closed, locked door, a percussion from the defibrillator upstairs pulsed through the ether. The ghost lit up, flashed brightly, and blinked invisible for just a nanosecond. But in that gap when the ghost disappeared, a nimbus of chaos flashed bright all around it—the halo I'd seen before when doctors shot a jolt of electricity through Oscar's physical body. The halo I'd glanced when I salted Reginald. Only now, against the backdrop of the empty basement hallway, I got a better look at that halo.

And it was seething with habit demons.

It was just a flash. A glimpse. But that quick look was enough. I backpedaled quick, and Jacob—who couldn't see all the invisible gruesomeness overlaid on physical reality—smacked into my back. White light leapt from me to him. "Goddammit—don't touch me!"

"I'm sorry!" He sounded panicked—he couldn't have seen the flash of discharge, but he might very well have felt it. "You just stopped all of a sudden and I—"

"The pharmacy—it went in the pharmacy." Cripes—had *all* of them been heading for the pharmacy?

"I'll get Erin." Jacob turned on his heel and pounded back up the stairs while I stood ready on the balls of my feet and tried to cobble together a protective shell of white light. He didn't mean to steal it. I knew that intellectually. But the thought of my defenses being whisked away in proximity of the thing that used to be Oscar scared the living crap out of me.

Frankly, part of me was relieved that I couldn't go after that ghost. Okay, all of me. Like, really freaking relieved. Because the last thing I needed was the habit demons stuck all over it to decide I was a tastier target.

I had resigned myself to dredging up some sort of expression of disappointment that wouldn't sound too obviously contrived when the pharmacy doorknob turned. I froze, horrified, and backed away. But it wasn't the contaminated ghost that pushed the door open. It was Dr. Bertelli.

At least, I hoped it was. I'd better check. "Oscar?"

Bertelli did a double-take at me. "What's that? Wait, never

mind. What are you doing down here when I explicitly requested you stay on the first floor?"

It sure as hell sounded like Bertelli. "Code Blue Star," I told him—as if that had any bearing at all on what was going on. "I'll need to access the pharmacy."

"Under no circumstances can I allow any unauthorized personnel unsupervised access to our patients' medications. Just think of the liability! No, it's impossible. It would put our patients at risk—and our patients always come first."

While my sidearm was a comforting hardness against my ribs, and while I would've loved nothing more than to bully my way into that room, real-life law enforcement isn't like the movies. You can't just wave your gun around like a disgruntled headcase at a preschool. But body language speaks just as loud as a weapon. I got right up in Bertelli's face and said, "If you don't open that door right now, I will cite you for obstruction."

Since I was no longer a cop, I couldn't cite anyone for anything. But he didn't know that...and like a good white-collar asshole, he was suitably impressed by my stance. Oh, he hemmed and hawed all right, something about the board and something else about indemnity, but he opened the damn door.

I dragged down another volley of white light—did I feel that in my eyeball? Cripes, I hoped not—and rushed into the pharmacy.

Where I was entirely alone.

I sucked even harder at the white light, since a cagey ghost can camouflage itself better than a raisin in a chocolate chip cookie. Was what remained of Oscar flickering just outside my range of vision? I pulled harder, and looked. I didn't think so. But I had to make sure.

Jacob and Erin joined Bertelli in the doorway. "I need a few minutes in here," I told Jacob. "And I need to concentrate."

"Alone?" Bertelli cried. "Only authorized personnel have access to the medication—"

"Erin can stay." I looked at her to see if she had any qualms about me volunteering her as my babysitter. She was pale and her eyes were wide behind her thick glasses, but she gave me a shallow nod of agreement.

Bertelli wanted to complain, I could tell. But he could hardly object to me being in there if I was monitored by the person in charge of the pharmacy. I gave Jacob a meaningful look, cut my eyes to Bertelli, then glanced at the far end of the hall. He nodded and said, "Let's give Agent Bayne the space to do his job," and then herded the complaining administrator a short distance away.

"Why do you need to see the pharmacy?" Erin asked. Her voice shook.

"You probably don't wanna know." I drank down white light as she let me into the workroom, then opened up the vault and the storage locker too. "You'd better stay by the hall."

I'll give her credit. She didn't jump to the conclusion that I was just out to pocket some Valium.

I took stock of the workroom. No ghost. I pulled harder at the white light and approached the climate-controlled bunker where the medication was kept. No ghost there, either. Finally, I checked out the equipment storage. The cluster of disused medical goods was chaotic, all jumbled up, sideways, backwards, upside down. Poorly lit, to boot. "What's the deal with this?" I asked Erin.

"It keeps the outdated stuff out of everyone's way."

"Why don't they just get rid of it?"

"Liability, I guess. Someone could hurt themselves with it and trace it back to us." I pondered the jumble of crap, and she added, "Dr. Bertelli caught the last pharmacist taking naps in there."

A roomful of clutter was the last place I'd personally want to nap. Still, I couldn't see why anyone would care about a bunch of decrepit medical equipment.

I backed up, and took stock of the rooms as a whole. Nothing. If the suite hadn't been locked to me, I could've seen exactly where the ghost went. If he disappeared through a particular wall, for instance. Or sank through the floor. Or if he just stopped in the middle of the room and flew apart. Thanks to Bertelli's ghostly cock-blocking, I'd never know.

Of course, there was always the chance that Oscar Valdez hadn't left the pharmacy at all. "Remind me—how many refills do I get on my last prescription?"

"The painkillers? None. That's pretty standard—the team would have to write you a new scrip. Why, is your eye bothering you? I can page someone."

"I'll be fine," I said, and waved off her concern. If whatever was left of Valdez really was possessing her, he would've made a surprisingly good pharmacist.

I did one more sweep of the pharmacy, and then headed back upstairs. The bleating of all the monitors had died down, and everyone was distraught and hushed. And the form in the emergency bay that was once Oscar Valdez was now just another sheet-covered body.

Someone on staff, a woman, was crying. These guys'd had zero casualties up until a week ago, so I wasn't surprised they weren't as cavalier as the folks at LaSalle General. And Jacob had taken advantage of the opportunity to do some comforting. This was good. The more we could get the staff here to think we were on their side, the better off we'd be. Not that we *weren't* on their side. More like we needed to do whatever it took to stop Kick from spreading. But when Jacob turned to avail himself of the nearest box of tissues, I realized that it wasn't some random nurse he was comforting, but Carolyn.

I'd never seen her cry before.

I didn't know what to make of it.

Carolyn went out to the car to collect herself. It took her nearly an hour before she could pitch in and do her share of the work. It turned into a long, grueling day. We questioned a bunch of people, including the Stiff half of Oscar's PsyCop unit, to retrace his steps. But frankly, chances were, he scored the Kick off-duty, so no one was surprised when his coworkers turned out to be a bust.

Still, we had to try.

What was it that had inspired Oscar to play psyactive Russian roulette? Was it the missing kid he found—abducted, but alive? Or the kid he was still trying to locate?

He should have known better.

Not because he was a precog...but because he was a cop. He refused to acknowledge his limits and he insisted on using just one more time. And now? Not only was the kid he was looking for languishing in some sick bastard's bed—or maybe a shallow grave out by the landfill—but so were all the other kids Oscar would never have a chance to bring home.

Selfish. That's what it was, him trying to force his talent open with Kick. Just plain selfish.

And now look where it got him.

The ride home that night was pensive. Jacob and I were both rattled over what happened. Losing a brother in blue always hit hard. Losing a fellow PsyCop was positively brutal. Not only that, but I'd lost a really solid ghost to a locked door— a ghost who could've given me solid intel on the source of the drugs.

When we got home, I gave Darla another call, but her voicemail was still the same. Damn it. If only I could have her for half an hour, we'd get a shot at contacting Valdez and breaking this case wide open.

If only I could figure out how to call a ghost long-distance myself.

Note that I had no doubt of my capacity to reach past the veil. After all, Darla got only the vaguest twinge of an impression where I saw a full-blown repeater. It was my *ability* in question. The fact that I didn't know what the hell I was doing.

Or the fact that I was naturally focused in a particular direction. Visual where Darla was auditory. Physical where Darla was etheric. Could a medium even train themselves to shift from one focus to another, given enough time, effort and patience, in the way a right-handed person might learn to write left-handed if they had no other choice? Or was it as futile as trying to change your facial features by simply thinking about them?

I'd been standing there in the vestibule staring at Darla's number on my phone for who-knows-how-long when the sound of something breaking in the kitchen brought me back to present-day reality with a sudden jerk. I headed in, and found Jacob standing amidst the carnage of a dropped container of chili. And since we were transitioning from plastic storage containers to glass and our kitchen floor was ceramic tile, not only were there globs of saucy ground beef and beans all over, but shards of broken glass, too.

I refrained from observing that it reminded me of a week-old murder scene I'd once worked. Judging by the look on Jacob's face—a look that was entirely out of proportion with the dropped chili—he wouldn't have found it even remotely cute. I grabbed a plastic bag out of the drawer and said, "We're all upset about Valdez."

Jacob gave a little start as if he hadn't even registered that I was there. "I didn't really know the guy. Only in passing."

O...kay. I knelt just outside the splatter zone and picked out the biggest, most dangerous-looking hunks of glass, though everyone knows it's the sneaky little shards that'll get you. I grabbed a spatula, hoping to avoid finding said shards the hard way, and started shoveling the fragment-studded chili into the bag. Jacob grabbed a serving spoon and followed suit. When we excavated down to the tile—hooray, our grout work was now orange—he said, "You stopped so suddenly."

"Stopped...what?"

"If I could've avoided touching you, I would have. Give me *some* credit. I do know how this all works."

Wow. We'd both been ruminating over the death of Oscar Valdez, but for entirely different reasons. His, a lot more personal than mine. "I know you do."

"Just because I can't actually *see* it like you can—"

"Jacob—I know. I didn't mean to snap at you. You just surprised me, is all." In a stunningly dangerous moment, I might add, though pointing that out would only make things worse.

"Put yourself in my shoes. I lost Kamal's trail and can't figure out where the hell Patrick Barley came from. Laura hardly even speaks to me. I used to think I was good at being a Stiff, acting as the right-hand man to a high-level Psych. But I felt that energy jumping between us and there was nothing I could do to stop it. You think training is sparse for mediums? It's nonexistent for...whatever it is I've got."

I was supposed to be the one with the inferiority complex. Not him. "Hey." I grabbed Jacob's hand and squeezed it against the handle of the spoon. Nothing extrasensory leapt between us. "Even with whatever support the Program can give us, this is a bigger case than either of us is used to tackling. The stakes are high. Plus, it's personal. It's bound to be frustrating. And of course we want to do better. But, heck, even if we weren't psychic, we'd just feel daunted in some other way. Cut yourself some slack."

He nodded, then nudged off my hand to delve beneath the

sink for some liquid cleanser with bleach. I yanked off a wad of paper towel and swabbed up all the liquid and the remaining few beefy crumbles. Jacob squirted on the cleanser and pushed it into the grout with our kitchen sponge.

Despite the talk, he still felt shitty about grabbing my white light, I could tell. And I still felt shitty for barking at him.

Some things just had a tendency to leave a mark.

CHAPTER 26

When I climbed into bed with my Mood Blaster app, it was tempting to take a little cruise on Calming Comet. But while part of me was eager to remedy my perpetual sleep deficit, another part—the one that liked to bask in its own self-perpetuating anxiety—was convinced I'd need to snap to in the middle of the night and deal with a scary-assed ghost.

I settled for the Down to Earth mode which, according to the info, oscillated at a low-alpha high-theta frequency designed for calm relaxation. It wasn't exactly like valium...but I didn't hate it. And, again, though I was suspicious any effects these binaural beats might've been having on my state of mind were mere placebos, I did find myself thinking about our current case in a more constructive way than I might have otherwise.

As I directed soothing, slow-motion meteor showers toward the surface of the planet, I thought about Darla and how it might feel for her to reach out for a ghost who's long since left the physical world. As far as I could tell, all she had to do was try. Like searching for an elusive memory...though that analogy was no big help, since I was lousy at remembering things, too.

If only I could initiate a long-distance connection myself, just once, and see how it felt. But it seemed like I'd need a boost of some kind to help me get over that hump.

Yoga? I hadn't been able hit on the right sequence of moves without the yoga lady from Jacob's gym—the gym I was banned from.

Binaural beats? I had a sneaking feeling that all they did was tweak my level of alertness.

A psyactive? Herbs and powders were hit-or-miss, and the prescription goods were off the market.

But there was one particular tool I had at my disposal that I knew, without a doubt, actually did something. A tool people had killed and died for.

The GhosTV.

Jacob wasn't sleeping any more than I was when I said, "I'm gonna need your help with something."

He rolled over to face me and nodded.

"But I'm not willing to do it here. We need to install the GhosTV at The Clinic...and we need to do it on the down-low."

In her bid to challenge the finality of death itself, Jennifer Chance had cobbled together five GhosTVs that we knew of. The units that belonged to Con Dreyfuss and Dr. K had been confiscated by FPMP National. It wouldn't surprise me if the suits had grabbed the set from the evidence locker in Iowa, too. There was one TV at large. And another in my basement.

That particular set? I tried my best not to think about it. Because, frankly, it gave me the creeps. Even boxed up as it was in its locked protective crate.

Jacob was sorely in need of a win, and he latched onto the idea of successfully adding the GhosTV to our arsenal. "I'd call Jack to help us move it. Good thing it fits in his SUV." Good thing we'd purchased a heavy-duty dolly when we spotted one on sale, too. "If anyone asks, claim it's paperwork, a bunch of files, something boring no one would care about. Too bad they moved us out of the conference room and into an exam room. It'll be a tight squeeze."

"Will it? If Zigler and Carolyn find out about the damn thing, that puts them under FPMP National's microscope." Not that they weren't already. But things can always get worse. "Plus, Carolyn can't lie. If anyone asks her a random question—"

"Then it ends up on *their* permanent record, too. You're right. We need to keep this between the people who already know. I can deal with Carolyn. Tell her to steer clear since we need to do something she's better off not knowing about."

"She won't pry?"

"She knows better."

While he called and gave her a heads-up, I decided it wouldn't have occurred to me to be so direct. Maybe that was for the best. In my experience, that wasn't how the world worked. Directness just pissed everybody off, and then they did what they were going to do in the first place, regardless.

Monday morning, Jack Bly showed up bright and early with a big cup of coffee for each of us. Not because he wanted to slip experimental psyactives into mine, but because he lived with me undercover for the better part of a month, and he didn't want to run the risk of having to drink anything I'd made myself. As much as I knew what Agent Bly of the FPMP looked like, the sight of him in a well-tailored black suit caused me to do a mental double-take. I was used to seeing him in baggy gym shorts and old T-shirts now.

"Hell of a thing about Oscar," he said by way of greeting. I'd forgotten they knew each other as PsyCops. "Not that I expect any of us to live long enough to die peacefully in our sleep. But still, it was a lousy way to go."

We led him down to the basement to take stock of the situation. He sized up the crate as if he'd forgotten precisely how daunting it was. Can't say I blamed him. That was my typical reaction to the thing, too.

Jacob said, "Even if we claim it's something as tedious as files, people are still going to wonder."

"What if we kept it inside the case?" I suggested. "Thread the power cord through and keep it facing the wall. It's not like I need to see the screen for it to work its magic."

Bly said, "It might work, but only for short bursts. The old tube generates heat, and the padding inside the case will act as an insulator. If you kept it turned on in there for any extended amount of time, you'll risk burning it out."

Part of me wondered if that was actually such a bad idea. If I killed my GhosTV, I'd no longer need to worry about Big Brother coming to snatch it from my sweaty grasp.

Frustrated, Jacob said, "It's been sitting here for ages gathering dust. We should've had some sort of camouflage made for it. A vented casing that makes it look like something unremarkable. A bank of locked filing cabinets."

Oh sure. Now the useful ideas present themselves.

Bly shrugged. "Our stagers can make that happen—they'll do it without asking too many questions, too, if I give them the dimensions. But HQ is stretched thin with everything that's going on. Even if they dropped everything and started right now, it would take a few days. Have we got that long?"

I thought back to all the creeptastic ghosts we were dealing with. And my proximity to them. And the fact that I really needed to have the sharpest view possible if our illegal psyactive claimed another victim. If...or when. "We can't afford to wait," I said.

Even with the dolly, it was no treat wrestling the GhosTV into Bly's humongous Lexus. We followed him to The Clinic and met up in the lobby. Bly flashed an ID and told Troy, "We've got some equipment to transfer, so we'll need access to your delivery bay."

Troy was flustered. Apparently last night's episode of *Clairvoyage* wasn't offering him any clue as to how to handle the situation. But Jack Bly had the confidence of someone who didn't take "no" for an answer. Plus...as a high-level empath, he was able to predispose strangers to do his bidding.

Without waiting for Bertelli to invent some reason to tell him not to, Troy met us and our massive load of "files" by the service door. When we shoved our work table against the wall, we could wedge the crate into the room with us. Barely.

We removed the cover and situated the set so it was facing the wall with its protective shell toward the door. Any medical staff would see nothing but a nondescript black case, unless they took it upon themselves to come right up to it and peer around the back. It would've been a lot easier if there were casters on the thing so I could swing it away from the wall without Jacob's help when I needed to tweak the dials. But since its ungainly bulk would shield it from casual curiosity, it was probably for the best that we'd never added wheels.

Bly said, "If you guys don't need me anymore, I'm gonna head back to base. The collective anxiety level here is sky high." He gave the back of his neck a squeeze. "It's so bad I'm starting to sweat."

I could only imagine what it must be like to watch your patients drop like flies. Or, in the case of Bertelli, worry not that people were dying, but that he'd somehow be found liable for their deaths.

I had to perform a pretty acrobatic contortion to reach the outlet and plug in the set, but thanks to my long arms, I managed. "If someone croaks, we'll be ready for 'em. But we'll need to be careful not to burn out the tube."

Jacob said, "I'll monitor the temperature—I can slip my hand between the console and the case right there, see how hot it's getting. You call me, we keep an open channel, and let me know when to turn it on. Should we test it now?"

I nodded and Jacob turned it on. The channel was currently set to whatever it was that let me see people's talents. A webwork of red veins appeared on him. Or maybe it was more of a protective mesh. Whatever it was, it didn't spook me quite so much, now that I knew what to expect. "Is it working?" he asked.

"Yeah. It's working."

I was so distracted by the red lines of power coursing through Jacob, I nearly jumped out of my skin when a quiet voice behind me said, "Vic?"

I whirled around and found Gina in the doorway, looking alarmed. Or puzzled. Or maybe just baffled. But while she was obviously curious about our big black case, what she said was, "We have a new patient who was referred by LaSalle, and I think you'll want to talk to her."

"No Code Blue?"

"Let's hope not. Right now, she's listed as urgent. Not emergency. But according to a Dr. Gillmore who sent her here, there's Kick in her system."

An odd glow around Gina made me realize she was a precog, albeit a subtle one, and also reassured me that the GhosTV was playing. She led me to the room where a team stood ready. Some thin-skins flickered among the staff. Empaths. Not surprising, when you thought about it. Though I'd imagine the burnout rate was high.

A moment later, paramedics brought in the patient through the emergency door in the back of the building—on a wheelchair, not a gurney. I registered that it was a thin woman with long, dark hair. And that an oxygen mask was covering her face.

And that she was swarming with habit demons.

One of the paramedics gave the nurse beside me the low-down. "Bethany Roberts, age thirty-eight. Ingested a single dose of Kick approximately ninety minutes ago, then admitted herself to urgent care at LaSalle General fifteen minutes later."

I backpedaled until my shoulder blades hit the wall. The woman knocked the mask askew and the paramedic calmly replaced it. I knew her. The yoga lady from Halsted Fitness Club. Not only did I know her, but when she moved her hand quickly, it left a tracer behind.

I glanced down at my own hand and gave it a quick wave.

Just like mine.

"Listen to me!" She knocked her mask off again. "It takes food several hours to pass from the stomach into the small bowel. There's still time to purge it from my system."

There was a commercial for mosquito repellant, back when I was a kid, that showed someone sticking their bare arm into a glass box filled with mosquitoes. Looking at this Bethany woman within range of the GhosTV? That's what it was like. But substitute translucent, fist-sized blobs where the mosquitoes would normally be. Instead of plunging their built-in drinking straws beneath her physical skin, they were hooking into her with their etheric tethers. And every time she swept her arm for emphasis, most of them flew off, which only added to the boxful-of-mosquitoes effect.

The doctor helped her onto the exam table and said, "I take it you tried to purge unsuccessfully yourself?"

The nurses with thin skin both flinched as if the doctor had scolded them, and the habit demons swarmed in hard.

"I made a mistake," Bethany said coldly, in the same tone of voice in which she'd tell me not to lock my knees, back when she thought I was cruising her class in hopes of seducing a vulnerable stay-at-home mom. "Don't make me regret transferring my care here. I'm sure they'd be able to pump my stomach just as well at LaSalle."

She chafed her forearms and habit demons took flight. Not for good. They were still hovering around her, hoping for a snack. But it was obvious she wasn't gonna just sit back and let them feed off her. Whether she knew it or not.

Suddenly, the habit demons disappeared, and for a moment there, I thought Bethany had done it. Maybe with a mental yoga move in her arsenal that was my equivalent of white light. But then I realized that it was more likely the GhosTV was turned off. Hopefully just that, and not burned out and ruined.

I backed into the hall, shoring up my own defenses all the while. Causation or correlation—I wasn't sure if habit demons had a particular hard-on for mediums, or if it was just the mediums who were most bothered by them. Either way, I didn't want them to decide I was an easier target than Bethany. I turned up the wattage on my white light, then gave Jacob a quick call and asked him, "Did you turn off the TV?"

"I did. It felt pretty hot. Should I turn it back on?"

I wanted him to. But I also didn't want to lose the set over a bunch of...I'd need to start calling them something other than "habit demons" if I wanted anyone to take them seriously. I wasn't surprised to find them lurking around. They could even be the reason Kick was so addictive. Oh, sure, there was probably some neurochemical reward system in play. But that didn't mean the etheric body wasn't involved.

Gina approached and nodded for me to follow her. We stepped into an empty exam room, where she said, "They're going to administer activated charcoal to try and neutralize whatever drugs are still in the patient's stomach, and it can get pretty ugly. Some people vomit. And it looks like something out of *The Walking Dead* when they do."

I'd seen worse, but figured I shouldn't brag about it. Your average person doesn't need to know zombies are somewhat real, even if they aren't coordinated enough to chase you down and eat your brains.

Gruesome or not, I really needed to keep an eye on Bethany. Ideally with the GhosTV playing. "Say, Gina, would you happen to know if I could get...a fan?"

"Sure. How big?"

"There's more than one size to choose from?"

"Sometimes the exam rooms get a little stuffy, so we have a desktop model I could rustle up. Jill keeps a bigger one in her cubical she might let you borrow. I doubt you want the fan the janitors use to dry the floor."

Actually, I wouldn't be so sure about that. But in the spirit of not calling too much attention to the GhosTV, I said, "If you can snag me a couple of the desktop fans, that'd be great."

While Gina went off to find me some fans, I headed back over to see how Bethany was doing and found her lips were blackish, the doctors were now gone, and a PA was seated in the room doing active observation...or maybe just babysitting. Judging by the look on Bethany's face, she was none too thrilled about it.

"Do you mind if I talk to the patient?" I asked the PA. "Alone?"

"I should check with Dr. Bertelli...."

I gestured to all the monitors. "I'll holler if any of these alarms go off. I promise."

The PA wasn't entirely convinced, but since she knew I was a big federal so-and-so—and since I asked nicely—she did relent.

I left the door slightly ajar, just in case any medical

personnel needed to rush in, and said, "Ms. Roberts? Is it okay if I call you Bethany?"

She'd been glaring angrily at the wall, but her head snapped up when she registered that she'd heard my voice before. "Hold on, I know you. From the gym."

"Victor Bayne," I said, suddenly glad that unless she made me spell it for her, it wouldn't contradict anything I might've told her while I was undercover. I flashed my ID, long enough for it to look official, but not long enough for her to get too curious about the specific agency I worked for. I generally just refer to myself as a federal agent and let folks think what they will. I've never had anyone ask me to clarify.

I could have tried throwing my weight around and acting all important, but I'd seen Bethany in action and knew she preferred to be top dog. Since bossing her around would only shut her down, I tried appealing to her helpful side. "Listen, my boss wants me to figure out where the Kick is coming from and I'm having a really tough time. Any information you can think of would really help me out."

"I don't know what you're talking about."

"You're not in any trouble. I promise. This drug is dangerous, though, and we need to get it off the streets before anyone else gets hurt. Can you tell me where you got it?"

"I was at a party at a coffee shop, a bunch of us were, from work. Someone offered me an herbal supplement. I didn't know him."

I was eager to ID Bertelli once and for all. I called up his dossier on my phone and showed Bethany his photo. "Is this the guy?"

She shook her head. "No. I'd remember if he had such good posture."

I turned the phone around and wondered how she got "posture" from his cheesy headshot.

She added, "Plus, his BMI was higher."

That was awfully...specific. "About how old would you say he was? The guy with the Kick?"

"Oh, I'm terrible with ages. Maybe my age? But that's what I always think."

"And his race?"

"Definitely Northern European. Possibly Swedish, though he might've been Norwegian."

I blinked, then said, "And the supplement he was peddling—what did he claim it would do?"

Bethany crossed her arms and drew in on herself. It didn't make her smaller. It just made her angles protrude. "I don't see what difference it makes."

Carefully, I said, "Was it something...psychic?"

She gave me a piercing look to see if I was mocking her. My bland cop-face must've been reassuring. "Fail a psychic screening and forget it. Everyone acts like you're delusional if you think the findings are flawed."

While she spoke, the air around her blossomed with habit demons as Jacob tinkered with the GhosTV. I jerked away, then turned aside and tried to cover my flinch with a dry cough. Then I said, "Screenings can be pretty subjective. And they measure some talents better than others."

"Exactly! You know, I never would've pegged you for someone with an interest in esoteric matters. It just goes to show how far off-base a snap judgement can be."

Not necessarily. All things considered, I probably would be just the sort of guy to scoff at psychic ability, had I not seen the air around her swarming with nonphysical jellyfish. "If you don't mind my asking, what was it you thought would show up on your tests?"

"Astral projection. But since there's no empirical measure—since I couldn't do it at will—I was told I was probably just dreaming, thank you very much, goodbye."

I made a mental note to talk to Darla about adding another section to the Clinical Pre-Assessment for Mediumship.

Bethany uncrossed her arms and gave her forearms an absent brush. Habit demons recoiled.

"Tell me something," I said. "You had second thoughts about Kick just as soon as it hit your system. But if there was another dose right in front of you...would you be tempted?"

"Of course not."

"You sure about that? Just...y'know...in case you maybe didn't give it a fair shake?"

She frowned, and habit demons swooped down and sank in their tethers.

If I powered up my white light, could I knock them aside like so many cobwebs? Maybe. But then there was the chance that, just like cobwebs, they'd only end up sticking to me. Hastily, I added, "You made the right choice. That drug you took is highly addictive." The habit demons stirred, but remained stuck to her. "It's not an herbal supplement, either. It's as manufactured as they come."

A single habit demon dropped off. One out of at least a dozen. And it didn't even disappear—it just hovered nearby, waiting to reattach. How crazy would I come off asking her to do a visualization with me and walking her through a white balloon? She did that type of thing at the end of her yoga sessions, but that was yoga. This was urgent care. "Give me your hand," I said. She held it out, and I pulled the baggie of sacred salt from my pocket and tipped a small mound onto her palm.

"Is that...salt?"

"The crystal structure has a beneficial vibration. Clinically proven." I pictured white light flowing into it from the heavens, and thanks to the range of the GhosTV, it lit up to my inner eye. In an ideal world, the activated salt in her hand would be enough to send the habit demons packing. So, naturally, nothing of the sort happened. They noticed it, all right. The closest ones rippled, then sniffed at it. But it wasn't the abject fear I'd been hoping for, just curiosity.

I told her, "This will sound a little bit abstract, but you've got to center yourself. Whatever that means to you."

She was giving me a puzzled look that conveyed, *The awkward guy from the gym is telling me to do what?* But when she smoothed her long hair back, a few more habit demons detached. And then, one by one, they faded. Wow. All those years of yoga must have given her some phenomenal control.

"I found three fans—I hope that'll help." Gina walked in with a small electric fan in each hand and one tucked under her arm, power cord dangling. We all looked at the mound of salt in Bethany's hand. No doubt Gina had seen plenty of unusual things at The Clinic, since all the patients were certified psychics. Even so. I picked up a nearby trash can and held it up for Bethany, who wordlessly tipped in the salt with a self-conscious brush of her palms.

Once Gina handed off the fans with her blessing, Bethany looked pointedly at my ringless left hand and said, "How's your husband?"

The urge to keep up the charade was strong—but if private lessons could potentially be in my future, it would be inconvenient to make Bly come over and pretend he lived with me. "Things didn't work out," I said. Would she end up running into him again, too? Anything was possible. "Turns out he's straight."

CHAPTER 27

Jacob's ringtone sounded. His timing was great. By taking his call, I excused myself from having to go into my speedy divorce. "There's something you need to see," he told me. And while most people would think he simply had a relevant tidbit of information to share, I could tell from the amount of control in his voice that whatever it was he was onto, it was big.

Was the GhosTV doing something interesting? That hunk of electronics was a royal pain in the ass—and terrifying, to boot. It was about time for it to earn its keep. The dials were hardly exact, and something would invariably get knocked out of alignment in transport. Maybe this time around, I'd tuned it into something Jacob could see, or feel, or somehow tangibly sense.

I rapped on the door and he let me in, and now, seeing him with my own two eyes, I could tell he was practically bursting at the seams. "Take a look at this," he told me.

But instead of leading me to the GhosTV, he pulled up something on his laptop and spun it around for me to see.

Surveillance. From the pharmacy. I craned my neck to see if the GhosTV was playing without sticking my head between the console and the wall. But I was no longer leaving tracers behind and Jacob wasn't looking red and veiny, so probably not.

Jacob said, "Right there, at the timestamp I've marked. Bertelli pockets something."

Did he? I poked at the controls until I figured out the one that would let me step back. "It's kind of blurry."

"No, he's pocketing meds. I'm sure of it."

I checked the timestamp, and then my watch. All this had happened while Bethany transferred in and the staff was busy. I played back the few frames of video at normal speed, then half-speed, then normal speed again. He might have been pocketing something. Or he might've just had an itch.

"We need to see what he's skimming," Jacob said. "Antipsy-actives?"

"Why would he do that?"

Jacob looked at me knowingly. "In case his homemade psyactive goes wrong."

Did Bertelli strike me as an innocent man? Not by a long-shot. The guy was way too slick, and it was obvious he was hiding something. And of course I didn't buy his whole "liability" song-and-dance, either. He wanted to limit our access to the building. In fact, he would've preferred to get us locked out completely. And yet, I wasn't entirely convinced he had anything to do directly with Kick. "I showed Bertelli's picture to our latest guinea pig, and she says he's definitely not the one who gave her the drug."

"So he's not in it alone—there's another guy handling the distribution. It's not the footsoldier we want, anyway, it's the mastermind. All we need to do is establish possession of psychic pharmaceuticals."

"He's the director of a specialized psychic medical clinic."

"But he doesn't have an antipsyactive prescription—I've

checked. And I'm sure he doesn't have carte blanche to skim from the pharmacy while Erin is looking the other way. Someone's gotta search him."

If you've ever been targeted by a mall cop, you know what it's like to be forced to turn out your pockets. Lucky for me, I'd never been tempted by five-finger discounts. Once, back when I was in high school, a ruddy-faced security guard thought he'd pulled one over on me when, apparently, I'd spent too long hovering by the Teen Beat magazines. Thankfully, there was nothing in my old Wranglers that afternoon but a partially-sucked Gobstopper.

If we accused Bertelli of smuggling out meds, we really couldn't afford to be wrong. Even my teenaged self had been affronted over being accused of stealing—even as I was trying to cultivate the reputation of a tough mohawk guy.

Jacob said, "The longer it takes for us to bring him down, the more people will die. People we know. People like us."

True. All of it. And not only did I know the psychics who were dying...but they were leaving really fucked up ghosts behind.

Jacob stood. "If you don't take care of him, Vic, I will."

"No. I'll handle it. It's my investigation." That's the reason I gave him. Not the fact that if he was wrong, it would be like the Laura Kim murder accusation all over again. "Call HQ and have them send some experts to search his car and office. I'll confront him now, before he has a chance to ditch any evidence."

It wasn't in my jurisdiction to place a civilian under arrest. Not anymore. In fact, the only people I had any kind of authority over these days were already dead. But my findings carried more weight than they ever did when my paychecks were issued by the Chicago PD. If I pointed my finger at Bertelli, someone would show up and arrest him. And whatever he was charged with might actually stick.

At least...it should.

But the nearer I got to Bertelli, the more I second-guessed myself. In law enforcement, you need to pick a lane. Make a decision and follow through. But finding out that the legal system had failed me these past several years, that murderers I'd brought to justice had been walking free? It did a number on my self-confidence. And even though I knew Laura Kim would have my back, I was hesitant to confront Bertelli in a space where whatever happened would be his word versus mine. I paused in the doorway of his office and said, "Can I see you for a minute?"

He looked up from his paperwork. "I'm really very busy."

"It can't wait."

"Fine. But make it quick."

I fixed a surveillance camera in my line of sight. "Not in there. Out here."

Since he wanted nothing more than to get rid of me, he did as I asked. With a long-suffering look, he put down his pen and came to join me in the hall. I held out my hand and said, "Remove your jacket."

He looked at me like I'd asked him to take off his own head. "You're serious."

"Sir?" I said this in my coppiest cop voice. The one designed to elicit compliance. "Remove your jacket now and hand it over."

He wasn't used to hearing that kind of tone from me. Then again, no one on staff was...and a couple of the nurses poked their heads out of a nearby exam room to see what all the stern voices were about.

I thought Bertelli was going to keep on defying me to buy himself some time to ditch the pills in his pocket. People do it all the time. Pitch their stash out the window of a moving car, or at the very least, toss it in the back seat and hope the traffic cop who stopped them is phenomenally unobservant.

Very few people in this world enjoy submitting to authority, and bigwigs like Bertelli are particularly averse to being challenged. I was so sure he'd make a huge stink about it, it surprised me when he stood up, crossed the room and unbuttoned his blazer. I backed up a few paces to ensure he was well within range of the mechanical eye and he matched me step for step. He peeled off the jacket and presented it to me. As he did, he murmured, "I have no idea what you think you'll find, but I have no doubt you'll be sorely disappointed."

"Anything sharp I need to worry about?" I asked.

"Of course not."

Right pocket, cell phone. Left pocket, spare change. Fine. I was just covering all the bases before I got to the big reveal—the inner pocket. There was something in there, all right. Something substantial. I pulled out a palm-sized leather case, flashing back to all the times Con Dreyfuss waved a pill-minder under my nose to tempt me with yet another Seconal. His was cheap plastic. But Bertelli was too fancy for that, and I doubted he owned a cheap plastic anything.

I met his eyes just as my thumb found the latch to flick it open. And in that fraction of a heartbeat before I exposed him for all to see, I registered the tiniest hint of a smile.

The leather case? A business card holder. Nothing more.

Normally, I would just figure he'd stashed the drugs somewhere in his office. I still hoped that would be the case. But that fleeting glimpse of a smile made me wonder if whatever I'd seen on the pharmacy surveillance had been nothing more than a stray itch after all.

CHAPTER 28

WE CALLED IN THE cavalry, on the off chance that if Bertelli had indeed taken drugs from the pharmacy, he hadn't yet managed to dispose of them. Specialized investigators combed through his office, men and women who took finding things very seriously. A couple of them were even clairvoyant.

Nothing.

Bertelli was equal parts resigned and inconvenienced. But I had the sneaking suspicion he was also pleased.

The afternoon wasn't a complete shit show. On the upside, Bethany was stabilized enough to be released. As they wheeled her out the emergency door into a waiting cab, we exchanged numbers and I made her promise to call me if she remembered anything that would help me track down the dealer. I hoped I wouldn't regret it. She might start peppering me with details like his resting heart rate or his shoe size.

We were on our way home and I was lost in thought, replaying that video of Bertelli in my mind's eye. He really had appeared to be reaching in that pocket...the one that contained nothing but a business card holder. The specialists had even gone over the jacket to ensure I hadn't missed anything. I hadn't.

Jacob must've been processing the day too. Neither of us said a word the whole drive. The silence in the car was so profound that when the fuel gauge beeped, it startled me enough to make me flinch. We could probably squeeze one more trip to The Clinic out of it, but now was as good a time as any to fill up. Jacob veered off toward a nearby gas station before the beep got any more insistent.

While Jacob dealt with the pump, I wandered through the mini-mart. The coffee smelled amazing. You can always tell when it's fresh by jiggling the vacuum thermoses. Later in the day, you'll want the ones that are pretty full. Otherwise, there's a chance you'll end up with something that's been sitting around since noon. But even though I found a coffee that was good and heavy, given that I would need to go to sleep in a few short hours, I couldn't afford to indulge.

Were the brightly colored slushy drinks churning through their specialized machines crawling with caffeine? No idea. But since most things I knew to be caffeinated were brown, I was pretty sure the slushy was safe. At least in terms of keeping me awake, anyhow. I couldn't really speak for the brain freeze.

I grabbed one and went back outside. The car was gassed up, but Jacob had shifted his attention to the windshield. The squeegees at the pump are usually ragged and the fluid they're soaking in is filthy, but for some reason, Jacob was experiencing the urgent need to clean that window. He scrubbed at the remainder of a bug splat for all he was worth, then dropped the squeegee back into the slot, planted his hands on his hips and glared. I cut my eyes to the slushy and said, "Did you want some of this?" He's not usually big on processed sugar...but he seemed pretty put out. "Or I could get you your own."

"It really did look like Bertelli was pocketing something. What else would he be doing, standing there in front of the pills and rifling around in his jacket?"

I recognized that tone. It was the tone of someone unaccustomed to being wrong. "Sure. And just because we didn't find anything doesn't mean it didn't happen. Only that he was one step ahead of us."

"Don't say that just to make me feel better." Yeah, right. Like he'd rather have me simply agree that his idea didn't fly? "As if Laura's not leery enough of me already...now I go and blow the wrong whistle. Again. But here's the thing: no one audits a pharmacy that much unless they're up to something."

"Or he's got suspicions of his own." Though if he did, he'd throw his own staff under the bus in a heartbeat. My gut told me Bertelli had something to hide. But my gut's been wrong before—spectacularly wrong. And there was a good possibility I just wanted him to be breaking some law for the simple satisfaction of seeing him get caught.

"I just don't get it," Jacob said. "Not only is our new surveillance useless, but we go through all the trouble of taking the GhosTV off mothballs and it doesn't do us a damn bit of good."

"Actually...before we zeroed in on Bertelli, I did notice something." I struggled to explain, and decided I just couldn't say "habit demons" with any chance whatsoever of being taken seriously. I trooped out the official F-Pimp term. "Nonphysical entities."

That grabbed Jacob's attention. "Ghosts?"

"More like...etheric...parasites."

I'd been trying to make the creatures sound less goofy, and I'd succeeded. In fact, I'd gone straight from ludicrous to horrific. As I scrambled to backpedal so as not to burden Jacob with any new nightmares, a shiver played across the back of my neck. Initially, I attributed the chill to the frozen drink...until I heard, "Hey, white boy."

I got my bearings. We were three and a half blocks from my old apartment.

Jacob had at least ten thousand questions about the etheric parasites, but as he drew a breath to begin asking them, I held up a pause-finger and said, "Hey, Jackie, what's up?"

"I seen some folks talking about Kick, over by the corner store. You know the one. With all the roaches."

Actually, yeah. When I lived nearby, I'd done my best not to shop there. And when I did, I only bought things that were really well sealed. "Was it just a conversation, or did something change hands?"

"Nuh-uh. Nobody hit that. You don't take nothing from a man without no street cred, you know what I'm saying? Who knows what he try to pass off as a good high."

"Can you describe him?"

"An old white guy."

"Right. I get it. Like me."

"Well...not *that* skinny."

"Would you say he was closer to sixty or forty?"

"I dunno. Y'all look the same."

"What about his hair? Was it long, short, dark, light?"

"You didn't say I had to memorize his hair!"

Jackie was getting pretty annoyed, and if I pushed the wrong buttons, she'd storm off and leave me standing there talking to myself. But the thing about businesses these days—even the tiny corner stores—was that they all had surveillance, and it would help if we could narrow our search window. "Listen, how about this—what *time* did you see him?"

"After dark."

Great. Since it was March, that would be fourteen hours out of any given day. "And what day was it?"

"You think I can go check my social calendar? I told you—a white man tried selling Kick at the roach store, he got shut down, and that's all I know. I should've known you wouldn't appreciate my hard work."

"Of course I appreciate it. If you could just narrow it down. Yesterday? The day before?"

Silence.

"Jackie? Jackie!" I swung around stupidly, knowing full well I wouldn't get a visual but not knowing what else to do. She didn't answer. I took an angry pull of my slushy, then muttered, "Goddammit."

We headed over to the store in question. It was doing pretty brisk business, despite the roaches. After the way Bertelli had panned out, Jacob was pleased to have something authoritative and useful to do. While I called down white light and did a quick scan of the store to make sure nothing worse than insect life was lurking in the nooks and crannies, he persuaded the clerk to surrender the past week's surveillance footage.

Jacob contacted the office, and fifteen minutes later, an on-call specialist showed up with a laptop to download the files. I knew she was a specialist because she did the whole thing in ten minutes flat. And I knew she was on-call because she was wearing high heels and bright lipstick, something you hardly ever see at HQ.

I felt bad for interrupting her date night. But as a fellow one-trick pony who got sent out to look at murder scenes any time of the day or night, I could relate. When she was done, the specialist tucked her laptop under her arm and told us, "Both of you will have full access to the footage, and our team will get to work on identifying the salient parts."

"We're looking for a white guy over thirty-five." Of which we'd seen at least half a dozen come and go in the time we'd been standing there. "After dark," I added.

She didn't seem too put out by my lack of intel. Then again, surveillance in general was nothing if not tedious. It took a special kind of patience to maintain that kind of focus…a patience I sorely lacked.

I dropped my half-full slushy into the trash and climbed into the car. I said, "There's gonna be a mind-numbing array of white guys buying scratch-off lottery tickets in our future. And what are we even looking for, anyway?"

Jacob shook his head. "Hopefully I'll know it when I see it."

"If only we could narrow it down to a specific night." If I had Jackie's phone number, I'd call her, try to make nice and encourage her to scour her memory for anything at all that might be of use. I glanced at my phone—not that I actually thought I could call her, but purely out of habit—and realized that I might have a way to contact her after all. If the case Bob Zigler dug up for me was the right one, anyhow.

I tapped my email and opened the attachments, scrolling immediately to the shots of the crime scene. I never thought I'd be grateful for the experimental psyactives I'd sucked down in my morning Starbucks, but in that time, I'd had my one visual of Jackie. And it was gruesome enough that I'd never forget. A matted wig. A sparkle tube top. And an ugly shank protruding from her breastbone.

I'd heard the anecdote from Jackie several times before. She's the type of ghost I'd come to think of as a complainer—someone who dies before they've had a chance to come to terms with it, usually from someone else's negligence or malice. Back when I worked homicide, complainers were my bread and butter. They were the ones who couldn't wait to blow the whistle on their own murderers.

Hearing about it and seeing it—by the bright lights of the crime scene photographers—were two different things.

Jackie's fatal injury was bad enough on its own...but the photos were something right out of a horror movie. I imagine at the time the whole thing went down, it was dark and shadowy, tucked away between the back porch of an apartment building, a telephone pole, and a dumpster. For the purposes of the photographers, though, the whole thing was lit up bright as day.

A stained, bare mattress slumped on the ground. Either it was too heavy to make it into the dumpster, or it was light enough to drag back out and help an enterprising young woman earn her twenty bucks. That gnarly old mattress would probably have been awful enough...even if it weren't saturated with blood.

My red slushy churned in my belly as I flicked through the photos. It was a stunning amount of blood for such a small knife. Arterial hits can really bleed, and normally that's what I would've figured—until I saw the angle of the crime scene photos took special care to focus on the victim's legs, splayed wide, with her short shorts shoved to the side and a massive stain of crimson blooming onto the mattress under her bottom.

I was gonna be sick. I rolled down the window and gulped some air until I got it under control.

"What is it?" Jacob asked. He looked for somewhere to pull over, but it was dinnertime and we were too close to a restaurant to even dream of finding a spot.

I closed my eyes, clapped my palm over them, and turned the phone face-down in my lap. But none of those things could obliterate the image that was now seared into my memory of Jackie bleeding out from between her legs. Jacob managed to find a hydrant and pull over by the time I lost the battle with my gag reflex, and I got the passenger door open before I decorated the interior of Jacob's car like the crime scene photos. It wasn't a full-on hurl, though, just a couple of wet heaves. And the slushy tasted the same coming up as it had going down.

I straightened back up and Jacob had his arm slung across the headrest. He massaged the back of my neck. I hadn't realized how tense it was. When I finally felt I could talk, I said, "It's the case report for Jackie's murder—and it's bad. Not just what she suffered, how rotten her life was, either. But how I've treated her. I don't think I ever thought of her as an actual person. Not until now. And...I feel like a real asshole."

"Can I see?"

I turned my phone over and angled it so we could both have a look. Jacob narrowed his eyes, and I could practically see the search engine churning in his mind. Crimes like these straddled both our areas of expertise, and he wondered if he was already familiar.

He scrolled through quickly, getting an overall impression of the scene, then went back to the beginning and zoomed in on the report. Sometimes it helped to read about things in cop-speak. Dry. Factual. Even clinical. The facts themselves were bad enough. They didn't need all the dramatic narrative my brain wanted to add.

Jacqueline Mason had been twenty-three at the time of her murder, some two decades prior. That would put me in my last few weeks at the Cook County Mental Health and Jacob fresh out of the Police Academy. Cause of death, blood loss.

Maybe it was splitting hairs, but this finding pissed me off. "Who the hell was Medical Examiner back then? This is a prime example of blaming the victim. She didn't die because someone fucking stabbed her, but because she'd bled out after it."

Jacob agreed. "That *is* a weird finding,"

If I found the perp, all these years later, would the FPMP make things right? Well, there was no making it right, not really. But if I told Laura it would rid the world of one more ghost, how could she resist pulling some strings?

Jacob zoomed in closer on the report. "Vic, take a look at this."

Decedent had a four-inch serrated knife protruding from the right of the sternum three inches below the collarbone at a depth of 53 mm, piercing the right lung.

The damage inflicted between her legs, however, was determined to have come not from the guy who'd stabbed her, but from a baby born only two hours prior. Detectives had indeed located Jackie's assailant. There was a significant amount of investigation put in to ascertain the timeline, too, because when they tracked down the perp, covered in Jackie's blood, they wanted to try and charge him for a double-homicide. Jackie had been trying to turn a quick BJ. Her customer decided he wanted something more.

The guy, who had a history of erratic behavior, denied any knowledge of a baby and claimed he panicked when he shoved her shorts over and found a maxi-pad full of blood—way too much blood for a period. In the end, they could only charge him with aggravated assault, which could see him walk in as little as a year. I would've gone for assault with a deadly weapon at the very least, but maybe it was comforting to know that *my* collars weren't the only ones getting away with murder. On the bright side, he managed to hang himself at the county lockup before he even received his slap on the wrist.

The newborn infant was found dead in the basement of an empty apartment building nearby that was undergoing renovations. There was no way the crews could have heard its cries over the floor sander and vacuums.

It was a girl.

CHAPTER 29

NOT ONLY WAS I an asshole all these years for glossing over the fact that Jackie had died horribly.

I was a complete dickwad for thinking of her as a "complainer."

Jacob flicked back to the crime scene photos. "That garage in the background...that's across the alley from your old apartment, isn't it?"

He'd zoomed in in such a way that Jackie's body wasn't visible, though you could still see a splatter of blood on the blond brick. The graffiti was different twenty years ago. An exuberantly colorful DJ tag instead of the word "fuker." But the distinct sag of the doorway was already well underway.

I'd always figured the baby in the basement had a sad story. I'd never realized it would hit me so hard.

Back when I left my car at the mechanic's, I'd grabbed everything from the glovebox and center console, shoved it in a shopping bag, and tossed it in the trunk of the Crown Vic. I retrieved the bag now and pawed through it, looking for the old keychain I'd so recently rediscovered in my glovebox. I'd turned in the keys to my apartment when I moved out. But I'd been short one of the keys to the outside door, and given that no one ever closed the things properly anyway, management charged me twenty bucks for the inconvenience and called it good.

The corner store we'd just exited had a pretty esoteric selection of goods: ramen from halfway across the globe, tamarind soda from south of the border, and faded air fresheners from 1972. They also sold prayer candles, cheap incense, and Hoyt's Cologne, an alternative to Florida Water that was just as stinky, albeit in its own special way. Hoyt's is usually used by people hoping for a run of good luck. I imagined Jackie and her daughter were long overdue to turn their luck around.

I bought a handful of white prayer candles, a bottle of Hoyt's, and a regular tub of iodized salt, then rejoined Jacob in the car. He was still reading through the police report in detail, but the gist of the story was enough for me—more than enough. Part of me was worried that he'd try to talk me out of what I needed to do. Jackie had the potential to help us with our current case. Did it really make sense to lay her to rest now? After all, she'd been plying blowjobs in those alleyways for nearly twenty years. What difference would it make if she stuck around just a little while longer?

Thankfully, there was no hesitation at all when he drove us back to the scene. And thankfully, my key still worked.

Jacob made to tap me on the shoulder but drew back at the last minute, worried he'd steal my white light. But I wasn't charging up just yet. "Should I wait in the car?" he asked.

"No, you're fine. Stay." A knot of unease rested in my belly over the notion of revisiting my least favorite basement—one I thought I'd never need to see again. "I could really use the company."

Other than a different padlock hanging off the storage

locker that used to be mine, the basement hadn't changed. It smelled like cheap laundry detergent and damp concrete. I found the spot where I'd seen the ghost baby—Jackie's baby— but there was nothing there. But given that I'd just encountered Jackie in the vicinity earlier that evening, I had a strong suspicion it was only a matter of time.

Prayer candles will burn for a week, so I lit them right away and placed them around the perimeter. I'd been taught to find magnetic north and form a compass, but it's been my experience that ghosts aren't necessarily that particular. Maybe it wasn't the ghost's preference that made the difference, but mine. I didn't put much stock in which direction I was facing, but I felt less inadequate with a handful of salt and a snootful of cheap cologne.

"It'll be a while," I told Jacob. "I've only seen it—the baby— really late at night."

"However long it takes. I'll stand over by the stairs and make sure no one disturbs you."

It probably wouldn't make any difference if I had an audience or not, but I appreciated the chance to get my head on straight. Guilt isn't a very useful emotion. It's distracting and it puts me off my game. I sat between two of the lit candles on the cold concrete and thought about Jackie. I wouldn't have been able to help her back when she was alive. I was too young. Not only did I have no authority, but I had no autonomy, either. By the time anyone saw fit to give me a gun and a badge, the deed had already been done.

I could've helped the dead baby's ghost when I first saw it, though. I'd been too much of a coward. The cold seeping into my sit-bones through the fabric of my slacks was hardly penance enough for my failure to take action.

Even with Jacob standing sentry at the foot of the stairs, it was hard to focus. I could hear someone's TV through the floorboards, a schmaltzy sitcom soundtrack, and every time a toilet flushed, the pipes rattled. I slipped in my earbuds with the sole intention of drowning out the noise...but soon realized that Mood Blaster did a lot more than block out the TV. Would the right binaural pulses magically pump me full of white light? Unfortunately, no. But they did help me stay in the right frame of mind to fill up my reservoir myself.

I didn't need a watch to tell me when the time was near. My skin prickled in anticipation and my senses were drawn to the spot on the floor I was always so careful to avoid. The time for avoidance was over, though, and now I had to face it head on and bear witness.

I was as full of light as I could really hope to be without a psyactive in my veins and a GhosTV in the background. And when the baby appeared—Jackie's baby—I was watching.

It waved its fists and gave a thready cry. Normally, this was the point where I'd talk to the ghost and urge it to cross over. I couldn't usually hear repeaters. But sometimes I did. Hard to say for sure that the baby was a full-fledged spirit and not a repeater, since she couldn't talk back, only cry. I wasn't sure how much words actually mattered anyhow, at least with the way my particular brand of mediumship worked. I visualized the veil, somewhere over by the circuit breakers, and then imagined the baby being drawn toward it.

Highly evolved spirits are usually the ones to take earth-bound souls and help them find their way, but the crossing guards of the dead tend to station themselves at hospitals and cemeteries, where they'll get the most traffic. There was no one like that here. Just me.

I pocketed my earbuds and knelt awkwardly on one knee about a yard away from the apparition. Jacob was watching, and he drew closer. His face was earnest. I imagined he was practically flooding the area with his earnestness. But I only sense the manifestation of his ability when it's thieving the white light I've so fastidiously gathered.

It was hard enough to try and figure out what to say to a ghost baby without someone else listening in, but I did my best to draw support from Jacob's presence instead of embarrassment.

"It's time to go," I told the baby gently. "I know you weren't here for long. And I can't say for sure if it's on to the next thing, or if you'll get some kind of do-over. But this plane is for the living and you need to move on."

The newborn infant whimpered and squirmed.

I should've imagined the veil in closer proximity. Ideally directly beside the tiny spirit, so all I'd have to do is nudge her over, then jump back before I got pulled in behind her. But, no. The wall by the circuit breaker was the first thing that popped into my head, and now the position was fixed in my mind's eye. For all I knew, I hadn't summoned it, but simply noticed it. I glanced from the baby to the unseeable portal and gauged the distance. A good three, three and a half yards.

I knew what I had to do. But I didn't like it.

I glanced up at Jacob and wondered exactly how I should phrase it. *If you see me start to die, you should probably grab me before my spirit drains out.* Yeah, that would go over really well. "Wait for me to the right of the breaker box. I'm feeling a little-...woozy. So catch me if I fall."

He seemed to buy it. And why not? It wouldn't be the first time I pushed hard enough to make myself sick.

If it came down to it, was I ready to cross? No. I had way too much unfinished business. Not only did I need to get Kick off the streets, but I had to put a ring on that big lug over there watching me with such palpable concern. I pulled harder at the white light and gathered myself up, and hoped to all hope that there was some kind of intelligence to the other side that would bounce back a clumsy medium who wasn't ready to go. I'd seen plenty of dead folks, though, who were no more ready than I currently was...which I did my best not to think about.

I shuffled forward on my knees and murmured, "No more concrete floor and rattling water heaters where you're going. Just puffy white clouds and lullabies." Even more white light—my capacity expands when I'm terrified—and I reached down to take her.

My hands passed right through.

It surprised me. I was so hopped up on light, it seemed like I should have at least felt a chill. I shifted my focus to my subtle bodies, my etheric form, and I tried again.

Nothing.

It just goes to show that even I have my moments of overconfidence. I should be good at exorcisms by now, I reasoned. But when I thought about it, did I really experience sensation in my etheric body? Other than the occasional chill, no. My technique involved reasoning, cajoling and begging. But how does a person do any of these things with a newborn?

Maybe I should've hit a yoga class while I was waiting for the baby to appear instead of sitting here watching the prayer candles flicker. Fat lot of good that realization did me now. I took a deep, centering breath, and tried to scoop up the baby again.

It was no good.

"How can I help?" Jacob asked. He might not have been able to see the ghost, but he knew what I looked like when I floundered around ineffectively.

"Just gimme a sec."

I pictured all my rainbow chakras spinning, took a deep, cleansing breath, and opened up the top of my head to the white light. Not sure if the edge of desperation was a hindrance or a help. Only that I must've really expected to succeed, given how distressing it was to fail.

I couldn't tell if I was powering up anymore or not. For all I knew, the psychic power was only passing through, like a spent scoop of coffee, with all the caffeinated goodness long ago filtered from the grounds. I might very well be at capacity. I took up the bottle of Hoyt's Cologne and sprinkled it around the baby, then anointed my own hands. It smelled like pumpkin spice flavored aftershave.

Hopefully getting the olfactory senses involved would give me some kind of edge. I sat with the stink of cloves for a long moment, and then I reached, yet again, for the squirming half-seen baby.

Still nothing.

It hardly seemed right to pitch a handful of salt and try to command the spirit, but I was running out of options. And if that wasn't bad enough, a tickle at the back of my throat seemed to suggest that maybe that baby would be safe on the other side by now, if only I had access to a half-dose of Kick.

My anxiety ratcheted higher still.

Jacob edged forward and said, "This isn't all on you. Let me help."

"Fine. Let's do the salt." He brought it over, pried up the flimsy metal chute, and dumped a big mound into my palm. White light...white light...white light. It seemed like the salt should light up to my inner eye, but it didn't. I was too weak.

I could probably see it if I was on Kick.

No, goddammit. The only thing I'd accomplish by taking that drug would be landing myself in the ER. Or worse. Besides, I didn't even have any.

Jacob settled his hands over the top of it and his kinesthetic energy prickled through the crystalline structure. I felt it as the slightest brush of magnetism, like when a synthetic sock fresh from the dryer wants to cling to my polyester hoodie.

Between my mojo and his, the salt was as ready as it would ever get.

I poured it in a thin circle around the baby and tried to imagine my power was amplified. If it had any effect at all, it was so subtle, it might be wishful thinking. Since I was visual, I tried to visualize her floating up off the cold basement floor and into the warmth of the light.

Nothing happened.

Frustrated, angry—and most of all, disappointed—I stood up and brushed off my knees. "I'm sorry," I said. To the baby. And to Jackie.

"For what?"

I spun around, but as usual, there was nothing to see. "Jackie?"

"What're you doing down here?" she said, and all the things I associated with her, the hustle, the stubbornness, the edge of desperation...all of that was gone. She sounded quiet, and young, and phenomenally sad.

"I'm trying to help your baby."

A long pause. Then, "Her name is Trinity."

"Okay. Trinity. She needs to cross over. You both do."

"I was gonna come back for her, y'know. I just needed money for the train. Twenty dollar will get you to St. Louis. I heard of a women's shelter out there where we could start over. Then my baby girl and me, we'd get on that train...and we'd be free."

My heart went out to her. To both of them. Not that Jackie wouldn't have bled out anyway in the train's bathroom halfway to Peoria...but at least they would have been together. And maybe Trinity would have survived. "Forget about St. Louis. You can be free now."

Silence.

"Jackie?"

"Is she gone?" Jacob asked anxiously.

I put my finger to my lips and held my breath, and just when I thought we'd really blown it, Jackie spoke again.

"I was gonna get my life together. For Trinity. Stop using. Get a job, a real job. Find us a place to live, just the two of us. No one would ever raise a hand to her. Ever. You know what I'm saying?"

I considered how much I could realistically promise her was on the other side of the veil. I'd only had a glimpse myself, and from that glimpse, it felt more like inner peace than St. Louis. "Whatever's over there, it's got to be better than this. And the two of you will be together, just like you wanted."

"No, we won't," she said sadly. "Trinity is pure, but I got too much sin on me. I was gonna try to make things right. To be a better person. But I just ran out of time."

"Tell her the man who stabbed her was convicted," Jacob demanded. "Tell her he came to justice."

It wasn't about justice, I realized. It was that Jackie couldn't move on because she didn't feel worthy of heaven. And before I could reassure her that whatever she'd endured on this earth must surely be punishment enough for anyone, something very subtle rippled through the ether. Whatever small window of visibility Trinity possessed was done for the night. The baby was gone.

And so was Jackie.

CHAPTER 30

No wonder Jackie was lucid one minute and desperate to turn a twenty-dollar trick the next. She was subject to the same mysterious etheric rhythms as her daughter.

In her case, I wasn't sure which was worse. Knowing she was dead, or not knowing.

Once the prayer candles were cool enough to handle without dripping wax all over ourselves, Jacob and I packed up our gear and headed home, and got back to the cannery well past midnight. Jacob kept trying to wrap his head around the situation as best he could, but I had precious little explanation to give him.

Jacob was desperate to reassure me. Or maybe to reassure himself. "We'll try again—we'll be better prepared next time. Carl would come help if we asked. Or we could bring the GhosTV."

Which, if I were telling the God's honest truth, I didn't even know how to use. Other than showing me that Jacob's power was pulsing under his skin in red, ropy veins, even the TV might not do us a damn bit of good.

Frustrated and disillusioned, I climbed into bed with my

earbuds and phone, hoping to get enough sleep to function the next day. I chose Calming Comet from the Mood Blaster menu and an amber-tinted galaxy opened up. Maybe all the orange was to counter the "blue light" that supposedly kept people awake…or maybe just an aesthetic choice. Not only were the graphics and the music different from Perky Planet, but the game was different too. Instead of bouncing, bursting action, I guided my comet through a soothing flow around and between planets. When I hit a celestial body, there was no fiery explosion. The comet just nudged it aside. Not much of a challenge—and maybe that was the whole point. As the music droned along and the *whub-whub-whub* of the binaural pulses slowed down, I felt my eyelids drooping. By the time the comet tucked itself into the Milky Way with a happy sigh, I was drowsy enough to fall asleep with the lights on.

Sleep comes in many stages. If I was willing to wear a fitness tracker, no doubt it would tell me which stage I was in when my phone rang. And it would probably be a deep one. I snorted awake and scrabbled around for my phone, then realized it was right there at the end of my earbuds. It was 3AM and I didn't recognize the number, but since I'd given out my card to anyone at The Clinic who would take it, I picked up.

"Bayne."

"Agent? It's Dr. Gillmore. I just got a call there's an overdose on the way to LaSalle. And it sounds like Kick."

Thankfully, Jacob drove, because I was still half-asleep. We turned into the parking lot on two wheels and screeched to a halt in a handicap spot—and I damn near had a heart attack thinking Jacob had mowed down a big fat pedestrian…until the guy flickered and reappeared halfway through our front bumper, clutching at his left arm.

I opened up the top of my head and groggily sucked down white light. The repeater staggered, fell, then reappeared in our bumper. Oh well. As long as he didn't try to follow us, I probably didn't need to worry about him. But even though I knew the likelihood of a repeater sticking to something was minimal, Jacob's car definitely had an exorcism coming in its near future.

Plenty of folks on the daytime staff at LaSalle know me from all the time I spent throwing salt on the victims of the hospital fire that had been doused some eighty years ago, but to the night guards, I was just another groggy guy in a rumpled suit. While Jacob peeled off to square us away with the guards, I found Dr. Gillmore pacing by the emergency bay. "Where's your usual partner?" she asked.

"Zigler? He's home in bed with his wife, I presume. Zig stayed on with the police department when I left. Jacob's FPMP."

We watched as Jacob said something that left both guards suitably impressed with his credentials...and I realized Gillmore was checking out more than just his body language.

I couldn't help but brag a little. "He's also my future husband." I must've sounded like I was being a smartass, judging by the look she gave me. "If the crises ever stop coming long enough for us to tie the knot, anyhow."

"Huh." She unabashedly scrutinized his butt. "Some folks say work and pleasure don't mix. But I can see where you'd make an exception."

Whatever brief moment of bonding had just occurred, it came to an abrupt end as an ambulance peeled up and the paramedics scrambled out to grab the gurney. "Madeline Cruz," one of the paramedics announced. "Fifty-six. Found unconscious by her stepdaughter."

I was accustomed to getting a general feel for a person at a quick glance—gender, race, age, weight, height and clothing— and no way would I have pegged this Cruz woman as a day over 40—not until I got a look at her hands. She'd had work done on her face. Expensive work. Even her pajamas screamed *money*. How the hell had someone like her ended up on Kick?

"BP 160 over 90, pulse is 110 and erratic. We thought we were looking at a seizure...."

"But there's no history of seizure," Gillmore guessed. The paramedic confirmed it. On the gurney, the woman twitched—a spastic flap of her hands while her heels drummed arrhythmically. My skin crawled, and I realized that in my grogginess I'd totally been neglecting my white light. Damn it. I focused on my third eye and pulled.

"Let's get her started on an IV—"

Whatever Gillmore was about to say, she was cut off by the appearance of a brick shithouse of a guy from the waiting room with a bloody towel pressed over his eye. "What about me?" he demanded.

The paramedics flinched away—he was really formidable, and he was angry, too—but Gillmore stood firm. "Sir? Go back to your seat and we'll call you just as soon as—"

"I've been here an hour. You want me to lose my eye?"

Up until that point, everything had been moving fast. But it was a controlled speed. Now, though, with an angry bleeder gearing up for a tantrum, things turned chaotic. The guy with the eye was clearly scared, and guys who've found that bluster and intimidation are the quickest way to get what they want were unlikely to take a "no" answer sitting down. Everyone's attention was on the eye guy except the paramedics, who were busy transferring Cruz to a bed. I flattened against the back of the emergency bay to stay out of their hair. "On three," the leader of the team said. "One, two...."

As they hoisted the woman over, her twitching intensified into something more like flailing, and one of the paramedics took a diamond ring to the cheekbone. And now we had two bleeders.

"I'm fine," he declared as he grabbed a wad of gauze from a nearby stock of medical supplies. He'd probably need a stitch or two, or at least a butterfly suture bandage. But while his partner was looking at him and mentally assessing the damage, something small clattered to the floor and landed directly between my feet.

A contact lens case.

Ask me if I ever developed a cop instinct and I'll deny it up and down. But even before the tiny plastic case hit the floor, I knew there was something inside it other than contact lenses. I don't need to wear contacts myself, though I've dated guys who have. And every one of them kept their lenses by the bathroom sink...not in their pajamas.

I pocketed the case, then glanced around to see if anyone noticed. Jacob's attention was on the yelling eye-bleeder guy. The security guards', too. The paramedics were distracted by the bleeding cheek. Cruz was twitching on the bed. With no one looking, I reached into my pocket and gave the case a subtle shake. Something inside rattled...suspiciously like a pill.

I eased my hand out of my pocket.

Somehow, Gillmore managed to explain to the eye guy that it was his eyelid bleeding, not his eyeball, which calmed him down enough for the team to turn its attention back to Cruz. They started a drip and pumped her full of saline, anticonvulsants and sedatives, and the twitching stopped.

At least, *her* twitching did.

My foot was tapping on the linoleum as if I'd been watching a jazz combo, not a potentially fatal drug reaction.

Again, I realized my white light was low, and I made an effort to fill my tank. If Cruz shed her mortal coil and tried me on for size, clearly neither of us would be too keen on the results. Would it be weird of me to slip in my earbuds and play a few rounds of Perky Planet to top up my light levels? Probably so.

The lens case felt heavy in my pocket, despite the fact that it weighed almost nothing. Because I was tampering with evidence? Hardly. Authorities already had samples of Kick in analysis, and any prints on the case would be from the victim. While there was a precog in the FPMP's employ, the hits she got were so random and obscure, they tended to throw investigators off the scent. The cases where she consulted took twice as long to solve. No, it felt heavy because I knew that if I needed to boost my white light, a cruise through the galaxy on my new app would certainly be noticed, but I could turn aside and swallow a pill with no one being any the wiser.

The pill in my pocket might not be Seconal. But I felt that old, familiar yearning at the back of my tongue nonetheless.

The team stabilized Cruz well enough to transfer her to ICU, where her hysterical husband was waiting. Gillmore stepped up beside me, planted her hands on her hips and scowled at the empty emergency bay. "Guess I jumped the gun in calling you in. It'll be a while before she regains consciousness."

"You did the right thing," I murmured...and patted my pocket to reassure myself that the pill was safe and sound.

CHAPTER 31

THE RIDE HOME WAS middle-of-the-night quiet. No one was around but us, some bakery delivery vans, and a dozen or so intersection repeaters.

"I'll need to question Cruz when she wakes up," Jacob said.

"She has a teenage stepdaughter, doesn't she? Start there." Hopefully it was just some stray pills the kid brought home from a party and not a whole new pipeline of deadly recreational psyactives.

There was the opportunity to get another two and half hours' sleep that we really couldn't afford to blow off. Jacob was out within ten minutes of his head hitting the pillow. It's not that the shit we'd seen at the hospital didn't affect him. It was that working sex crimes had been so much worse that in comparison, this new gig could sometimes be a relief.

Would it help for me to break out my new app and pledge my brainwaves to whichever fraternity would promise to send me off to dreamland?

Maybe.

But a good night's sleep doesn't come without a cost, and I strongly suspected the reason I had trouble holding onto my white light was because of my sojourn earlier that evening with Calming Comet. I'd need to be on my game in the morning. No two ways about it.

But was that really an issue, since I had a psyactive at my disposal?

The rational part of my brain tried to shut down that idea just as soon as it took form. But that's the thing about thoughts. It's impossible to unthink them.

I'm all for better living through pharmaceuticals, but I couldn't recall a time when psyactives have ever done me much good. Usually, they'd need to build up in your system for weeks, kind of like antidepressants. Those were the kind Roger Burke dosed me with. They didn't enhance my working capacity at all—they just made the entire spirit world eager to slip under my skin. And then there were the horse pills Con Dreyfuss supplied. Effective at helping me drag Jennifer Chance across the veil? I suppose. But given the physical toll they took on my body, I wasn't keen on trying them again. Not with my own MRIs so fresh in my mind.

But Kick wasn't formulated from the horse pills. It was the safe-ish one, with something extra added to sidestep the need for weeks of buildup. And I was perfectly fine now. So if I did end up turning to a little chemical support, there'd be nothing to worry about.

A little voice told me Kick was only fatal the third or fourth time around, so actually, the fact that I'd probably taken its precursor made it *more* dangerous, not less...but I decided that had nothing to do with me. It was a good long while since Burke slipped those psyactives in my coffee. Any psyactive sensitivity would've worn off by now.

Never mind the fact that those drugs had probably been tested on me back at Camp Hell, too. Though that was years ago.

Years and years.

And back then, I'd had so many drugs coursing through my system....

The memory floated to the surface of my mind. Just a fragment at first—the scenery skimming by the window of the van I was riding in—then another memory, and another. Faun Windsong staring out the opposite window like she'd forgotten what a tree looked like. In the row behind us, Richie whining, "Stop it. I mean it! Stop!" followed by Dead Darla's quiet snigger.

And the look on Krimski's face when he swung around from the front row and said, "Do you think this is a game?"

Krimski was the administrator who took over Camp Hell once the first director went on a permanent vacation. He was a middle-aged guy with deep creases in his face that most definitely weren't laugh lines. I would've gotten a dangerous vibe off him even if I hadn't seen the spirit of the previous director strangled in his office.

Darla blinked innocently. No doubt, she had the same impression of Krimski. Even at that young age, she was adept at reading a room. She also knew exactly how far she could get away with pushing.

Richie, though? Clueless. "Her hand is on my side of the seat," he whined.

I had no doubt she'd put it there on purpose, too. Satisfaction was hard to come by locked in your room all day. And baiting Richie was surprisingly satisfying. I could attest to that myself.

Krimski shot him a glare, then turned toward the windshield, muttering to the driver. "Gets on my very last nerve."

The driver shrugged. With a barely perceptible accent, he said, "I can sedate him for the drive back."

Not just a driver, then. Something more.

I remembered that particular field trip. And I remembered who was on it. Heliotrope Station's four mediums. Director Krimski. And the guy who never spoke a word to any of us as he jabbed us with needles or pumped us full of pills...a wizened little wrinkled-up guy who looked uncannily like this particular rubber monkey I bought from a dollar store with my birthday money when I was ten. A chimpanzee, I think it was. Actually, maybe it was plastic, not rubber, since it melted really quickly in the microwave.

Anyhow, in those later days of Camp Hell, the policy was to keep all info on a need-to-know basis, and apparently Krimski decided we lab rats didn't need to know much of anything, including the name of the guy who kept us flying high. In my mind, I'd called the guy in the driver seat Monkey Man.

Orderlies came and went, and they schlepped us from place to place, but no drugs were ever administered without Monkey Man's direct supervision.

Right. Because he was a doctor.

Dr. Kamal.

The more I prodded at the memory, the more details came back to me. Kamal and Krimski hadn't been taking us on a leisurely Sunday drive that afternoon. They'd hauled us off to some small suburban community out past Joliet where a kid had gone missing. I remembered the intensity in Darla's voice when our wardens left the van and we could speak freely. "How much do you wanna bet he's not specifying what sort of psychics we are? Letting the kid's parents think we're precogs or telepaths. Like there's any way in hell their missing kid's not lying in pieces somewhere at the bottom of a dumpster."

"Death is nothing more than a different state of being," Faun Windsong said loftily.

"Yeah? I'm sure that'll be a huge fucking comfort." I remember Darla said that, specifically, because Richie took to calling everything a "huge fucking comfort" until eventually Darla told him to shut the fuck up or she'd spit in his Jell-O when nobody was looking.

Good times.

Krimski yanked open the door of the van, fixed us each with an icy glare, and said, "Line up next to the shed. Eyes forward. No talking." He gave Richie an extra glare. "Not a word. And when you get there, roll up your sleeves."

Fear crept down my spine as I climbed out of the van and assembled in the family's yard with the other unfortunate mediums. Part of me was eager to see what they were going to inject me with, because even a queasy high would break up the monotony of my days. But another part of me—one I tried not to think about, because it wasn't very punk rock—wondered exactly how thoroughly this stuff had been tested and precisely how safe it might be.

Both Darla and Faun had something to prove, and they waited for their injections without comment. But Richie? He was like an amoeba trying to avoid pain, and once he realized a syringe was involved, he flipped out. "I don't feel good. I wanna go home. Please! I wanna go ho-o-ome!"

Dr. Kamal slid Krimski a look that implied he'd been serious about the sedation. Krimski grabbed one of Richie's arms and told me, "Mr. Bayne, hold down the other. And if he manages to hit me, expect consequences for you both."

Funny how little I appreciated the status quo until someone threatened to take what little I had away. We're not talking smoking privileges or junk food, either. In a stark room with nothing to my name but a few boring textbooks, all he could withhold were things like food or blankets. One time, Movie Mike mouthed off and had his door removed for a week. His *door*. So when Krimski told me to grab Richie, I did what he said. "It's worse if you move around," I told Richie. "Unless you stay really still, the needle can break off in your arm."

Even back then, Darla and I were a lot alike. She took up the story and ran with it. "And then the tip will travel through your veins. When it gets to your heart, you die."

"That's ridiculous," Faun said.

"Maybe, maybe not." Darla fixed Richie with a smirky eyeliner look. "But do you really wanna take that chance?"

Other than some really fierce headaches, the intravenous psyactive didn't yield any results that day. Later, I heard through the grapevine they found the kid alive. In retrospect, that poor kid was probably never the same. And also, in retrospect, they're lucky none of us came back to Heliotrope station with a ghost under our skin. Though even if anything were to hitch a ride, no doubt it would vacate the host body just as soon as it got a load of our living conditions.

They didn't make fast-acting psyactives like that anymore. But maybe with the addition of the second drug, the one that went into Kick would be something like that early taste of psychic enhancement?

There was one way to find out.

I banished that notion just as quickly as it reared its ugly head. Of course I wouldn't subject myself to something as dangerous as Kick just to satisfy my idle curiosity.

Not when I only had the one dose...and I might need it later.

As Jacob rolled over and dragged half the covers off me, I eased out of bed, blew my nose, and crept over to where my suit coat was hanging off the back of the door. With the contact lens case so cleverly concealed, hopefully I could get some rest.

The next morning was a real doozy, even with the help of Perky Planet and three and a half cups of strong black coffee. I felt like I'd been running myself ragged...probably because I had. And Jacob was no better. His eyes were squinchy and he spoke only in monosyllabic grunts. We needed to wrap this case. Or at least sneak off for a decent nap.

We shed our cobwebs quickly enough when we pulled up to The Clinic and found a pair of men in black standing sentry at the front door. "Are those our guys?" I asked.

Jacob said, "I don't recognize them. And if reinforcements were coming, someone would've told us."

We both checked our phones, and neither of us had a message waiting. Jacob cut the engine and said, "I'll go see what's going on."

Better him than me. Just when I think I'm over my distrust of stern alpha types, the world conspires to put that newfound tolerance to the test.

I got Laura on the phone while I watched Jacob through the windshield. Could I tell if his body language was projecting any alarm? Hard to say, since his standard M.O. is to present a cool and unruffled front. "Please say you've got good news for me," she said. "Dr. Bertelli kept me on the phone last night for nearly half an hour, going on about the disruption my agents were causing in his clinic."

"Did he? What did he say?"

"Something about wild accusations being flung and liability—basically you guys really ruffled his feathers—but I think I managed to calm him down."

Outside, Jacob turned and began walking toward the car. Judging by the look on his face, I wasn't so sure exactly how successful Laura had been.

I should've known Bertelli wouldn't give up so easily. Searching his office had been an outright challenge to his authority, and we were on his turf. And he was about to pull out all the stops to make sure we knew it. When Jacob turned back to the car, his expression was grim. I knew in my gut that whatever was happening, it could hardly be construed as good news. "Hold on just a sec," I told Laura, and carefully muted the call.

Jacob climbed into the car, worked his jaw a few times, then said "Those guys are FPMP all right, but they're not ours."

"What do you mean?"

"They're FPMP National."

CHAPTER 32

To say Laura was distressed that FPMP National had been called in would be putting it mildly. And the fact that they'd shown up without informing her? Nothing short of a grave insult. She said, "Stay out of there—both of you. Don't even so much as look at those guys funny. Not until I find out who authorized their presence and why."

I muttered, "You don't have to tell me twice."

"And, Vic? I won't have the leverage to get rid of them unless we handle this whole Kick fiasco."

I'm no good with authority in general. Back before I joined the Program, I was none too fond of my regional F-Pimp office. But the next level up the food chain was downright scary. Even Con Dreyfuss gave them a wide berth—and despite all his best efforts, they'd roughed him up and confiscated his GhosTVs. All of them...except the set he'd left with me.

The set that was currently inside the building surrounded by Big Brother.

Once I hung up with Laura, Jacob looked up from his phone and said, "Carolyn wants us to meet her at the Fifth.

She's got something to show us."

I glanced up at the agents standing ramrod straight beside The Clinic door. It's a cold day in Hell when it's a relief to head over to my old precinct...but that day had most definitely arrived.

The Fifth Precinct was the same as it ever was. Black-and-whites in the parking lot, a ranting guy at the front desk, and an old woman at the switchboard who should have retired twenty years ago. Betty greeted me with a big smile and a thorough once-over. Aside from the bloody eyeball and the lack of sleep, I must've looked pretty good, what with a real haircut and a suit that actually fit. Plus, I was doing my best to walk with my head high and my shoulders squared. Chances were, I would run into someone eager to cut me down to size—some swaggering asshole like Jeff Raleigh—and I wanted to make sure I was ready for him. So, when I rounded the corner, the guy I nearly blundered into wasn't one of the mean kids after all...but instead, Brett Warjovsky.

Warjovsky and I had seen some stuff together, stuff most normal people are blissfully unaware of. "Agent Bayne!" he said brightly. "Wouldja look at what the cat dragged in! What happened to your eye?"

"It's really nothing...."

"Beating up the bad guys." He threw a couple of mock punches my way. "Same as ever."

One thing was for sure, he'd changed all right—no more Chicago PD uniform and bulletproof vest. He was wearing a suit. Not a tailored suit like me, but the type of off-the-rack number that fits a cop's budget. "What's up with you?" I asked. "Going in front of the judge?"

He seemed pleased that I'd asked. He unhooked something from his belt and held it up proudly. A new badge—a detective's shield. He was beaming. "I wouldn't have sat for the test if it wasn't for you. When I saw you handle the Body Snatchers. Boy oh boy."

Body Snatchers, huh? I guess it had a better ring to it than Zombie Basement—plus, the only ones who knew the corpses were *moving*, other than the folks responsible, were me, Zigler...and Zigler's therapist.

"That was such a crazy chase—remember? We went right through that woman's house! And then we found all those bodies!" He shuddered, but gleefully. The way Jacob used to, back before he'd seen just a little too much. "The way you were willing to do whatever it took to catch those sickos...something clicked in me that day, and I knew that was what I wanted. To be that guy. To get the job done."

Better him than me. Slimy defense attorneys wouldn't be able to turn a gullible jury against a sturdy, all-American kid like him quite so easily.

"Are you here to see Zigler?" he asked.

"As a matter of fact...."

"Wow. What I wouldn't give to be a fly on the wall in that investigation. Anyway, good seeing you. And if you ever need anything, just gimme a holler." He gave me a manly clap to the shoulder and headed off to right wrongs and fight crime.

How old was Warjovsky—late twenty-something? He seemed so damn young and earnest...in a way that I'd probably never been. At any age.

If running into Warjovsky in plainclothes was weird, finding my old desk occupied by Carolyn Brinkman was downright bizarre. There had always been a disused quality about that battered metal desk, back when it belonged to me. But Carolyn looked like she was using that thing within an inch of its life. New blotter. New computer. Pictures of her kids and a small potted cactus. But that was just background for the really impressive stuff.

For the work.

Her desk butted up against Zigler's face to face, and they both had their computers shoved far to one side so an array of printouts could span both of them. Pictures, not words. The images were all grainy and low-resolution, but a couple of them were close enough that there was no mistaking who was on camera: Troy Malone. Apparently he did more with himself than just watch TV.

Did he realize he was about to land a starring role in our investigation?

Zigler walked us through the timeline. "This shot was taken from a traffic cam at the intersection of Irving and California just a few blocks from the party where Tammi Pauls acquired her last dose of Kick. Malone lives over two miles away." He pointed to another printout. "Here's Malone a block away from a party our second victim, Reginald, was at."

I said, "But wouldn't he have recognized Troy?"

"Reginald was a longtime patient at Mid North, but he hadn't been there since Patrick Barley quit." Zigler pointed out another photo. "Here's Malone by the ATM across the street from the cafe where Bethany Roberts was approached. And we've got a preliminary match on the prints from one of the pill bottles. Alone, the prints wouldn't mean much. After all, Troy is the guy who hands drugs to every Psych in the city."

I nodded. "But placing him at multiple scenes...." Troy. The whitest white guy I knew. Indeterminate age and hair color, average height, average weight. And Bethany was right. His posture was nowhere near as good as Bertelli's. "I can barely recognize him from this security footage. How did you figure out it was him?"

"Because he's a liar," Carolyn said. "Who lies about what they've seen on TV? Other than someone who just wants to seem like one of the gang so they'll play along with the conversation, I mean. Troy was initiating the conversations, though. He wanted us to think he was home every night, glued to the set."

Jacob considered the accusation and added, "Maybe it was even more than that. Troy Malone is fully aware just how many people have tested positive for psychic ability. He deals with them day in, day out. It takes a pretty big mental adjustment to get used to the idea that a telepath might pick up on what you're thinking." He must've been referring to all the years in which he didn't yet know about the psychic off-switch in his brain. Somehow, he managed not to be too smug about it.

Carolyn's frown deepened. "So you're saying that not only is Troy trying to misdirect us into his movements verbally, but he's sending up a psychic smokescreen to block out telepaths?"

I filed away the technique for future reference. It would be a lot less fishy for me to think about a TV show than to constantly sing the alphabet song whenever a strong telepath was in range.

Jacob said, "I've got a team trying to place Bertelli in the footage we just obtained last night. I'll have them look for Troy instead. What else can we do? Have you got a warrant?"

Zigler shook his head. "Not so fast. We like Malone for distributing the Kick, but looking at his history—the guy was a business major who took the bare minimum science requirement for his bachelor's—I doubt he's compounding the drug himself. Before we go for him, we've gotta figure out who else he's working with."

Bertelli. Jacob and I locked gazes. We were both salivating to take that guy down.

Carolyn said, "Erin Welch would be the obvious suspect. If someone supplied her with Palazamine, she'd have the skill and equipment to reformulate it. She knows about my talent.

Maybe she figured a way around it when we questioned her."

I shook my head. "She's not the only one in that pharmacy. Bertelli 'audits' her every ten seconds. Do we know what kind of doctor he is?"

Zig had the info at his fingertips. "A psychic neurologist."

Oh. I'd figured him to have a Doctorate in Pompous Obfuscation. "Then I'm betting he's way more familiar with psychic pharmaceuticals than your average joe."

Jacob balanced his laptop on the corner of Carolyn's desk and called up the footage we'd both watched and re-watched umpteen times before searching Bertelli's office...and coming up dry. He said, "Whatever Bertelli was up to during his audits, he did it outside camera range. Erin helped us plant additional surveillance."

Carolyn and Zig crossed their arms and watched the clip of Bertelli opening a bottle and pocketing something. Or scratching an itch. Or brushing away a stray bit of lint. Neither of them was willing to say with absolute certainty that he was skimming meds. Zigler said, "We all know how far people will go to save their own skin. If the pharmacist is working with Malone, maybe the whole reason she planted that camera was to position it where she wanted and buy herself some time to skip town."

It surprised me how attached I was to the idea that Erin really was on our side—especially since she was usually so prickly toward me. But if she wasn't doing anything wrong, she'd stand up to whatever scrutiny we might throw her way. "The Program can have them tailed—all three of them, Erin, Troy and Bertelli—and monitor their banking in case anyone gears up to run by making an unusual cash withdrawal."

I paused to let Carolyn voice what I would've been thinking if I were still a cop. Must be nice to have all those resources and no red tape. But she didn't say anything, so she must not have had any objections. I stepped away to make the call, into an out-of-the-way spot over by evidence that was always good for a little privacy, and put in my requests with Surveillance. By the time I was done, Jacob found me, and took the opportunity to check in with me alone.

"Is there something about the pharmacist you didn't want to say in front of Carolyn?" he asked. "If Erin confided in you, we need to know."

"Nothing like that." I didn't know how to explain it. I was also worried about being completely wrong.

"She really is the logical suspect. You know as well as anyone how charismatic a person can be when they're trying to win you over. Roger Burke, Patrick Barley—"

"I'm a lousy judge of character. I get it."

"Not just you. They had everyone fooled." How Jacob managed to refrain from mentioning that he'd always thought Roger Burke was fishy, I had no idea. "For all we know, the three of them are in it together—Erin, Troy and Bertelli. Or maybe it's someone else at The Clinic we haven't even considered yet."

Holy hell. What if all this time, my buddy Gina had been baking up more than just brownies?

Jacob took me by the upper arms and said, "Listen to me. We both know you have a thick skin. If you need to compartmentalize, do it. And if it turns out that someone's been playing you, it doesn't make you gullible. Trusting people isn't a weakness."

Like hell it's not, if you trust the wrong ones.

A text came in from our Surveillance team, a group of men and women who got paid to watch TV all day—whose job I wouldn't touch with a ten-foot pole. They had tentatively ID'd Troy at the roachy store, and did I want to see the frames? Yes, I did.

Video surveillance captured only three shots of the guy, since they were all trained on the register, and our subject hadn't actually bought anything, just walked past. They weren't very clear and the guy was mostly turned away, plus he was wearing a baseball cap. But slap that same hat on Troy and turn him at just that angle? I'd wager a modest bet that it was him.

We rejoined Carolyn and Zigler. They were conferring together quietly, Zigler jotting notes while Carolyn talked something through with a scowl on her face, and I realized what a good fit they were. Zigler, methodical, tenacious and smart. Carolyn, just as smart, and brutally honest. With Zig scarred from his run-in with the "Body Snatchers" in the Zombie Basement, he needed someone he could really trust. And Carolyn couldn't so much as placate him with a little white lie. An easy partnership? Probably not. But definitely solid.

They looked up when we approached. Zigler said, "The more I re-watch that clip of Bertelli doing the audit, the less sure I am that he's palming drugs. We need to interview him."

Jacob said, "I already did. He's evasive. And since he has access to Carolyn's medical records and psychiatric testing, he'll know exactly how to get around her telepathy. Carolyn's first shot at him is critical. We can't blow it. He's had weeks to practice responses to anything we might throw at him. What we need is a piece of evidence he doesn't know we have—something to shock him out of any response he's rehearsed."

Zigler smoothed his graying mustache and nodded. He wasn't the type of guy to feel threatened when someone came up with a better idea than him. He just added the technique to his arsenal for next time. He looked at me and asked, "What about the pharmacist? Sounds like you're pretty close to her. How likely is it she's working with the other two?"

I gave an uneasy shrug. "Maybe she sees the end coming

and she's setting up Bertelli for a fall. But she's never said a word about Troy. Even if we can't place the two of them together on the outside, they work in the same building. There's gotta be a good dozen spots they could do a drop, from the break room to the parking lot. And they both have access to Carolyn's records, too. They'd be ready with a canned response. We're gonna learn a lot more from Troy if he doesn't know we're on to him, and we need to see exactly what Bertelli's doing. I'll recruit Erin. And while I'm at it, I'll plant the seed that if she's in over her head, maybe the best thing for her to do...is flip on her partners and save herself."

CHAPTER 33

Since I really didn't want to go anywhere near The Clinic while the goons from FPMP National were there, I called Erin and convinced her to meet me offsite. She grudgingly agreed to see me at a shop in Chinatown where she sourced certain herbs. I suspected that if she weren't low on botanicals, I'd have been shit outta luck.

Chicago's neighborhoods change quicker than I do with a lapful of sloppy joe, and Chinatown is a colorful beacon in an otherwise bleak South Side expanse of warehouses and train tracks. A several-block stretch of Wentworth Avenue is lined solid with exotic shops where I could buy anything from a cheap knockoff handbag to a leathery whole smoked duck. Really. They were hanging right there in the window. A smell lingered up and down the street that might or might not be food. I decided not to overanalyze it.

I had to double-check the address Erin gave me, since the shop's name was in traditional Chinese. From the outside, it was hard to tell what they sold. The window was full of sun-faded boxes of small appliances and kitchen gadgets, and lots and lots of dust.

Well, if it was a dummy address she'd given me, at least I could grab some steamed dumplings before I headed up north again. And maybe an electric rice cooker.

In my youth, back when I was a snotty teenager with tattered jeans and a bad attitude, store owners tended to follow me with their eyes. Since nowadays I'm a middle-aged guy in a suit, I don't usually elicit much more than the "hey, that guy's pretty tall" look. Today, though, the old woman minding the cash register watched me warily from behind her colorful magazine. I had a bag with me, and I hoisted it just a little bit higher so she could clearly see I wasn't using it to smuggle out any of her merchandise.

The store was cramped. Its narrow shelves were crammed floor to ceiling with seemingly random items, from soap to slippers to salad tongs, and they were all either weirdly expensive or disconcertingly cheap. I made three whole circuits around the store and was debating whether to text Jacob about those dumplings or just multiply my usual order by three when I heard the gentle rise and fall of female laughter. I craned my neck around the nearest endcap and found the old woman with the magazine scowling pointedly in my direction, so it definitely hadn't come from her. And then I noticed a curtained-off door among all the mishmash of wall hangings. There was a sign above it in Chinese. Hopefully it didn't translate to KEEP OUT.

I slipped behind the curtain. The room beyond was dim. It smelled of resins and herbs, plus the whiff of old buildings you'd still find in the cannery, as if it was just too big for Jacob and me to force our own scents into every last crack and crevice. There were two women in the room, Erin and an Asian woman about her age. Their heads were bent together over a phone as they laughed over something—an autocorrect doozy, or maybe a cat meme. At my intrusion, their smiles died and they both looked leery, even as Erin said to her friend, "This is the guy I told you about. Can we have a minute?"

The friend gave me an especially cool look, then unlocked a door on the far wall and slipped through it, leaving us alone.

"How are you holding up?" I asked. "I'm sure Bertelli's been a real delight since we had his office searched."

She seemed surprised I wanted to know how she was doing. "I've seen less of him, actually. He's been busy with those new agents."

F-Pimp National doesn't exactly check in with us regional guys and tell us what they're doing, so I had no idea if they were interested in stopping Kick, stopping us, or stopping the staff from showing up on a syndicated talk show telling the world at large about the existence of the FPMP.

I said, "Listen, I hate to ask you for another favor—but whatever Bertelli's doing, we need to catch him in the act."

"Isn't that why I planted your camera?"

"We need a better view." I placed my bag on the counter. "This bluetooth speaker will grab a 360-degree view of the pharmacy. Just place it up as high as you can. And it'll stream your music, too."

I could tell she was ruing the day she ever stuck my air freshener to the wall. It wasn't in my nature to try to scare people—probably because I've done so much of it inadvertently just by being a medium—but I couldn't risk her siding with Bertelli over me.

"We both know he's up to something. And when it comes time to throw someone under the bus, who's that gonna be?"

"Fine." Erin snatched the bag off the counter. "You're just lucky I like podcasts."

I headed back up to the Fifth. The team was watching Bertelli chat with our agents from National through The

Clinic's security feed. Carolyn looked particularly peeved. "I hate not being there in person. Watching these people talk without being able to pick up on extrasensory clues is disconcerting. I feel like I'm just watching TV and these people aren't even real."

If it was TV, at least we'd have some dramatic music hinting at who the villain was.

Something pinged on Jacob's laptop and he said, "Looks like Erin's plugged in her new surveillance." He moused around. It wasn't a solid 360—that's impossible to get without mounting something in the middle of the ceiling—but it was still pretty damn good.

We watched as Erin put away her Chinatown purchase. Some herbs and tinctures went into refrigeration. Others in a series of glass jars. Then she sat down at her computer, pulled out her receipts, and started logging everything in.

Good thing I'd never aspired to being a pharmacist. Her job looked incredibly boring.

While Erin typed stuff on her computer and counted pills, Bertelli cycled through the building and Troy manned the reception window.

I switched her feed over to my phone so Jacob could focus on Bertelli, marking down who he talked to and when, scrutinizing all his movements. Jacob watched the guy so hard, he probably could've told you exactly what Bertelli had for breakfast, when he'd crapped it back out, and everything he'd done in between.

Meanwhile, Zigler and Carolyn scrubbed through old footage to build a timeline for Troy. That guy was busy, to say the least, hopping from party to party—most definitely not watching TV. When my attention wanders, I'm not necessarily aware that it's happening. And my attention isn't the only thing that wanders. I hardly see myself as someone who needs constant entertainment, but faced with several hours of watching someone work on spreadsheets was so mind numbing, the coffee machine and water fountain called my name every ten minutes. And once I processed all those fluids, the men's room entered my rotation of distraction, too.

Since I know full well there's nowhere good in that john to put your phone while you've got your dick in your hand, I'd left it on Zigler's desk. And when I came back, he and Jacob and Carolyn were all staring at it. Hopefully, I hadn't made myself look bad by letting my battery run down. I shouldered into the group of them and said, "What?"

Carolyn said, "Is this something she normally does?"

Erin stood very still in the center of the room with her head slightly cocked, staring. I'd probably look the same if I was trying to determine whether a distant speck was just a stray wad of dust or it had antennas and legs—and if so, what I should swat it with. "Can we see what she's looking at?"

"That's the thing." Jacob moused the 360-degree cam and it swung around to her line of sight. "There's nothing there."

He pulled up the feed from the air freshener on his laptop, and now we had two views. One of Erin staring, and another of the blank wall she was staring at. This whole process had taken at least a minute, maybe two. And in that time, Erin hadn't moved. Possibly hadn't even blinked.

Stress makes people do funny things, and her job had been nothing lately if not stressful. Didn't I often find myself wandering into another room with no recollection of why I was there? If I'm able to get lost in thought, surely anyone can.

It was when she finally got moving again I really started to worry.

Erin shuddered. She ticced a few times, then turned away from the wall and lurched a few steps to her right. Jacob followed with the camera.

"What's that door?" Carolyn asked.

I scrambled to remember. "Storage."

Erin pulled out her keys and unlocked the door. It took her three tries, but finally, she let herself in. Jacob tried to aim the speaker-cam to see what was inside, but the angle was all wrong.

"We need to see what's in there," Jacob said.

I scanned our group. Zigler hadn't said a word and he was the color of ash. He'd seen the way Erin was moving...and whatever was going on, he was definitely not equipped to deal with it. But me? I didn't see how I had any other choice than to try and handle the situation.

I said, "Zig, you and Carolyn stay here with the bird's eye view, and get us some backup." I turned to Jacob and said, "Let's go."

CHAPTER 34

JACOB GRABBED A SQUAD car and drove like a crazy person. Even though it was a straight shot up Lincoln, The Clinic was still a few miles away. Far enough to make it impossible to avoid giving voice to what we were both thinking.

"It's Jennifer Chance," I said grimly. "And one guess as to who brought her in."

Jacob swerved around a driver who'd panicked at the sight of the police lights and just stopped in the middle of the road. "This is not our fault."

"How can you say that? We were the ones to troop out the GhosTV—at her last place of employment, no less. It must've been a ginormous, honkin'-assed beacon. She went sniffing around the tuner, then jumped into Erin. And now we're fucked."

"Regret is not helpful, Vic, not now. We have to move forward. Focus—what do we need? Florida Water? Salt?"

"We should've thought of that before we grabbed a squad car. All we've got are road flares and an assault rifle." Could I use those road flares in lieu of candles? Not without burning the whole building down. I zeroed in on my crown chakra and scrambled to suck down as much light as I possibly could. As we roared up Lincoln, I envisioned myself as a whale cutting through the water with my mouth open wide, scooping up the krill of psychic energy. But unlike Moby Dick, I was only cut out to hold so much mojo.

Okay. What else was at my disposal?

I blundered out my phone, which was still streaming the air freshener channel. The spycam showed nothing but an empty pharmacy. If it were planted an inch or two to the right, it might show the door Erin had gone through. As it was, I could see one of the hinges. But unless it could peer through metal and wood, it wouldn't have made a damn bit of difference.

I flicked back to my menu and saw the Mood Blaster app. I should have done more with it, I now realized. Tested it methodically to find out what expanded my white light capacity and what knocked me out cold. Now I couldn't risk dialing in the wrong binaural pulse and deadening my psychic edge. On top of that, I suspected my earbuds were still on Zigler's desk, tangled up with a charging cable.

Of course, there was always the Kick. I didn't need to touch the tiny plastic case in my pocket—I could feel it against my hip with the pill gently rattling around inside. Part of me wondered if I should take it now. Give it a few minutes to sink in. But the thing about the fatal seizures was that they only happened to people who'd done it more than once. And me? Maybe I'd never done Kick...but my body was no stranger to experimental psyactives.

To flush out Jennifer Chance and send her back to Hell where she belonged, I'd need to pinpoint that critical moment before the seizures took hold. I couldn't risk it happening in the car.

We squealed to a stop in front of The Clinic in a loading

zone. Thanks to the sirens, four agents from FPMP National had come out to meet us. Four black-suited thirty-something white guys with tactical stances and expressionless stares. The one at point position stepped forward. I took him to be the senior agent. I climbed out of the squad car and headed for him. He'd know what the M-5 on my ID meant. Hopefully that would be enough to make him hear me out.

But when I swung out of the vehicle and reached for my ID, things took a crazy turn. First, the agents—from my *parent agency*, mind you—thought I was going for a weapon and drew on me. Jacob reflexively went for his weapon, too. I forgot all about my laminated card and stuck my hands in the air. My marksmanship wasn't bad these days, thanks to long, tedious hours on the range with an instructor who took great pleasure in pointing out my flaws...but I knew I'd never pull the trigger.

Not while I was so distracted by the way the agents from National all sprouted a flickery third eye in the middle of their foreheads.

Telepaths. Within range of the GhosTV.

I had no idea why it was playing...but at least it meant it was still here, and not in pieces in the back of an unmarked van. I might regret it later, but for now I'd take all the help I could get.

I eased behind the dubious protection of my open car door, keeping my hands where everyone could see them. I'm not a hundred percent sure how strong telepathy works. Psychs who were used to the world being an open book might take none too kindly to encountering a True Stiff. But if their talent was anything like high-level empathy, they should be picking up enough from me to know I was really hoping bullets wouldn't fly.

Either that or they were wondering how I knew they were all telepaths.

Shit. Maybe I should take a play out of Troy's playbook and just think of the last TV show I saw. Though I usually only watched the news. And that always led in with a report about someone getting shot.

I decided to act as professional as I could and reason with the guys, Psych to Psych. "Agent Victor Bayne, fifth-level medium. We've got a situation inside with a nonphysical entity that I need to deal with. Pronto."

The lead agent made a hand signal and his guys shifted to low ready. He holstered his gun and said, "I'll make a call."

"There's no time for that. How about this? I'll leave my sidearm with you." As I spoke, I did my best to project, *Scary ghost! Right now! Really!* But who knows what the hell telepaths actually hear?

The lead guy already had someone on his phone. A quick exchange, and then he said, "Sorry, Agent. I'm not authorized to let you in."

He had no idea what damage Jennifer Chance could do inside a human host. She could insert a dose of Kick into all those prescriptions. She could murder someone just to prove a point. Hell, she could tell everyone Morganstern was definitely not in Japan!

"I'm talking ghosts," I said desperately.

One of the guys in back flinched, but the lead guy repeated, "I'm not authorized."

Jacob tried to reason with him, but I could tell we were dealing with a guy who wasn't about to risk his career over the word of a couple of regional agents. We operated differently in Chicago than they did in DC. Con Dreyfuss hadn't hired agents for blind obedience, and Laura Kim didn't micromanage us. Our culture wasn't about asking permission. We thought on our feet—hell, we had to, given that the scariest shit we came up against was usually something no one had ever dealt with before.

And then we did whatever it took to handle it.

If the agent wasn't authorized to let me in, I realized-
...someone inside most definitely was. "Jacob? Call The Clinic's
emergency number."

With his eyes on the agents, he asked, "What should I say?"

"That one of their high-level patients is having an emergency." And before I could second-guess myself, I stepped to
the side and slammed my hand in the car door.

CHAPTER 35

OH GOD. THE PAIN.

I was bent over double and couldn't catch my breath. One good thing about my hand-slam. It made Jacob sound really convincing when he called in my emergency. He ran around to my side of the car and demanded, "What the hell were you thinking?"

That it was just my hand. Which, I could totally see now, was beyond blasé.

Someone in scrubs burst through the door with a wheelchair—Gina. I almost didn't recognize her with her skin glowing like an Instagram filter. Did she even know she was a precog? No clue.

It speaks volumes about how stunned I was that I actually climbed on. It was easier than arguing—and besides, my vision was starting to tunnel. The goons from National gave us a wide berth—and one guy actually held the door. But the lead asshole moved to intercept Jacob. "The medium is the Psych with the medical emergency, Agent. Not you."

Trembling with adrenaline and bursting with red veininess, Jacob ground out, "I am his emergency contact."

"You heard him," Gina said in her most authoritative mom-voice. "Agent Marks has the legal right to accompany his fiancé. Now, get out of his way."

We banged past Troy Malone's window and into the fluorescent-lit hallways of The Clinic, and the closer we got, the more the GhosTV's signal hummed through me. I stole a glance at my hand. I'd nailed myself just above the knuckles, and all four fingers were swelling up and turning a mottled shade of purple.

The pain wasn't a steady thing—it was a throb. And through my blurred vision, I saw the ghostly outline of my etheric form making a fist, squeezing and releasing, in time with the throbs. I tried to force my subtle body to stay still, but no luck. My physical brain might be begging it to stop clenching, but my etheric brain (if such a thing even existed) was operating with its own agenda.

Gina pushed me toward the exam rooms at a good clip. "The doctor's on his way," she told me reassuringly.

"Gina, wait!"

She didn't quite stop, but she did slow enough for me to tumble out of the chair beside the stairwell door and land in an ungainly crouch.

"But your hand—"

"There's no time to explain. C'mere." I grabbed her keycard on its springy lanyard and swiped open the stairwell. When I released it, the card snapped back and bapped against her thigh. "Now go to the break room, grab me all the salt you can find, and bring it to the pharmacy. Quick!"

Gina dashed away, and we headed in. Jacob thundered down the stairs with me fast on his heels, and together, we spilled out onto the basement level: conference rooms, janitorial, storage, and pharmacy. If begging the white light to come down and fill me up was effective, I should be lit up like a jack o'lantern. But between the throbbing in my hand and the GhosTV broadcast buzzing in my head, it was hard to know for sure.

"Keep your gun holstered," I called out as we careened down the hall. "You need your hands free."

Jacob lurched to a stop outside the pharmacy door. Whatever channel the TV was on, it made him look big and scary, even without a weapon in his hand. I lowered my voice and said, "We can't fuck this up—not like we did with Jackie and Trinity. I shove Chance out of the body and you drag that monster to the veil. Got it?"

"Got it. Let's go."

At the last minute, I realized I should've held on to Gina's keycard—but thankfully, when Jacob gave the pharmacy door a good, solid tug, the overhead lights flickered, and it opened.

He paused just inside the door. "This doesn't feel right," Jacob growled. I'd be surprised if it did. "Do you feel it?"

"I don't feel anything but my goddamn hand." Besides, my feelings were the last thing I trusted. I took a look instead.

The room was just like I'd seen it last, cramped and cluttery, with a new bluetooth speaker up on the shelf. One thing was very different, though—an unassuming door that had always been closed now stood ajar.

And there was movement behind it.

White light—white light—white light.

The pharmacy might be filled with clutter and stuff, but the room beyond was a freaking nightmare. It was narrow, cramped and dimly lit, and stuffed to the gills with discarded medical equipment. And thanks to my time at Camp Hell, just the sound of a gurney was enough to bring on a panic attack. Let alone a bunch of medical surplus with a big fat ghost inside.

"Erin?" I called out.

Something shifted in the dimness.

I turned to Jacob for reassurance. He was so pumped up he hardly even looked like himself anymore—unless you counted the set of his shoulders, which was totally him. Maybe the GhosTV upstairs wasn't just *showing me* his talent. Maybe it was *enhancing* his talent.

I took a centering breath, wrapped myself in white light, and tried again. "Erin...come out where I can see you."

Erin peered out from the gap in the door. And when she spoke, she sounded stilted and strange. "Well. If it isn't Victor Bayne. It's been a while."

Nowhere near long enough. "I'm onto you. Whatever it is you think you're cooking up here, it's not gonna happen."

Half-seen, Erin twitched and shuddered. "But...it already has."

A frantic knock on the pharmacy door made me jump. Jacob hauled the door open and Gina burst in, reading glasses swinging on her bright beaded chain. She clutched a cardboard tub of table salt in one hand and two smaller plastic shakers in the other.

I'd sorely underestimated how terrified I was of Jennifer Chance, so when I saw the salt, I made a grab for it. Unfortunately, my left hand was so swollen now I couldn't close my physical fingers. Oh, my etheric fingers made a valiant effort. But it didn't mean squat in the physical world. I boffed the salt out of Gina's hands and the tub fell to the floor and rolled into the shadowy room. With Erin...and the thing inside her.

"Give me that," Jacob said, and grabbed a salt shaker from Gina. He twisted off the top with a crunch, then jammed it into my good hand while she struggled to open the other shaker. There was a jolt when his fingers brushed mine, but the white light didn't jump over to him like it usually did. More like a weird combination of resistance and catalyst. My etheric arm recoiled, and my physical hand went clumsy. The salt dropped and scattered.

Luckily, Gina had her shaker open…though I couldn't be entirely sure my light wouldn't jump over to her if we touched. I gave my arm a shake to align all my subtle bodies. "Careful," I said, and took the salt shaker very gingerly from her outstretched hand.

Just my luck. It was practically empty.

"Stay back, Gina," I said, then turned to Jacob and pointed at the salty floor. "Can you activate this yourself?"

"I'll try." He dropped to one knee and slapped his hand down on the spilled salt. The floor lit up to my inner eye.

I've always thought optimism was a crutch, but in that moment, seeing him bursting with psychic energy and able to actually channel his power? I felt a tentative surge of hope.

Unfortunately, we weren't the only ones scrambling around for an advantage, and our fumbling with the salt had given Erin time to break out the big guns. When the door creaked open, she had a syringe in her hand—an old-fashioned glass-and-metal syringe with a bead of fluid glistening at the tip. She smiled all wrong and said, "Don't worry. You'll hardly feel a thing. I've had plenty of practice."

The confusing thing about possession is that the voice still belongs to the poor schlub who's got a ghost puppeteering their body. I'd convinced myself I was dealing with Jennifer Chance, so it took me a moment to register the lilt of the accent. And then I got a load of the way Erin held that needle. Not like Chance, but an entirely different doctor, one from my distant past. Visions of drug-addled field trips with Faun and Richie and Darla bubbled up from my memory.

I was dealing with someone I hoped I'd never see again, all right, but it wasn't Dr. Chance. And once I made the connection, another face flickered briefly over Erin's features—the wizened face of an old man.

In a dry whisper, I said, "Dr. Kamal."

Erin bared her teeth. I'd never once seen her smile. But if I had, I'd wager it didn't look anything like that.

Jacob scrambled to his feet and looked frantically around, as if he'd somehow managed to miss a fifth person in the pharmacy. "Kamal? Where?"

I pointed at Erin and said, "Stay back."

But Kamal wasn't intimidated by me. Never had been.

Reflexively, I backed up a step and did my best to power-charge the salt shaker in my hand—the one that contained maybe half an inch of salt.

"What's the matter, Mr. Bayne?" Kamal asked through Erin's mouth. "You've always taken the needle in stride." With a jerk of the arm, he elbowed the door wide. It smashed into the old medical equipment with a thunderous clatter. Suddenly, knocking the ghost out of Erin's body seemed a hell of a lot more daunting than it had as a sketchy plan. Spilled salt rasped under the soles of my shoes as I scanned the room, scrambling to locate the veil.

"What's happening?" Gina demanded. "Should I call a doctor?"

Jacob got bossy. "No doctors. You'd only put them at risk. Now get back!"

Gina shuffled backwards, muttering fragments of a prayer—I think it was the type of blessing you'd say at mealtime. I took a step sideways, placing my body between Erin's and hers. No doubt Kamal could just blow right through me to get to her if he wanted...especially since mediums were a lot easier to displace from their physical bodies than anyone else. Hopefully he wasn't after Gina.

I gorged so hard on white light I probably popped a vein in my other eye. And when I was bursting with as much as I could hold, I felt the telltale pull of the veil.

It was in the shadowy room full of creepy, disused medical equipment.

Of course it was.

"The veil is in there," I told Jacob, and while Kamal thought I was still dithering about what to do, I launched the contents of the salt shaker in his direction. It hit Erin's body square in the lab coat. She lit, briefly, with a sickly bluish aura—an aura filled with slithering movement. It was so horrid, it left an afterimage in my mind's eye...and I made sense of the squirming nimbus only after it disappeared.

It wasn't just Kamal we were dealing with. It was a metric shit ton of habit demons. Not just tethered to him either, but *merged* with him.

And the salt had been scarcely more than an annoyance.

Before I could warn Jacob, he was striding across the salty floor like he was hell-bent on tackling Erin. "Wait," I called out. "Kamal's not alone."

Maybe not. But Jacob? He was all Hulked out on his Superstiff equivalent of white light, and before I could stop him, he lunged forward and batted the syringe out of Erin's hand. The tube shattered on the floor, spraying the salt with broken glass and whatever drug cocktail Kamal had been hoping to stick me with.

The sight of Jacob going in for the jugular broke open something inside me. That stupid, secret part of me that doesn't know when to admit defeat. I opened my white light capacity even harder, and hallelujah, there was that spike of pain deep inside my head that told me I was doing it right.

Hopefully I wouldn't stroke out before we got rid of all the parasites.

My sight shifted, and the wispy forms of nonphysical entities tugged around the periphery of my vision. Erin was covered in habit demons like a sunken ship crusted in barnacles and seaweed. Once I focused on them—once my brain figured out what I was trying to look at—they took on substance and form, until they were so thick I could hardly see Erin anymore at the center of them all.

"How do I grab him?" Jacob shouted.

I stepped up to guide him...or at least I tried to. Gina caught me by the back of the jacket and tugged hard enough to almost unbalance me. "Wait!"

Major liability.

I swung around to bark at her to get the hell out of there. She blinked back at me with a look of utter confusion, and said, "You have flowers. Oh god. What am I saying?"

Then, thankfully, she spun on her heel and dashed out the door.

Once I was sure Gina was good and gone, I turned and found Jacob grabbing Erin by the upper arms and shoving her back into the storage room. Since Kamal was still in her, at least it would bring his ghost closer to the veil.

But the habit demons were in an uproar.

The ones who weren't stuck to Kamal dive-bombed Jacob like a mass of angry bees. Big, gelatinous, etheric bees the size of oranges. That was how they described tumors, wasn't it? By comparing it to fruit? Jesus Christ, he was being swarmed by etheric tumors.

I scanned the floor, hoping to scoop up whatever salt I could. But thanks to the broken syringe, not only was it littered with shards of glass, it was spattered with fluid, so it would only stick to me if I tried to toss it. I reached for the etheric fairy dust I often conjured in my panic, same as always...and nearly blacked out from the pain. Here I'd thought I was so smart, slamming my left hand in the car door. My non-dominant hand. The one I don't use for writing, or shooting, or wiping my ass.

Not considering that it was the hand responsible for all the fairy dust and ectoplasm.

No Florida Water. No salt. No fairy dust. But there was still one ace up my sleeve....

A dose of Kick rattling around in my pocket.

I whipped out the contact lens case and flicked it open with my thumb.

My first thought? *Wow. Kick looks just like those belchy multivitamins in our medicine cabinet.*

And then...realization dawned.

It *was* one of those belchy multivitamins. And the real Kick?

It was coursing through Jacob's veins.

CHAPTER 36

"WHAT THE HELL WERE you thinking?" I demanded. Probably because that's exactly what Jacob yelled at me when I fucked up my hand.

"That I'm sick of being the most useless one on the team."

"You? But you're a human shield!"

"Not good enough," he said through gritted teeth. Apparently I wasn't the only one who felt like a one-trick pony—and evidently Jacob had no compunctions about going through my pockets, and he wasn't particularly deterred by a used tissue. "I can feel the veil now."

No no no. I crunched across the broken glass to make sure he wasn't getting sucked in. And now that I knew he was not only on GhosTV waves but a volatile, fast-acting psyactive? No freaking wonder he was bulging with red energy fit to burst.

Me? The TV enhanced my panicked white light, and I saw the veil too. Or I could tell where it *would* be if I could see it, judging by the way a couple of the free-floating tumors got sucked in. But the more deeply I peered into the etheric, the worse it got. The whole room was thick with habit demons. Ever see a microscopic video of sperm battering an egg? That was those goddamn etheric parasites struggling to attach to Jacob.

Every Psych who'd come through The Clinic's door covered in those things had been heading right here, to some nightmarish etheric spawning ground, drawn by their habit demons, pulled by some nonphysical resonance. And at the center of it all was Dr. Kamal. Seething with symbiotic monsters, feeding one another on siphoned etheric energy. Pumping out experimental drugs even after he was dead and gone.

The drugs attracted habit demons. The demons rode to The Clinic on the dying psychics, whose energy was released with their death. That power generated more demons in an orgy of stolen psychic mojo.

And Kamal? He soaked up all that power, took over Erin's body and made a fresh batch of Kick…and the vicious cycle started again.

From my vantage point in the doorway, I pointed to a gap between an exam table and a banged-up gurney. "There, Jacob! There's the veil."

Jacob shoved Erin toward the spot. But while the demons couldn't quite snag Jacob, the parasite-riddled ghost in Erin was clinging to her hard. When the veil pulled, the parasites doubled down, drawing up against her like a protective etheric shell. Jacob shoved her, head and shoulders, into the distortion where the veil seemed to be…but all the etheric trespassers just squeezed in tighter and stayed right where they were, sealing Kamal in.

Jacob had to let go. Hell, neither of us should be touching that, juiced up or not.

I scrambled for something to throw, and my eyes fell on a neat row of glass apothecary jars—jars that had just been refilled with fresh roots and petals and stems after Erin's trip to Chinatown.

You have flowers.

When I redirected some white light toward the botanicals, a jar of tiny brownish petals blazed bright. I grabbed the jar and dove into the storeroom. As I vaulted over a fallen IV stand with the jar tucked tight against my body, a few potential outcomes flashed through my head. One, the habit demons scatter and Kamal is jarred loose. That was probably the best-case scenario—despite the fact that those etheric tapeworms would all burrow right into me.

But judging by the sharp, stabbing pain in my head, the other (more likely) result would be that I accompanied Kamal across the veil personally...right as I stroked out.

I wasn't ready to go. Not by a long shot—not with a wedding on the horizon and my permanent record mostly untapped.

No, I wasn't eager to play escort...but better me than Jacob. "Let go on three," I called out. "One...two...."

I yanked the top off the apothecary jar and heaved the contents in their direction. A cloud of tiny dried flower petals billowed out. When it touched Erin's body, a kaleidoscope of habit demons erupted. A lot of them got sucked into the veil—unfortunately, not all. But the habit demons, scary as they might be, weren't my biggest concern. They couldn't reason. They couldn't think. We could clean up the psychic jellyfish later.

Once we got rid of Dr. Kamal.

I charged forward and gave Erin a shove to the sternum, fully expecting my etheric body to ram straight through. But my dominant hand felt awkward and strange when I was focused on my subtle bodies, and all I managed to do was push her into the table. She smiled—just a fraction of a second after the old-man face shimmering on top of hers did—and whipped out another antique syringe from her pocket.

I backpedaled, a knee-jerk reaction to playing the lab rat, and tripped over the IV stand on the floor. My arms wind-milled to stop me from wiping out completely, and I teetered there helplessly, right within his reach.

I lost the battle with gravity and toppled—or maybe it was Jacob shoving me out of the way. Our auras struck together like an etheric thunderclap, but he didn't steal my energy this time. He was way more hopped up than me, and for once, he was the source and I was the vacuum. His energy hit me like a punch to the gut, so stunning I hardly felt myself hit the ground, and all I could think was, *Holy hell, if I just stole his shield, I will never, ever forgive myself.*

I tried to shove myself up from the ground but only floun-dered on my crushed hand. Though even if I hadn't, no way would I have managed to stop Jacob. He was already in mo-tion. Palm forward, he smacked Erin in the forehead like a faith healer. As he struck, the dim lights flickered. It wasn't his physical body that collided with hers, I realized, as Erin's physical shell did little more than rock on its feet.

But her subtle bodies?

An explosion of them blew right out the back of her. Most of them were hers—shadowy, half-seen forms that looked more or less like slight variations of her physical form. But one of them was a wrinkled old man.

The subtle bodies that belonged inside Erin sprang back into place.

Kamal's didn't.

"He's there, behind her," I called out. But Jacob already felt it. With both hands out, he gave a massive etheric shove. The lights flickered again like we were in a brownout.

Kamal's ghost made a grab for Erin, but he was no more successful in latching back onto her than I was in getting to my feet. A pharmacy timer bleated, then fell silent. The electronic locks clicked like castanets. A bright worklamp flared to life beside me, dazzling my physical eyes. The bulb popped. I was locked onto Kamal too solidly to be deterred, though, and I gathered up my white light and willed him toward the veil for all I was worth.

My talent might have distracted him. But it was Jacob's final push that drove him through the veil once and for all.

His expression was somewhere between horror and dismay as habit demons swarmed him...just as his wrinkled face was pulled across the veil.

In the room behind us, a random pop song burst through the bluetooth speaker for a few seconds, then crackled to a stop. Something left a buzzing noise behind, and the faint stink of charred electronics tickled my nose. Jacob staggered back, dazed.

Erin looked around frantically. "What's going on?" Her face crumpled as tears forced their way out. "Ohmigod...it happened again."

Now there's something you never want to hear from a formerly possessed medium.

I grabbed a handful of dried flowers from the floor and tried to pitch them at the roiling habit demons—who were whirling around the room like a frog in a blender—but I couldn't gain any meaningful velocity. "Jacob—can you feel them? The etheric...things?"

He shuddered. "They're like nails on a chalkboard!"

Or guys folding paper and whispering about it on YouTube. "Quick, before the veil disappears—the more we can shove through, the better." I commando-crawled to the door on my elbows and knees to try and stop them from getting away. The fact that they could go through walls, floors and ceilings wasn't lost on me. I was a physical guy in a physical body, but I had to at least try.

Erin offered me a hand up and I took it—white light didn't jump between mediums—and I focused until my headache throbbed in time with my swelling hand. The damage was physical, I reassured myself. I'd deal with it later. Right now, the etheric was all that mattered. And as I understood the distinction, something cold spread across the palm of my left hand.

Normally, ectoplasm freaked me out. But at the moment, it was actually kind of soothing.

My hand filled with fairy dust—and since it was nonphysical, that stuff went exactly where I tossed it. It was like corralling a bunch of panicked birds. Somehow, though—together—Jacob and I managed to coordinate our energies, to sweep the room and herd the majority of the little bastards through by the time the veil faded. Part of me felt chagrined that I'd been nowhere near as slick as I'd thought when I palmed the contact lens case. But the rest of me realized I might've just dodged a major bullet. The flock of habit demons was half merged with what was left of Kamal. I'd hate for a psyactive to loosen me up so they could get their hooks into me.

Erin was a smart lady, and she'd done exactly the right thing: backed away from the chaos and presented the smallest possible target. Sure, she was shaking like a leaf and riding the brink of hyperventilation...but she hadn't fumbled into my path or disrupted our half-assed exorcism, so I counted that as a win.

"It's okay," I told her. "He's gone."

"Who's *he?*" she asked. But any real explanation I could dredge up would make things worse.

"You're safe. We're all safe."

She stared at me, the hollow-eyed stare of someone who's seen too much—an unwitting casualty of Psych, like Zigler and his PTSD, like Jack Bly and his insomnia. She'd need help. From Darla. From me. Heck, maybe even from Faun Windsong, who'd at the very least make all the unseen shit around us seem a lot less horrifying than I would.

"Erin?" I asked, as gently as I could. "It's over. Do you understand?" She didn't speak. Didn't even nod. "Are you with us? Say something."

She raised a trembling hand, pointed at me, and said, "What's that thing on your neck?"

I slapped at my throat and managed to slime myself. And then my hand throbbed hard. "What? Where?"

Erin gestured wildly. "A giant transparent flatworm wrapped around you like a scarf!"

Sonofabitch.

I scrabbled at it harder, which made a cascade of half-buried desires roar to life. The urge to swallow a painkiller. A Valium. An Auracel. But most of all...a Seconal. If I so much as suspected my old dealer was holding, I'd drop what I was doing, commandeer the squad car and drive there right this second. Hell, I might even do it just to prove to myself he wasn't.

But before I could so much as turn toward the door, Jacob was on me—and when he went for my neck, it wasn't to mark me up with love bites. Whatever had been tapping into me, it felt him coming a split second sooner than I did. And for that brief, shining moment, I realized that while I might be obstinate, in the end, time meant nothing to the parasite that was feeding off my addiction, and eventually it would outlast my stubbornness. As it recoiled from Jacob, its pull was so strong that I groped in my pocket for the nasty vitamin. Or some lint. Or even the contact lens case itself. Anything to quell the urge to stuff something in my gob and swallow it.

And then Jacob's hands closed around something. Not my neck...but the thing around it.

I felt the tether tear free as a catch in my throat. My eyes teared up and I spluttered, coughed, and swallowed. If not for the GhosTV, maybe I wouldn't have actually seen the entity. After all, Con Dreyfuss had been trailing around fingernail demons for ages and I'd been none the wiser. But we were still in range of the signal—lucky me—and when Jacob tore the squirming creature from around my neck, I saw it. The tether was long and wormy, topped by a fat, bloated head. Its tail whipped back and forth, searching for something to sink into and anchor it in the physical.

The crimson channels of power that threaded through Jacob's being swelled as he did his True Stiff equivalent of sucking white light. Except, his energy didn't beam down from the heavens—it drew up from the ground. I may be the poster boy for visual understanding, but I felt the power just as much as I saw it, rumbling up into him like a seismic tremor.

The psychic remora twisted and thrashed. Jacob gave a guttural roar...and tore the thing in two.

The etheric body collapsed in on itself and oozed through Jacob's fingers as it fell to shreds. I searched for the glisten of ectoplasm on his hands, but there was none. Maybe, though, I caught the smallest glint of fairy dust as the red veins gently faded away.

CHAPTER 37

Habit demons don't come with histories attached, so it was anyone's guess how long that goddamn parasite had been tickling the back of my throat. I didn't think it was a long-term stowaway. Maybe it had been hovering around my dealer in that dive bar waiting to hitch a ride. Or maybe I picked it up when I saw Angelica in the treatment center. Either way, it was gone now. I probably should've felt relieved. But really, I was just phenomenally tired.

The demon might be gone, but I was still an addict. I'd always be an addict. One who wasn't currently using, thank God. And one who could turn down a tasty pill, albeit with a pang of wistful longing.

I'd have to settle for that.

Zigler and Carolyn had been monitoring the live feed on the security cams, and they'd grabbed another squad car and hauled ass to The Clinic just as soon as things went south. They showed up as we were picking our way across the broken glass.

After I reassured everyone that we had things under control, I said, "How'd you manage to sweet talk your way past the goons upstairs?"

Zigler shook his head. "I didn't. By the time we got here…they were gone."

Which makes you wonder what exactly FPMP National was doing there to begin with. "What happened to your hand?" Carolyn demanded.

"Long story," I said, but I changed my mind when I realized who I was talking to. "Actually, no, it's not. It's just fallout from a phenomenally shitty judgment call."

If I was in rough shape, Jacob was even worse. His muscles were cramping up and he kept chafing sweat off his forehead. But neither of us was willing to be seen at The Clinic. Sure, there was a chance that a confused ghost would be wandering the halls of LaSalle General, but I'd prefer that to whatever habit demons were still lurking inside The Clinic's acoustic drop ceiling.

Dr. Gillmore might come off as a hard-ass, but when she saw Jacob and me limping through the lobby together, she managed to slot us into adjoining emergency bays. "Good thing the two of you chose midday to beat yourselves up," she said. "After sundown, you'd still be in the waiting room."

Since I was waiting for a hand consult, it left me free to hover anxiously over Jacob while they hooked him up to an IV and tried to get his electrolytes straightened out. When Gillmore heard what he'd done, she made no effort to get me to go back to my own bed. "I've heard of couples who go for matching sweatshirts," she said, "but the matching subconjunctival hemorrhage takes the cake."

I couldn't say for sure when Jacob popped his eyeball capillaries. At the time, I'd been seeing him as a big webwork of red veins. I'm guessing his struggle with the habit demon had something to do with it.

Gillmore squared herself up with Jacob and nailed him

with her most piercing stare. "I'm well aware how easy it is for law enforcement to get their hands on whatever contraband they set their mind to—and, hell, Kick isn't even technically illegal yet. But believe me when I tell you, the next time you take it could very well be your last."

"I understand," he said, though his tone was tinged with *you're not the boss of me.*

At the other end of the ER, a controlled commotion burst through the door. As the paramedics rattled off the patient's stats, I picked out "multiple GSW." Maybe the city would chill out now that its requisite daily gunshot victim was out of the way.

"Don't either of you go anywhere," Gillmore said icily, and hurried off to check on someone way more critical than a couple of ex-PsyCops who'd just taken an etheric beating.

It had been tempting to harangue Jacob about switching out that pill while I was asleep, but Gillmore's warning brought everything into a new and terrifying focus. "Jacob...that wasn't your first rodeo. Maybe Kick's got a grace period where people bounce back from the first time they take it. But, Jesus. You've taken other psyactives. What if it technically wasn't your first time?"

He gave a bitter laugh. "Me? My psyactive consumption is nothing compared to yours."

"I *know* my limits."

"That's bullshit." He shoved himself up off the bed, snagged me by the lapel, and dragged me over him so we were face to face. "Think, Vic. Not only the drugs we got from Dreyfuss, but the ones Roger Burke laced your coffee with. That had to be Palazamine—just like in Kick. Not to mention Camp Hell—who knows what they pumped into you at Camp Hell? For all we know, whatever damage those things do, whatever physical pathways they alter, there's no expiration date. Do you seriously think I'd stand by and watch while you took one for the team?"

"But, Jacob...if it's ever a choice between me and you...it's gotta be me."

He knew exactly what I meant. If someone's gotta go.... "Why would you say something like that?"

"You have a family."

He balled my jacket in his fist. "Damn it, Vic, so do you. *I* am your family."

We sized each other up with our bloody eyeballs, Jacob and me. Each of us aching to throttle the other. Both of us breathing raggedly, waterlogged with emotion. When our mouths crashed together, it was more in desperation than love. A realization that neither one of us was invincible.

And neither was expendable.

———•———

According to the hand guy, I was lucky I didn't need surgery. Given that I'd have months of physical therapy in my future, *lucky* wasn't exactly the word I'd use to describe myself. Plus, no modern removable brace for me. I'd be stuck in a hard plaster cast for the next three to six weeks, depending on how well I healed. The nurse cautioned me to duct tape a plastic bag around it when I showered. Fine. I could do that. But I wasn't sure how it would hold up to ectoplasm christening it from the inside.

Jacob got a clean bill of health, though he wasn't really sure what the social worker who came to talk to him made of the whole situation. He held onto the stack of drug addiction pamphlets only as far as the trash can beside the exit. The remark Gillmore made about us having access to things like Kick was true enough, but I wasn't concerned that Jacob would be compelled to seek out his next dose. The way those habit demons bounced right off him, they'd never stood a chance.

We spent a while hunting for the Crown Vic before we realized it was still back at the Fifth. We found the squad car we'd ridden in on right where Zigler left it, though. And a woman huddled in her winter coat was leaning against the driver side door.

Erin Welch.

It was a relief to see she wasn't behind bars. Lincolnwood PD had pulled up just as we made our grand exit, and it would only be a matter of time before they approached her with an arrest warrant. I'd need to have a serious chat with my boss to keep Erin out of the clink...and hope she didn't end up in an undocumented cage at the FPMP instead. Hopefully Laura would be glad to have a newly discovered medium to train—...once she got over her visceral fear and loathing of possession, anyhow.

Erin's nose was red from the cold, or maybe she'd been crying. Her glasses sat a little funny. One of the arms, I saw, was held on with medical tape. She looked up at the two of us miserably and said, "They took your TV set."

Ah. And now we knew the real reason FPMP National got involved.

"Gina thinks it's her fault. She plugged it in. Those new guys checked that room half a dozen times and didn't notice it—Gina had a bunch of fans sitting on top, so I guess it just looked like a table. But maybe ten, fifteen minutes after she plugged it in, while we were all in the pharmacy, they hauled it out the door and took off. She's really sorry. She has no idea why she even did it."

I'd wager a guess. And it would go something like, *It's supposed to be plugged in. I don't know why.*

Was I dismayed the goons from Washington made off with

the GhosTV that Con Dreyfuss had left in my care? Probably, though the full ramifications would take a while to sink in. Mostly, I was insanely freaking relieved that, thanks to Gina, it had been broadcasting the etheric channel when it was, and the Feds hadn't found it until we'd dealt with my stowaway. Otherwise, there'd still be a psychic parasite around my neck, and we'd all be none the wiser.

"My boss is gonna get in touch with you," I told Erin. "And whatever suggestions she makes, follow them to the letter to make sure you don't take the fall for anyone else."

"What do you mean? I didn't do anything wrong."

"Just...listen to Laura. She's good people."

Erin nodded. She might not particularly like me, but she did trust me. And that was a start.

It was late by the time Jacob and I picked up our car...late enough to take another stab at setting something to rights that we should have handled long ago. We swung by the grocery store for salt...so much salt that the cashier asked if we were brining a turkey. And then she noticed our bloody eyeballs and decided she really didn't want to know.

We gathered the prayer candles and Hoyt's Cologne from the trunk and let ourselves into the basement of my old apartment. I'd been gearing myself up for a sad and heartfelt goodbye. But all the washers and dryers were going full-tilt, and I had no idea if Jackie would even hear me over the noise.

Jacob closed the door and jimmied it shut using the rubber stopper people normally kept it open with while they hauled laundry in and out. Since the washing machines were all coin-op, the controls were nonexistent, just the slots that ate the quarters, a button to pick the water temp, and nothing else. I could shut them up by pulling the plugs, but we couldn't risk a first-floor tenant realizing we'd interfered with his laundry stirring up a huge ruckus.

I put the noise out of my mind and lit the candles. "Are you still feeling the psyactives?" I asked Jacob.

"Maybe. Hard to say."

"You can't see the nonphysical. That's obvious. But you feel it. Right?"

Jacob shuddered. He hadn't come out and said what it felt like when he tore the squirming parasite in half, but I'd wager he wouldn't forget anytime soon.

I held salt awkwardly on my fingertips where they protruded from my cast. As I imagined white light infusing it from the heavens, I thought about Jacob's energy, the red, ropy, veiny power, and how different it was from mine. "What if we each power up from a different chakra?" I blurted out. I was clearly talking out of my ass and deserved to be laughed right out of that basement.

But when Jacob looked up sharply, he wasn't laughing. "How can that be? Everyone knows the crown chakra is the one that corresponds to psychic ability."

"Maybe, maybe not. When it comes to Psych, I've never put much stock in what 'everyone' knows. When you were powered up on GhosTV waves and psyactives, it wasn't white light you were mainlining. It was…earth energy." I'd heard that phrase recently. Where? I cast my mind back…to the chair yoga guy on YouTube. Who'd been lecturing us about the earth, and balance, and grounding. Just as Jacob was hammering away at my ass.

My base chakra.

No wonder I'd come away with my extrasensory talent stunted. It had nothing to do with the yoga, but with Jacob and me. I'd been stockpiling crown chakra energy, then we went and neutralized every last bit.

Part of me was horrified. But how bad was it really, when afterwards, I'd had such an amazing night's sleep?

I held out the salt to Jacob and said, "Try pulling from the ground up. Maybe it'll be easier than you think. Darla says the reason salt amplifies energy is the crystalline structure. But there's no reason it has to be my particular brand of energy."

We sat quietly together. As we each did our best to activate our salt, I noticed movement on the floor. We hadn't summoned the baby with our blundering actions. It just so happened that the nightly window of time—the one in which she intersected with the physical world—had finally arrived. The spot where the veil had been last time felt dry. Or maybe I was just too overextended to sense its presence.

"You've got this," I told Jacob. Not because I wanted to stroke his ego—which was surprisingly vulnerable in places I least expected. But because I truly thought he'd be just as likely as me to set things right. "Where's the veil?"

He looked around. His brow furrowed in frustration. I wanted to walk him through it somehow—me, the guy with a level so high that even when I lied about half the stuff I saw, I was nearly off the charts—but our talents were too different. Hell, it took some figuring to find common ground with Darla. Jacob's ability and mine were practically opposites.

Jacob took a deep breath. I'd expected him to pass the baton back to me, but instead...he closed his eyes. "There." He pointed toward the storage lockers. "I feel the veil."

Once he'd pinpointed the location? So did I.

"Now what?" he asked.

I scattered my salt and focused on it, all those tiny little crystals purportedly amplifying my psychic mojo, and I imagined the white light surrounding Trinity and floating her toward the veil.

Nothing happened. Unless you counted the throb deep inside my head growing more pronounced.

We were in uncharted territory. I saw things, but Jacob felt them. When he grabbed a possessed medium, he could hold the spirit inside. And he'd gotten a good enough grip on the habit demon to tear it in two. "If the baby can't get there herself…maybe you should help her along."

Jacob groped on the salty floor. "To the right. No, the other right." His struggle was agonizing. I wished I could take his hand and guide it, but I couldn't risk touching him. Our energies might short each other out. "Jacob, no, the other way."

It was no use. As the Kick ebbed from his system, helped along by all the fluids Dr. Gillmore had pushed through his veins, Jacob just wasn't cut out for this kind of task. Without the GhosTV, he'd need to settle for being impervious to psychic scrutiny and possession. And frankly, after going around with a habit demon suckered onto my throat for who knows how long, I'd trade places in a heartbeat if I could.

He stood from his crouch. Giving up so soon? Maybe he was right—we were tapped out for now and should just come back another day. I tried to figure out how to say as much without coming off as patronizing, but he piped up before I could find the words.

And when he spoke, I realized, it wasn't me he was talking to. "Your daughter needs you."

How long had Jackie been there?

Jacob's arm hung at an odd angle, and my vision shifted. I couldn't see Jackie plainly, not like the ghosts I usually dealt with. But when I didn't look at her straight on, I caught glimpses from the corner of my eye.

Jacob was holding her hand.

"You're the only one who can do it," he said gently. "Be strong. For your daughter."

Although his eyes were closed, with Jackie at his side, he went directly to the spot where Trinity fussed on the floor.

When Jackie hesitated, I said, "You can't just leave her

there, Jackie. Pick her up."

Apparently, it wasn't the time for tough love. Jackie flickered and tried to bail, but Jacob refused to let go of her hand. He said, "It's okay, Jackie. It'll all be okay, but you need to do this. You, not us. Bring her to the veil."

All the mediumship talent in the world won't help if you don't know how to deal with people. And Jacob? He knew people...and he knew how to get his way. He held Jackie there beside her baby long enough to gather up her courage, but not so long that her resolve could erode.

"Do it...for Trinity."

And with that, he released Jackie's hand.

When Jackie took her newborn baby in her arms—for the first time in decades—the room filled with light so bright it dazzled me. Not my physical eyes, but my second sight, though I tried to orient myself by blinking away nonexistent afterimages. It took a few seconds. When my vision finally cleared, the baby was gone.

"Jackie?" I called out.

No reply.

"It's over," Jacob said. "She's finally at peace."

CHAPTER 38

THERE'S PROBABLY A MEDICAL reason why the day after working a bunch of heavy etheric lifting, every last part of my physical body hurts like hell. We'd left a message with Laura that we'd debrief her at noon, just as soon as we got a decent night's sleep. So I was surprised when my phone woke me with the announcement, "You have a text message that may be important."

It had never done that before. But since it periodically revealed new features I'd never okayed, I wasn't particularly surprised.

"Read it out loud," I told the phone.

"Meet me at the newspaper boxes on Western in half an hour."

"Who's it from?"

"I'm sorry. That number is blocked."

"Are you going?" Jacob mumbled, half asleep.

I considered whether or not it was FPMP National angling to haul me away, and decided they'd be more likely to batter down the cannery's door than to have me meet them in a public place. In all likelihood, one of our witnesses had something to tell me off the record. Whatever it might be, since the Kick pipeline was shut down now, I figured it could wait. Then I considered if there was any likelihood I'd get back to sleep, and noticed daylight filtering in through the tiny window above the bed. I sighed. "Apparently I'm up now. I might as well go."

I must've been expecting Jacob to offer to come with me, because I was surprised when he didn't. Then I saw he was already out cold again. He'd done some heavy etheric lifting, too. Maybe more than his share.

Newspaper boxes were scarce in the city these days, since you'd have to go around with a pocketful of quarters heavy enough to pull down your pants to afford a single daily copy of the Tribune. But the Brown Line station was a busy hub that connected this neighborhood to the rest of the city. On the terrace outside, a line of metal coin-op boxes stood together in a brightly colored row like a chorus line of aging showgirls waiting to blow kisses at Ravenswood's daily commuters.

There was no one lingering anywhere nearby that I could tell. Then again, I was probably early. I considered taking a Chicago Reader to reacquaint myself with the city's cultural scene...or at least scan the goings on and reflect that I never did anything fun anymore. When I was young and surly, it's where all the punk rock happenings were listed. And though I hadn't been to a concert in years, I figured it couldn't hurt to look.

Unfortunately, the box was empty.

The intersection had plenty of foot traffic streaming by, but when I was bent over the box, someone paused behind me, casting a shadow across the metal front. I whipped around, probably too fast, cursing myself for getting so sloppy. For all I knew, the guys from the Washington office were hoping to use me as a channel guide for their new TV.

For all I knew, it was an assassin.

But, no. The face I encountered, with its weary expression and its once-blond mustache faded to white, belonged to someone I'd shared a precinct with for more than a dozen years. And he'd never once tried to kill me.

"Sarge," I said stupidly.

Warwick scanned the pavement, squinting. Spindly trees. A bike rack. A stream of normal pedestrians heading to their normal jobs. "So. We turned up a big stash of expired Palazamine in the pharmacy storeroom. Your new boss strongly suggested to us and to the Lincolnwood PD that we don't press charges against the pharmacist for her involvement in this latest shit show...but she wouldn't elaborate as to why."

"It wasn't Erin's fault."

"For...psychic reasons?"

"You could say that."

"Uh huh." Not only was Ted Warwick an early adopter in the PsyCop program, but he'd had a Psych in his own family...a beloved nephew. If Warwick didn't buy it, I could only imagine what would happen if Erin ended up front of a random judge. Or even worse, a jury.

Not that I could blame them. The explanation that she was possessed by a ghost powered by habit demons who were luring in additional psychics to sop up their etheric resonance wouldn't have convinced me. That was the best we could figure, anyhow. And I was still trying to wrap my head around it.

Warwick said, "I can take care of Welch if she cooperates. Any reason I shouldn't let the DA throw the book at Troy Malone?"

"The receptionist?"

"When we confronted him, he made himself out to be the mastermind of the whole operation. At least until we leaned on him hard enough for him to implicate the pharmacist."

I said, "At least tell me he flipped on Bertelli."

"Bertelli wasn't involved."

"But all the video evidence—"

"Showed him adding drugs to the pharmacy, not stealing them. Not psyactives, either—painkillers. He'd been skimming them for his own recreational use, we can't say how long—there's still a lot of video to process before we have a definitive timeline—and when our investigation zeroed in on the pharmacy, he started scrambling to make sure the numbers all jibed. Zigler was the one who noticed he made Welch open up a new batch to fill your scrip instead of letting her use what was already open. We think he's been substituting counterfeit meds to make up the shortfall."

But I'd never once seen Erin interacting with Troy. "So Bertelli wasn't even playing the go-between?"

"No. Malone found the Kick alongside his own prescriptions."

Hold on a sec. "Troy got prescriptions from The Clinic? For what?"

"Neurozamine. Apparently, he's a low-level telepath."

No wonder he'd come up with such an elaborate way of keeping his mind from being read. According to Warwick, Troy thought Erin's total lack of verbal acknowledgement about their venture was just her being cautious. She only communicated via notes tucked in with the pill bottles. He'd just figured she was avoiding all the security cams. He went along with it because he was secretly smitten...and infatuation can make us do some pretty bizarre things.

I said, "If you need proof that Erin wasn't exactly herself, at least for your own peace of mind, you could check the handwriting on the notes against hers."

Warwick watched as a couple wandered past, arguing in a language I couldn't readily identify, then crammed his hands in his pockets and said, "I already have."

"And?"

"The notes don't match Welch's writing. But they do match this book that Zigler turned up in the storage room." He drew out a battered notebook and handed it to me. It was old and water-stained, and the pages were yellowed. I flipped it open. The writing was in cursive, with lots of cryptic abbreviations and words I didn't know. The dates on the entries went back some fifty years. The numerals were foreign, with ones that looked more like sevens, and sevens with a bar through the middle.

"Did that belong to a certain Dr. Kamal?" I ventured.

"How much do you know about him?"

"It's been a few years since I've had the displeasure." In the physical, anyhow.

"Seems that a US Military sniper took him out one day on his way home from work...and a cleanup team made sure the body disappeared. And it seems that they did it on the recommendation of one Constantine Dreyfuss."

The stunningly truthful conversation I'd had with Dreyfuss so long ago in the astral plane came rushing back to me. *Once we took care of Kamal....* I hadn't recognized the name, at the time. But now my brain slotted it in like it had been there all along. Freaky. *Once he was gone, yeah. Once we'd cleaned house, at least I didn't have to worry about getting plugged by my own team.*

More implications than I could shake a stick at.

I hefted the journal. "What's the gist of it?"

"Records. Initials and dates. Some kind of...genealogy." Sarge's pale-eyed gaze went icy as he stared out over traffic. "My nephew's in there. With an entry that he's been terminated."

My heart hammered hard. Alex Warwick died just before I checked in to Camp Hell. "And me?"

"Not that I saw. But you should go through it anyways and

make sure for yourself."

I accepted the tacit agreement that neither of us would mention Warwick allowing me to make evidence disappear, and tucked the book into my overcoat pocket.

I walked home in a daze, begging myself not to get my hopes up. But if this was Kamal's work and it spanned his Camp Hell years, I had to be in there somewhere. I was one of his guinea pigs, after all. In fact, given how far back it went, it might shed some light on my past.

On my family.

I crept upstairs. Jacob was still out for the count, sprawled on his side diagonally with the comforter balled up on his arms as if he'd caught it trying to run away. I stripped out of yesterday's suit, grabbed a spare blanket, and climbed back into bed with him. He might be asleep, but his presence made me feel strong enough to open that stained, yellowed notebook and take a good look inside.

If I'd been hoping for entries like, "Dear diary, today I thought of a great new project. I think I'll call it Heliotrope Station…" I was shit outta luck. Like Warwick said: it was all initials, numbers, dates and charts. My knowledge of science is limited to high school biology and secret underground FPMP labs, so if scientific method was in play, it was lost on me. If anything, the diagrams reminded me of a sports playoff bracket, where you start a bunch of teams, the winners play each other, and finally the list gets winnowed down to one winner.

Or, in this case, the "subject."

The subjects were numbers and dates. Birthdates. All of them a similar year to mine, give or take five years. One of them must've belonged to Alex Warwick…one of the entries that also listed a death date.

The subjects weren't in chronological order, either, so I had to do a lot of flipping around. My birthday wasn't listed, but I was jaded enough to presume my birth certificate wasn't accurate—either because I'd been left on a cold basement floor, like Trinity, or because someone like Kamal had walked into a hospital and swapped my records with someone else's.

Jacob gave a gentle snort, and I glanced down at his sleeping profile and resisted the urge to stroke his hair. Strikingly good-looking, albeit with stray whisker growth around his goatee and deepening crow's feet at the corners of his eyes...and no red bulging psychic veins in sight. Good thing mediums were the only ones who saw talents by light of a GhosTV. Otherwise, those telepaths from Washington would've known that he was more than just a highly trained NP.

Bad enough having me on everyone's radar. At least one of us could sleep soundly.

I went through the notebook again, studying the birthdates of each "subject" to try them on for size and see if a date might somehow fit me. It was then that I noticed I knew one of those birthdates.

Not because I thought it was mine.

But because it belonged to the man at my side.

Jacob might come off like he thinks he's the center of the universe, but obviously he wasn't the only human being born on that particular date. That's what I told myself. Then, I looked at the playoff bracket above his birthdate and saw initials, JM and SL. Jerry Marks and Shirley....

I gave Jacob a nudge. "Hey. What's your mother's maiden name?"

"Larson." He was quiet a few moments, trying to fall back asleep, but then his curiosity got the better of him. "Why?"

I considered telling him I was just trying to retrieve a password. It was bad enough going through Camp Hell myself, but at least I'd been cognizant of the fact that I was there. Him, though? What if it turned out that all these years, he'd been part of some grand psychic experiment and not even known it?

I'd always envied his normal life...I hated to cast a pall over it now. But, in the end, I decided that whatever this was, it was too big for me to sweep under the rug. And besides, he deserved to know.

"Well, mister?" I gave his hair that caress I'd been holding back. "Rub the sleep out of your eyes. You're gonna want to see this."

ABOUT THIS STORY

I DID A RE-listen of the earlier PsyCop audiobooks to prep for Bitter Pill. While it was a huge treat to spend so much time with Gomez Pugh (whose Vic voice is just like I hear it in my head), it was also bizarre to be transported back to a time when poor Vic didn't even know how to salt a ghost. I think it's definitely possible to get so close to the top of your game that there's not much left for you to learn. That's not to say Vic won't continue to evolve, just that some of the tricks he picks up in these later novels are more interpersonal and social than psychic.

I know a lot of writers who use binaural pulses to up their productivity. I generally don't like any of the sounds that pull me up into the higher (beta) frequencies. I'm more like Vic, I prefer the stuff that brings me down. There's a site/app called brain.fm that uses binaural and other tones to entrain brainwaves. I bought a lifetime membership some time ago but find I only use it when I need to drown out barking dogs. Of course, it would be amazing if brainwave apps were a magic bullet. Slip on the headphones and fall right into inspired productivity.

Alas. There is no magic bullet. Not that I've yet discovered, anyhow.

I was pretty excited to have Vic team up with Zigler again, even though Zig's not exactly a flashy character. To me, he represents the everyman, the non-psychic who finds extrasensory stuff understandably scary. But whenever he's the one whose investigative work turns up something important, I always do a little "hooray" for him. There's something to be said for being tenacious and smart. (I found it funny that in Body and Soul, Vic's initial reaction was "I hate this guy.")

I was promoting Among the Living recently and was shocked to realize I'd started this series 13 years ago. When I revisit the early stories, I generally only notice it around the technology. The other day I saw a guy at the grocery store whip out a flip phone, and I thought, "Thank God Vic's not the very last holdout!" No doubt a decade from now, Vic's current smartphone will seem just as quaint as his flip phone.

With a wedding looming and now Kamal's notes in play, I'm eager to see where the next PsyCop will take Jacob and Vic.

Don't miss the next PsyCop adventure.
Sign up for JCP News
at www.psycop.com/newsletter to
receive all the latest writing
announcements and goodies!

www.ingramcontent.com/pod-product-compliance
Lightning Source LLC
Chambersburg PA
CBHW051651180726
48284CB00006B/1956